Also by Arthur Wenk

Axel Crochet:
Musicologist-at-Large

Quarter Note Tales #3

ARTHUR WENK

iUniverse, Inc.
New York   Bloomington

Axel Crochet: Musicologist-at-Large
Quarter Note Tales #3

iUniverse books may be ordered through booksellers or by contacting:

iUniverse
1663 Liberty Drive
Bloomington, IN 47403
www.iuniverse.com
1-800-Authors (1-800-288-4677)

ISBN: 978-1-4620-5586-9 (sc)
ISBN: 978-1-4620-5588-3 (hc)
ISBN: 978-1-4620-5587-6 (e)

Printed in the United States of America

iUniverse rev. date: 10/04/2011

For Patti

Preface

THE DEFINITION OF "MUSICOLOGY" IN the *New Grove Dictionary of Music* runs to some twenty-seven pages, including a bibliography. The definition offered by my next-door neighbour is rather briefer: "I dunno, something to do with music, I suppose." Readers who prefer a lengthy exposition are referred to *The New Grove*, whose erudite treatment of the subject may lead them to read all twenty volumes of this monument to twentieth-century scholarship. Readers attracted to my neighbour's definition may find cause for amusement in the rather less ambitious work that they hold in their hands.

My graduate training in musicology took place at Cornell University, which offered me a University Fellowship to begin studying there in 1965. Such was the system of benevolent paternalism in those days that when the University Fellowship expired, one of my professors, without my knowledge, arranged for me to receive a National Defense Education Act Title IV Fellowship to cover the remaining four years of my doctoral program. (A former military man, he may have concluded early on that he could best contribute to the nation's defense posture by keeping me at a safe distance from our armed forces.)

By 1970, when I was ready to enter the job market, the great period of expansion that had characterized higher education in the Sixties was drawing to a close, and the only job offer I received came from Chihuahua State College in California. Faced with the choice between Chihuahua and unemployment, I thought my course was clear. This pattern was to prevail throughout my career: having once opted for musicology, I never had to make another choice.

The series of *Quarter Note Tales* traces my musicological career from California to Boston to Pittsburgh to North Carolina to Bloomington to Québec City through the eyes of my alter ego, Axel Crochet. In British notation, a quarter note is a crochet, and in French, a *croche*. Claude Debussy, the composer to whom I devoted my scholarly career, wrote music criticism under the *nom de plume* of Monsieur Croche, anti-dilettante. The family name Axel comes from a play, *Axel*, by the composer's friend Villiers de l'Isle Adam, from which Debussy hoped to produce a theatre-piece.

While I recognize a certain kinship between myself and Axel Crochet, I must observe that he is even more naïve than I and a good deal more reckless, particularly when it comes to rushing headlong to the rescue of a female companion or colleague.

Regarding this new set of *Quarter Note Tales*, no one to my knowledge has plunged from the tower at Wellesley College (The Cloister in "Die, For I Am A-Dying") although I did lead legions of undergraduates up its steps for instruction in playing the carillon. My tenure as a Visiting Scholar at Duke University (Magnolia University in "Prime Suspect) has been shifted from 1976 to 1990 in order to permit the computer shenanigans. My year as a Visiting Professor at Indiana University (Frangipani University in "Tarry Awhile") saw no deaths, but that was not due to any absence of clashing egos or petty jealousies. And while I have team-taught a course in "Faust in Literature and Music," the pattern of my life hasn't imitated the structure of *Faust* the way Axel's does in "Tarry Awhile."

Those interested in the first two volumes of *Quarter Note Tales* can read excerpts from each novella at www.axelcrochet.com, along with the text of the first and only review of a work of fiction to appear in the Music Library Association *Notes* for *The Quarter Note Tales*.

Axel Crochet, Musicologist-at-Large

Phyllis the bright, when frankly she desired
Thyrsis, her sweet heart, to have expired;
Sweet, thus fell she a-crying,
Die, for I am a-dying.
(John Ward, *The First Set of English Madrigals*, 1613)

DIE, FOR I AM A-DYING

Chapter 1

BOSTON BOASTS THE GREATEST NUMBER of colleges and universities per capita of any city in the United States. It also has the country's oldest subway system. Both facts pertain to the story I am about to relate.

In the late 1950's the M.T.A. or Metropolitan Transit Authority (an institution immortalized in the song of that title by the Kingston Trio) decided to expand the so-called Green Line out toward the suburbs. Two main alternatives came under consideration: southwest to Waban or northwest to Riverside. Proponents of the Riverside option pointed out that several dozen trains ran daily between Boston and Waban whereas Riverside remained unconnected by public transit to the city described by Oliver Wendell Holmes as the hub of the universe. This argument carried the day and the Green Line pushed its way northwest.

Then the Boston and Albany Railroad, citing declining revenues as America's postwar love affair with the automobile made itself felt in Massachusetts, cut off rail service between Boston and Waban, leaving only one commuter run in the morning and afternoon. Waban became like an inland port, left high and dry when the river changes its course.

These decisions had an emphatic impact on The Cloister, an exclusive women's college located in Waban. The great social issues of the 60's and 70's—the student movement, the civil rights movement, the anti-war effort, women's liberation—brought together students from institutions both august and humble: Harvard, M.I.T., Boston University, Boston College, Tufts, Emerson, Huntington. But throughout these tumultuous times the young women of The Cloister remained, well, cloistered.

One could, in fact, travel from Boston to Waban, as I did twice a week during the 1973-1974 academic year. I would walk from my apartment near the Boston Public Garden to Copley Station, where I took the Green Line to Woodland and then waited for a municipal bus that would drop me a half mile from the campus of The Cloister. Occasionally I would see one or two students during my journey, but for the most part the population of The Cloister remained quietly sequestered, far from the fray.

I worked at The Cloister as an untitled replacement for a member of the music department on maternity leave, teaching a mandatory, non-credit course for music majors. Essentially my job was to detect any shortcomings in their overall musicianship and to correct these deficiencies in individual tutorials through whatever means I saw fit.

For the most part these young women came well prepared with keyboard and sight-reading skills. In order to challenge a fine pianist named Abby Fox, for example, I had her read Brahms symphonies with me four-hands at the keyboard. Another student, Penny Lapworth, proved remarkably adept at sight singing. When I asked where she'd developed this skill she described the daily regimen at the British choir school she'd attended for a year.

All the young women shared a virtual ignorance of music of the twentieth century, a deficiency I eventually attributed to the influence of Newton Falgarwood, the department chairman, who detested twentieth-century music yet insisted on teaching the course in that area as a mark of his broadmindedness. (Privately he held the opinion that western culture, especially music, had reached both its pinnacle and the beginning of its decline in the Renaissance.)

In exasperation I would complain to my students, "The twentieth century is nearly over, and you've missed it!" I assigned the music majors in my charge to play examples from Bartok's *Mikrokosmos* (they had never heard of it), to sight-read Stravinsky's modest dodecaphonic song, "The Owl and the Pussycat," (ditto) and then, having observed how it was put together, to compose a similar work of their own, often with charming results.

In order to obtain this position I was examined by the former department chairman and *eminence gris* Hubert Lamb, who required me to carry out a number of exercises that in the eighteenth-century would have been performed as a matter of course by virtually any keyboardist but which in the twentieth century could be considered academic tasks seldom encountered outside advanced musicianship courses in a conservatory. I had to transpose a chorale, read music written in the C clefs, and realize a figured bass at sight, translating the numbers written above the bass line into proper chords.

Early in the autumn of 1973 came the installation of Marjorie Clearwater as the tenth president of The Cloister. Ms. Clearwater, a robust, energetic woman who promised in her inaugural address to shake The Cloister out of its dreamy torpor (she didn't put it quite like that), had been particularly impressed by Jewitt Tower, the most prominent architectural feature of the campus. Upon learning that the tower housed a complete carillon, President Clearwater requested that the bells ring out following her investiture. The request made its way to the music department where it caused considerable consternation since no one there knew how to play the bells which, in any event, had not sounded in recent memory. Pleased to oblige, I mentioned my college bell-ringing experience and offered to take on the task.

In order to play the bells one had to climb six flights of stone stairs arranged in a kind of square spiral around a vertical shaft, in the fashion of the mission tower in Alfred Hitchcock's "Vertigo." (Just before the film's release, Hitchcock warned the sisters of the mission abbey where the climax of the film had been shot to expect a fair number of tourists looking for a non-existent tower. For while the mission itself was genuine, the vertiginous tower was strictly a studio fabrication.)

The top of the Jewitt Tower stairs opened onto a small chamber housing a practice keyboard, identical to that of the actual carillon but connected to tuned metal bars, somewhat like a xylophone, so that one could perfect a piece of music in private before inflicting it upon the entire campus community. A locked door, to which I had been given a key, gave access to a smaller spiral staircase leading to the actual carillon keyboard, situated at the bottom of the belfry itself. Pianists sit before their instruments, sousaphone players wrap themselves in their instruments, but only the carillonneur sits directly beneath an instrument weighing several hundred tons.

On the afternoon of the installation, immediately following the investiture, I mounted the six flights of stairs, unlocked the door to the belfry, climbed the spiral staircase, took a seat at the bench, about the same size and shape as an organ bench, and performed a program of more or less appropriate music, occasionally slipping in improvised variations on one of my old college songs.

In contrast to the hefty cylindrical rods—roughly the shape of rowboat oars—with which I had had to contend at Amherst College, the Cloister carillon offered a regular keyboard on which, after getting used to the somewhat stubby keys, one could play as if at a piano or organ. And in contrast to the nine bells whose narrow compass had severely limited my repertoire in college, the Cloister carillon had thirty-two bells (ranging in weight from 80 to 1,600 pounds) allowing one to perform a relatively wide range of pieces.

I guess I shouldn't have expected the carillon, that most public of musical instruments, to remain a secret. At our next tutorial Abby Fox told me she wanted to play the bells. Why not? Certainly her technical competence at the keyboard was beyond question. So at the end of the afternoon, following my last tutorial, we walked to Jewitt Tower and began the long ascent. A lithe, athletic young woman, Abby moved with the ease of a New England aristocrat, her blonde hair cropped short, her mind darting easily from one subject to another, completely at ease in the refined world of The Cloister.

Along the way I learned a bit about Abby's background. An only child, Abigail Adams Fox had been named by her mother, an ardent feminist who had died in an automobile accident when Abby was only five. Since that time she had been raised by her father, a retired military officer.

"I think he really wanted a son," Abby told me, recalling the endless series of camping trips, mountain hikes and other Outward Bound-like adventures of her youth. "Eventually he came to see that being a tomboy just wasn't my thing."

"But he appreciated your musical talent," I said.

"Yes, I'm grateful for that. I guess you could say that my parents endorsed freedom in the sense that a child of theirs could excel in the field of her choice."

"I didn't see your father at Parents Day," I said as we passed the halfway mark in our climb. Abby didn't reply but when she next turned toward me I saw tears in her eyes.

"Daddy's dying," she said simply. "Cancer."

"I'm sorry," I said, aware of the inadequacy of these words in the situation. From her earlier remarks I understood that Abby adored her father, and the prospect of life without her only parent must have looked bleak indeed.

Abby brightened as we mounted the final spiral staircase to the carillon console. I had brought along an album of Bach organ preludes and fugues for us to attempt four-hands at the keyboard, with Abby playing the soprano and alto lines and me taking the tenor and pedal parts. Actually these "Eight Little Preludes and Fugues" weren't by Bach at all (*Echtheit sehr angezweifelt* [authenticity highly doubtful], according to the editorial notes), but they provided useful exercises without any unexpected technical challenges.

Together we produced quite a sound—I could not have performed these works at the carillon unassisted—and when we finished Abby's eyes shone with enthusiasm, a spirit she must have communicated to her fellow music majors for at the end of my next teaching day a delegation of a dozen students declared their desire to "learn the bells," as one student put it. In the days that followed I led several groups of young women to the top of Jewitt Tower and eventually surrendered my key to Abby, the self-appointed director of the Guild of Carillonneurs, who began performing every evening according to a schedule that Abby organized and maintained.

On our descent from that initial collaboration I had told Abby about some of my bell-ringing adventures at Amherst. The great prank in those days was to break into the bell tower at night and play the "Mickey Mouse Club Song" on the bells. The campus cops would dutifully roll up in a squad car and wait for the miscreant to emerge, after which they would administer some minor penalty. One Sunday afternoon, the time I regularly performed, some freshmen living in the dorm beside the bell tower—whose afternoon studies I regularly interrupted—persuaded me to end my recital with the "Mickey Mouse Club Song." In an effort to mend fences I acceded to the request, never suspecting that they had tape recorded the piece. Come midnight, the sound of the familiar Disney melody chimed out over the campus. The patrol car eventually rolled up and the campus cops waited, but to no avail. The exterior of the tower enhanced the verisimilitude of sounds broadcast from loudspeakers of a third-floor dorm room against the stone surface. In these acoustical circumstances there was really no way to distinguish the original from the copy.

Evidently determined that no such shenanigans would occur on her watch, Abby refused to make copies of the carillon key, preferring to make the nightly ascent herself to insure that the door to the tower console remained locked when not in use. One could still mount the stairs to the practice keyboard, but nobody could activate the actual bells without Abby's consent.

One Tuesday in mid-October, just before mid-term exams, Penny Lapworth arrived red-eyed for her tutorial. Penny had black hair pulled back in a ponytail, exposing a high forehead. She wore rimless glasses and had a slightly upturned nose that she seemed to push unabashedly into everyone else's affairs, a distinction she probably would reject: everybody else's affairs were simply hers. But today she seemed so uncharacteristically withdrawn that I had to ask what the matter was.

"It's Abby," she said. "She killed herself." With these words Penny lost control and burst into tears. I let her blurt out the story as best she could and, at her request, excused her from our session together. Apparently Abby had committed suicide by jumping from the top of the stairs into the central shaft of Jewitt Tower. Abby's father had finally succumbed to cancer a week earlier, and Abby's distraught state at our tutorial on the day of his death—an appointment that she had refused to cancel—gave me no reason to doubt the assessment. Members of the Guild of Carillonneurs invited me to join them as we performed a series of Bach chorale preludes on the bells, the eloquence of Bach giving expression to our grief in a way that mere words could not.

Chapter 2

ON THE TUESDAY AFTER MID-TERM exams in October I discovered a flyer posted on the front entrance of the music building: "First Annual Autumn Appreciation Day. All classes are cancelled and the library is locked. Go out and enjoy the splendor of New England in the fall."

"What's this all about?" I asked a passing student.

"President Clearwater has decided to start a new tradition," she said. "Isn't it great? It means I don't have to take my counterpoint test."

"So there was no advance warning?" I asked.

"No. That's the whole idea. Nobody is supposed to know when it's going to happen."

"But presumably it has to be while the foliage is near its height. Otherwise you couldn't very well appreciate the autumn."

Another student joined the conversation. "I like the idea of a day off, but it's a good thing it didn't come during mid-terms. It would have messed up the whole schedule."

I couldn't help thinking of The Unexpected Hanging paradox. In a particular kingdom a man has been condemned to hang by the end of the week but the king assures him that the hanging will come as a surprise. The man, a competent logician, as people always seem to be in this kind of story, reasons that he cannot be killed. For if Saturday night arrived and he was still alive, he would necessarily have to be hanged on Sunday in order for the king's command to be fulfilled. But the king had also promised that the event would be a surprise, and if the prisoner knew he would have to hang on Sunday, the element of surprise would have been effectively removed. By the same reasoning, he reckons that he cannot be hanged on Saturday, because if Friday night rolled around and he was still alive, the element of surprise would again have been removed. Continuing to reason backwards, the man decides he cannot be killed at all, and consequently is completely surprised when the hangman appears for him on Wednesday. I didn't know whether President Clearwater was acquainted with the extensive body of literature dealing with this paradox, but I imagined that if she really intended this to be an annual affair, someone would eventually make the connection.

"Doesn't The Cloister already have an awful lot of traditions?" I asked the first student.

"Well the year begins with Flower Sunday, where each big sister gives her first-year little sister a bouquet of flowers."

"And don't forget Hoop-Rolling on May Day," said the second student.

"They really roll hoops?" I asked.

"Oh, yes," she assured me. "And the winner gets tossed into the pond."

"And she's supposed to be the first one in her class to get married," said the first girl.

As I entered the music building I recalled other traditions I'd heard about at women's colleges. Vassar had a 150-foot long daisy chain carried to commencement by the comeliest members of the sophomore class. Barnard had Midnight Breakfast on the night before final exams, where the faculty would prepare a repast for the students in the gymnasium. On May Day at Bryn Mawr members of the senior class would go to wake the president of the college. Smith College had Illumination Night, where the campus was lit only by colored paper lanterns. Mount Holyoke, where President Clearwater had served before coming to The Cloister, had held Mountain Day for more than a century. In the absence of local mountains, Autumn Appreciation Day would have to do as a substitute. But everybody at Mount Holyoke knew about Mountain Day. I had a feeling that the conservative music department faculty might be less enthusiastic about the unexpected interruption than the young women I had encountered.

Sure enough, grumbling about the unanticipated "tradition" filled the department meeting room. A sign on the faculty bulletin board announced a faculty meeting, made possible by the sudden suspension of classes. Unlike most music departments I had known, which generally held weekly, or at least bi-weekly meetings, the music faculty at The Cloister entrusted administration of the department to its chairman, Newton Falgarwood. Without a regular meeting time built into everyone's schedule, each meeting was essentially *ad hoc* and therefore exceedingly difficult to arrange, a situation that seemed to please everyone.

Professor Falgarwood called the meeting to order with a request that the agenda be approved and that the minutes of the previous meeting, which went all the way back to the preceding spring, be read aloud, a stultifying process that gave me ample opportunity to regard the head of the department.

Newton Falgarwood was the only chairman, nay the only musicologist, of my acquaintance to affect a goatee. *Affect* seemed to be the appropriate term, for combined with elaborately waved silver hair, the pointed goatee, along with thick eyebrows pointed up at the ends, contributed to the impression, presumably cultivated, of the scarcely-concealed sexuality of a cloven-footed satyr.

As for my own rather scruffier beard, my girlfriend Sheri Kimball had taken matters in hand shortly after our arrival in Boston by the simple expedient of observing men on the street until she found one whose beard pleased her and then asking him for the name of his hair stylist. This turned out to be Joseph (accent on the second syllable, *s'il vous plaît*), who worked at Continental East, a *haute couture* salon catering to girls who wanted to look like Yvette Mimieux, men who wanted to look like Mark Spitz, and peculiar women of indeterminate age who melted under Joseph's ministrations. During my visits I saw teeny-boppers hold pictures from Screen Gems magazine next to their heads and implore Joseph and his colleagues to make them into women; horse-faced farmer girls who came in looking like slatterns and went out with absolutely stunning coiffures resting somewhat uncomfortably on their horsey faces; and once in awhile, a truly beautiful woman coming in to become a goddess.

During one visit the woman in the next chair (not a goddess but definitely peculiar) hollered over, "How long does that beard last?" No answer. (How can you answer a question like that, anyway?) Then Joseph turned and inquired in a punctilious tone, "Were you addressing us, Madame?" "Isn't that awfully expensive?" she rasped. "The beard maintains its well-groomed appearance for about eight weeks, Madame." Once I had tried trimming the beard myself. Joseph did not approve. "You really butchered it on the side," he commented.

"I can cut it off, but I can't put it back on. Don't do that again, you hear?" Joseph took a proprietary interest in my foliage.

The minutes having been read and approved, the chairman disposed of a few lesser matters before coming to the actual reason for the meeting. The Flemish organist, Ton de Klerck, would be coming to the campus to perform an all-Sweelinck recital in December. Satisfied murmurs around the table greeted this announcement, for which I had difficulty feigning enthusiasm. I had sat through enough of these recondite presentations, including an all-Obrecht concert at an American Musicological Society meeting.

Next Professor Falgarwood announced that things were moving along nicely in the preparation of a Festshrift for Hubert Lamb, publication having been secured and a number of scholarly articles received.

"And what will you contribute?" asked Olive Earle, the only woman on the faculty. Her bright red hair might have led the conventional-minded to expect vivacity, even sensuality. Her stark white blouse, buttoned to the neck, and further fastened with a silver bar brooch just below the chin, seemed designed to squelch any such expectations before they had an opportunity to get dangerously out of hand. Miss Earle (no Ms. for her), although probably no older than forty, seemed determined to wear the old-fashioned designation of spinster as a badge of honor.

Falgarwood, evidently pleased by Miss Earle's effort to curry favor, smiled and said that he planned to offer a modest paper on "The Renaissance in Music: The Beginning or The End?" I had little doubt where his sympathies would lie.

Finally, the chairman asked us to consider a petition from the music majors asking whether the music library could remain open in the evenings during exam weeks. "Isn't the music library open every evening?" I asked.

"Of course not," said Miss Earle. "Miss Dunfuddle needs to get home to feed her aged aunt."

"Wouldn't it be possible to have someone else man the library during these periods, so that students could consult the books and listen to the records?"

"Miss Dunfuddle has a degree in librarianship," said Miss Earle in a tone clearly indicating that this should be the final word on the subject. I noticed that she didn't say "library science."

"Wouldn't such a measure require expenditures from the departmental budget?" another faculty member asked.

"I don't think we could expect volunteers to handle a position of this degree of responsibility," said the chairman. "Shall we put it to a vote?"

In the event, everyone in the department opposed the petition except for me. I had some learning to do. "The music department has a long-standing tradition of unanimity," Miss Earle instructed me in a correct but icy tone. I obediently changed my vote, allowing us to proceed to the principal business of the day.

"President Clearwater has requested every department in the college to consider long-range ideas," Professor Falgarwood said. "She will visit us later in the year to listen to the results of our deliberations. I consider this a forward-thinking move on the president's part and I invite your participation."

A substantial silence followed this invitation, the department having been administered under a form of enlightened despotism for so long that its members were unaccustomed to having their opinions consulted for anything beyond the most minor details. The counterpoint teacher finally weighed in. "I for one would hate to see us meddle with a curriculum that has served us well for as long as I can remember. I believe that my own courses form an integral part of that curriculum and I would frankly oppose any measure that might interfere with their continued success."

This speech set the tone for those that followed, as each member of the music faculty defended his, or in the unique case of Miss Earle her, domain, pointing proudly to long-standing tradition and their essential role in maintaining it. Miss Earle defended the traditional music survey course on the grounds that young women "find security in having everything in its place." (And here I thought that sexism was confined to porcine chauvinism of the masculine gender.) As Professor Falgarwood gazed about the table with a satisfied smile I felt impelled to speak.

"I do not wish to take issue with any of you," I said politely, "but I believe there are two areas in which the music department could serve its students better." Looks of incredulity about the table ought to have warned me to abandon this reckless line but I continued undaunted. "My experience with the music majors suggests that we should strengthen our offerings in twentieth-century music, particularly developments after the Second World War which seem entirely outside their ken. I also think that while we have strong offerings in Western music, our curriculum takes no notice of music of other cultures."

"I think you're talking about ethnomusicology," said the counterpoint teacher. "Surely this is a subject that properly belongs in graduate school, not in an undergraduate curriculum."

After the rest of the department had had a chance to voice their reservations and objections, Professor Falgarwood looked over to me with an air of sympathy and said, "While I admire your youthful enthusiasm, Axel, as an experienced administrator I need to point out that your ideas, compelling as they may seem to you, would require cutting out other portions of the curriculum, a measure I would be very hesitant to endorse. And of course in the interests of fiscal responsibility, I must point out that any such changes would involve concomitant expenses, and as the departmental budget has been fully allocated in carrying out our current mandate, I fail to see where any additional funding would come from."

Falgarwood would have adjourned the meeting then and there had I not called his attention to the last item on the agenda, "Other business." "I suppose you have a piece of business to introduce," he said, somewhat less sympathetically than before.

"I'm wondering whether the department plans any kind of memorial service for Abby Fox," I said. I could not have produced a more profound attitude of discomfort and embarrassment if I had openly broken wind.

"The young woman committed suicide, I believe," said that counterpoint teacher, as if this fact in itself sufficed to stifle all further comment.

"Surely this is not a departmental matter," said Miss Earle, looking to the chairman for confirmation.

"I believe you had Miss Fox as a student," said Professor Falgarwood, who knew perfectly well that I saw all the music majors in tutorial. "I can understand your personal feelings in the loss of a student, but as department chairman I have the responsibility of putting the interests of our beloved institution above personal feelings. The Cloister would not welcome any measure that might reflect adversely upon the college. Meeting adjourned."

Chapter 3

JANUARY SAW ME WATCHING THE mail each day for news of either a permanent position as a musicologist or announcements of opportunities to apply for same. I had left Chihuahua State College in California without a job but with a partner, and on balance felt that I had done well by the exchange. Sheri's sense of adventure—she had crossed the continent to be with me—and her easy sensuality, occasionally bordering on wantonness, had helped me overcome my feelings of insecurity at this interruption in my career path. Having completed my doctorate at Cornell only three years earlier, I still entertained the expectation that I would one day find my place in an Ivy League university.

One evening after dinner we sat in the living room of our apartment and opened the day's mail. Sheri, as was her habit after a day at the editorial office where she worked, wore one of my marathon T-shirts and nothing else, a pleasant sight that compensated for the negative news she shared with me.

Every week I received form letters from universities exclaiming how proud they were to have hired someone other than myself. Perhaps the most offensive such letter came from Washington University. In 1974, with Affirmative Action Plans and Equal Opportunity Employment in place, it seemed almost incredible that a major university would not only resort to the Old Boy Network to fill a position but publicly proclaim the policy. Nonetheless, there it was in mimeographed black and white:

> *The search process which led to the appointments in music history was not public; i.e., we did not advertise our openings. Nevertheless, we assembled a pool of about forty candidates, mostly through recommendations by individuals known to us in seventeen widely scattered universities with strong doctoral programs in musicology.*

Most of these candidates impressed our search committee as being indeed very highly qualified young music historians.

The letter went on for another paragraph without even the traditional ironic benediction ("We are confident that someone of your demonstrated talent will have no difficulty finding a position suited to your qualifications") and closed with the name, but not the signature, of the music department chairman.

One of my favorite movies, "A Thousand Clowns," stars Jason Robards, Jr. as a man incapable of fitting into the supposed norms associated with the grey flannel suit. Instead of working, he spends his days watching cruise ships depart from New York harbor, shouting to strangers on deck, "So long, Charlie, have a wonderful time!" His young nephew, who ended up sharing his apartment when his sister departed under suspicious circumstances, pleads with the Robards character to look for a job.

Evoking his response, I encouraged Sheri to "read me from the want ads," in this case the monthly job list published by the College Music Society.

"There's nothing listed for musicologists," she reported after looking through the listings, but there are a few openings for pianists."

"Then let's hear those," I said.

"University of Utica at Utica," she read, "Instructor, teach individual and class piano, perform in University Trio, tune department pianos and chairman's home piano. Terminal degree required. $7800. Address Mrs. Luella Simpson, Chairperson, Piano Committee, U of U at U, Utica, New York."

"I don't know how to tune pianos," I said. "What else have you got?"

"East Lansing Community College. Assistant Lecturer in Piano, two courses in history of piano literature, master classes for music majors and faculty wives; $4400 and membership in the Faculty Club; opportunity for private teaching to supplement income. Apply to the Chairman, Professor Harold Hill, ELCC, East Lansing, Michigan."

"'Supplement income' is right. Is there anything else?"

"There's one right here in Boston. BelCanto School of Voice, Number One, The Fenway, Boston, Massachusetts. Pianist to coach young singers, assist in voice classes, and accompany Miss Portlavois

BelCanto (Sr.) in recitals. ("The voice may have faded but the lack of musicianship remains intact."—*The Boston Globe*), salary negotiable, apply by telephone."

Even one of these unenviable posts would be an improvement over my experience during the fall, where I attempted to augment my income from The Cloister by accepting a call from Vocational Technical University to grade papers. The university paid $3 an hour to have a partially-employed college professor correct the several hundred papers that their fully-employed college professor was too busy to read. So I graded papers. The first few hours were amusing: one could take a certain perverse pleasure in learning that someone else's students were writing silly things in blue books.

Cesar Franck wrote 25% of the organ repertoire. (Two papers said this)

Ravel wrote masculine music, Debussy feminine.

There existed a Vicious Triangle (also a Triangle of Hatred) *among Verdi, Wagner, and Brahms.*

Debussy's orchestral prelude depicts a fawn chewing leaves beside a river bed. (Other papers had the fawn coming down the hill on its slender graceful legs. Never mind that Debussy's music was meant to evoke not a fawn, but a *faun*, or horny satyr).

The chromatic scale was developed by Wagner because no scale was good enough for him.

Berg later opened a school for twelve-tone music.

The whole-tone scale comprises the white notes on the piano. (There was almost universal agreement on this.)

The scherzo is when you play the piano by sitting on it. (Oddly enough, I really didn't think this was meant to be funny.)

Mahler had a thing about death and died shortly after the work was completed.

As I read on (and on and on), I discovered too much unanimity for this to be simply random errors on the part of the students. They were being fed lies disguised as half-truths by a professor who simply didn't know any better. When I got around to reading the essay questions it became a very discouraging assignment to separate obvious misconceptions from well-worded statements when it was clear that the students had not the slightest idea what they were saying. ("*The opening of the classical symphony is marked by a deep philosophical content.*")

Surely there must be a better way to keep a roof over one's head. If

I couldn't land a permanent position, I hoped to locate temporary part-time work. After all, January was the season when department chairmen looked for nickels to fill vacant slots in their faculties. You stuck a nickel in the slot and out came a semester's course offerings, neatly wrapped in plastic and conveniently divided into fifty-minute segments—just tear along the perforated tenure line. Of course, everyone pretended that not just any old nickel would do, insisting on seeking out the one perfect nickel to fill their slot. So search committees were formed and job announcements published, with pious gestures toward the Affirmative Action Plan and avowed preference for Indian-head nickels. Naturally standards had to be maintained; no pennies need apply.

But in the end, any old nickel would do; nickels were a dime a dozen. After all was said and done, music departments would grab whatever spare change lay at hand. The University of Wisconsin, for example, nominally an "Equal Opportunity Employer," after conducting a half-year search and interviewing dozens of women, blacks, Chicanos, and Canadian nickels, proudly announced that it had hired as dean the man who had been serving as acting dean during the six-month search.

Just before Christmas, Professor Fioratura of Huntington University decided that I was probably worth about five cents and suggested I fill his slot during his eleven-week sabbatical starting April Fools' Day. With an eleven-week sabbatical, you either work very fast or, as in the case of Professor Fioratura, entertain very low ambitions. But a Search Committee still had to be formed and women and blacks and Chicanos and French centimes interviewed, so it wasn't until January that Huntington University was able to announce that any old nickel— to wit, Axel Crochet, bearded musicologist—would do.

After Sheri finished reading the official letter from Huntington University announcing my eleven-week appointment she asked, "How are you going to make that fit with your job at The Cloister?"

"Huntington needs me Mondays, Wednesdays and Fridays. I've been meeting all my students at The Cloister on Tuesdays and Thursdays, so there won't be any conflict."

"What do they want you to do?"

"Professor Fioratura has two courses to be covered, Romantic Music and Twentieth-Century Opera."

"How much can you expect to accomplish in just eleven weeks?"

"Ah, you've hit upon the sweet mystery of the trimester system. At

Amherst our semesters were eighteen weeks long and even then you felt as if you were racing through the material. Eleven weeks is a joke. Happily I have no long-term accountability. Like a hired gunslinger, I just give it my best shot and then move on."

Outside the apartment horns honked and brakes squealed as drivers evidently succeeded in avoiding a collision. Probably just as well, although that combination of sounds always made me think of the half year I spent in Paris, where the prelude of horns and brakes was almost invariably followed by the satisfying crunch of metal and the tinkle of broken glass. Who cared? The automobiles, literally called lemons (*citrons*) seemed no more than fragile tin contraptions.

"So I take it you're going to put off working on your Debussy book while you prepare for teaching these courses?" Sheri said.

"No, I need to keep that going, too. The University of California Press has given me a deadline and I intend to meet it."

"But isn't this just your doctoral dissertation?"

"Mostly yes, but there are two chapters I didn't have a chance to write then that I'd like to include in the book."

"I don't know, Axel," Sheri said. "You seem to have changed since California."

"How so?"

"Well, it feels as if you work all the time."

"I certainly didn't get much work done in California. My last year in graduate school, even while writing my dissertation, I managed to read seventy-five books. The first year in California I read forty-five and my second year, only fifteen."

"That's amazing," Sheri said.

"Yeah, I know. I felt as if my mind was going to seed."

"No. I meant that you actually count the number of books you read."

"It seemed like a revealing statistic."

"So does that mean that the pile of books you keep by the bed is just like another assignment? You have to hurry through each one in order to get to the next?"

"I hadn't really thought of it like that."

"I think you were more fun in Chihuahua."

"I don't know. I looked at all those guys from Yale and Princeton— really productive scholars—who took jobs in California, discovered the joy of becoming one with the all, and for all intents and purposes stopped being scholars."

"Maybe they just found that there were more important things in life than publishing."

"You mean like hugging trees?"

"You're not planning to work anymore tonight, I hope."

"No."

"So you'll come and play with me?"

"Yes."

And so we did.

Chapter 4

FEBRUARY BROUGHT THE JUNIOR SHOW and the long-anticipated meeting with President Clearwater. Natalie Porter explained the Junior Show to me after one of her lessons.

"Students work on it all though their sophomore years and the first five months of junior year. I wrote a bunch of the songs for our show last year, but I know the girls who are creating this year's show and it should be a good one."

"What's it about?"

"Oh, they're always about the same thing. There's a typical student, called Clara Cloister, and the show traces her life through a school year."

"Beginning with Flower Sunday?" I asked, recalling the description I had heard in the fall.

"That's right, and going all the way through until Hoop-Rolling on May Day. But there are lots in between. Do you know about the Step-Singing?"

"Can't say that I do."

"That takes place twice a year. Each class dresses in its own colors and performs on the steps of the chapel, trying to out-sing the other classes. In between songs the girls who aren't on the steps shout out cheers making fun of the other classes."

"What else does Clara Cloister experience?"

"Well there's Marathon Monday."

"That would be Patriots' Day?"

"That's right. The Boston Marathon goes right through the campus—The Cloister marks the half-way point—so we set up the Cloister Scream Machine to encourage the runners. In our show we had Clara rush out of the crowd to kiss her boyfriend, who was running the race, only to have him disqualified because someone had touched him."

"Are the rules really that strict?"

"I don't know, but it brought a lot of laughs during the show. You know, a 'fatal kiss' and that sort of thing."

"What else?"

"I'm not sure if they'll include it this year, but we had a scene about the Class Tree. You know, each sophomore class plants its own tree in the fall. We made up our own words to the Johnny Appleseed song."

"Did Abby participate in the show?"

"Didn't I tell you? Yes, she was our pianist: a regular one-person orchestra. You really should come."

"I wouldn't miss it," I said, although as it turned out the event fell on the same night as Sheri's birthday and I didn't want a work-related event, no matter how inviting, to interfere with that.

President Clearwater's luncheon with the music department was, of course, a command performance. We gathered in one of the smaller function rooms of the Cloister Faculty Club, whose floor to ceiling windows looked out on a great rolling lawn which led eventually to the college pond. A fountain in the middle of the pond sent a jet of water skyward, each falling drop having the potential of becoming a tiny prism to catch the sun's rays.

President Clearwater arrived wearing a blue suit whose careful tailoring, along with her regal demeanor, conveyed the authority of a benevolent monarch. A neutrally-dressed underling accompanied her to take notes.

After we had filled a sufficient interval with small talk, the president invited the chairman to share the product of our departmental deliberations. "This is the last luncheon in the series," she announced, "and I have no doubt that your ideas will have been well worth waiting for," employing a verb tense I had never encountered outside of French classes.

Professor Falgarwood rose to his feet, adopted the demeanor of a favored courtier toward his liege, and began his prepared remarks. "Your Excellency ..." No, he didn't really say that, but everything preceding this moment led one to expect such a form of address. Falgarwood contented himself with "Madame President and esteemed colleagues." He extended a beatific smile in our direction. "The music department at The Cloister has a long and honorable tradition." I'll spare you the details of that long tradition, as Falgarwood did not. He wrapped up the speech with his vision of generations of music majors to come—their preparation identical to that of their predecessors—an unbroken line of halcyon harmony. (Yes, he even permitted himself that bit of high-flown, if indecipherable, alliteration.)

Ms. Clearwater seemed stunned by the utter lack of substance in the chairman's verbiage, essentially summarizing the department's decision to maintain our current program without the slightest alteration. An uneasy silence ensued while the president gathered her thoughts.

"This is really quite extraordinary," she finally brought herself to say. "Every other department in the college, without exception, has come to me with requests for additional funding for ideas ranging from the modest to the outlandishly ambitious. And yet you, in your quiet way, have managed to achieve perfection." (I didn't know the president well enough to assess the level of irony in her final sentence, but I earnestly hoped for it.)

Professor Falgarwood maintained the smug expression of a cat who has swallowed the canary, basking in the president's words of praise (ironic or not), secure in the knowledge that while other departments might engage in budget-busting pipe dreams, he (by which he meant the music department) remained loyal to the principles of fiscal propriety. Other members of the department looked upon their leader admiringly or even, in the case of Miss Earle, fawningly.

Finally I felt compelled to break the extended silence by pointing out that we had considered expanding our treatment of twentieth-century and non-Western music. The president had scarcely a chance to register interest in this breach of staunch unanimity before Professor Earle breathlessly interrupted me to say, "But we all felt these changes would be impractical at the present time." And that was the end of curriculum reform in the music department at The Cloister.

Chapter 5

On April 1st I took the Arborway branch of the Green Line to Huntington University and found my way to the chemistry lab where I'd been assigned to meet the 120 students in Professor Fioratura's Romantic Music course. I perched on the edge of the desk, next to the retorts and Bunsen burners, and made a quip about maintaining good chemistry between students and teacher. The class laughed. I made a crack about hoping to avoid any explosions. The class laughed again. Funny—it wasn't really that much of a joke.

Having broken the ice I decided to get down to business. I explained that each week we would explore a different genre—character piece for piano, song cycle, symphonic poem, etc. I would play and discuss a number of examples in class. Each week the students would complete a listening assignment—never more than sixty minutes—and then submit a one-page paper comparing the works they'd listened to.

At first my words met with giggles. The new professor really had a bizarre sense of humor. Professor Fioratura limited himself to puns whereas this guy could concoct full-blown fantasy. But when it finally dawned on the students that I wasn't joking, their mood began to turn ugly. Notebooks snapped angrily shut, pencil cases zipped fiercely closed, and backpacks scraped sullenly along the floor. Forty students packed up their things and stalked out of the lecture hall. I continued to sit on the edge of the lab desk and calmly asked if there were any other deserters before I began the day's lesson. Students looked at each other, murmured, and pondered their options.

Eventually I discovered that Professor Fioratura's Romantic Music course enjoyed a university-wide reputation as a roaring gut (Mickey Mouse course, easy A, snap course, whatever terminology you prefer). Why did I imagine that 120 students had enrolled in the course? Certainly the stolid, gray architecture of Huntington University did not inspire a sudden passion for Romantic Music. The standing agreement—

one might almost call it a covenant—required only that students attend the lectures and laugh appreciatively at Professor Fioratura's execrable puns, for which they were rewarded with automatic A's, there being no papers, tests or exams for the good professor to mark. I had not simply departed from tradition—I had broken a covenant.

I mistakenly assumed that the students who remained actually had an interest in Romantic Music. I should have known better. The departing students figured that they could take the course again when this imposter had left and the order of the world had been restored. The other students needed this credit in order to graduate, and were already calculating the disastrous effect of my supposedly modest assignments on their social lives.

Eventually the class got underway and the students dutifully turned in their one-page papers. What else were they going to do? I played some music, talked about it a little, and invited questions. No one raised a hand. It went on like this for eleven dreadful weeks. Every once in awhile I would throw out a question, some student's eyes would brighten and a hand would quiver a little. Then other class members would turn a hairy eyeball in that direction and the response would die. Still, the papers came in week by week, and got better and better. The students were learning, despite their absolute determination to stonewall the teacher.

Every Monday afternoon the music faculty would convene. The chairman maintained control by "raising the question to a higher philosophical level" (his phrase) whenever someone raised an objection. He liked to seek agreement "in principle" for ideas which could not withstand scrutiny "on a lower practical level" (my phrase).

One week the chairman was upstaged when Professor Fioratura himself came back for a visit. (When a sabbatical lasts as long as eleven weeks, you can imagine that a fellow gets lonely for his old buddies and the rough-and-tumble hurly-burly of a music department meeting.) What a great performance: he ranted and raved, declared the meeting illegal, threatened to report all of us to the dean, and finally claimed that he was going to persuade X, an old friend of his, not to accept the position of "Artist-in-Residence" that the music department had planned to extend to him. (I never did figure out what was eating him, and could only conclude that the prospect of actually producing something that could reasonably be construed as a "sabbatical project" had left him unhinged.)

The following week the music department granted me full voting privileges at faculty meetings and said I should consider it an honor. I blushed, stammered and scraped my shoe on the floor, which seemed to please them. The chairman liked to operate a democratic monarchy: everybody would discuss the issue and then he would announce a decision. Except when he felt threatened. Then he would argue people into the ground and place his foot triumphantly on their necks to be sure that they remembered who was chairman.

About two weeks into the course one of the students, Jessica Lansdowne, approached me after class. A round-faced, slightly freckled young woman, wearing blue jeans and a Huntington University sweatshirt, she asked if we could talk. The terms of my contract hadn't included an office—though I had difficulty picturing Professor Fioratura slaving away there—so we walked to the Student Union, a massive fortress of a building, where we were able to find a table in a quiet corner.

"Are you sure you want to be seen with me?" I joked. "I seem to be something of a pariah on campus."

Jessica looked embarrassed. "Actually, I'm enjoying the course," she said in a small voice, as if concerned that her words might reach the wrong ears. In fact, the students milling around the cafeteria seemed to be concerned only with filling their stomachs.

"Your first two papers have been quite good," I said.

Jessica blushed and looked down. Now her discomfort was making me uncomfortable. I tried changing the subject.

"Perhaps you have something else on your mind," I said.

She looked up, smiled hesitantly and nodded. I leaned back in my chair and tried to look open and sympathetic. We sat in silence for a few moments while Jessica apparently got up the nerve to speak. "They say that you teach at The Cloister," she said at last.

"That's right. I teach here on Monday, Wednesday and Friday and there on Tuesday and Thursday."

"And you see all the music majors," Jessica said.

"You're well informed," I said, and smiled at her.

"So you have ... or had ... Abby Fox as a student."

"Yes. I know teachers aren't supposed to have favorites, but she was one of mine. It's not just that she was an excellent pianist. She communicated a sense of being, I don't know, fearless. With some people self-confidence is off-putting, but her self-confidence made you feel comfortable to be around her."

Jessica smiled and nodded. "That's it exactly!" She paused for a moment and then continued. "Abby was my best friend in high school."

"Then I'm sorry for your loss. You must miss her."

"I do." Jessica began to tear up, but she brought herself under control by blinking rapidly, and then hurried on with what had evidently been a prepared speech. "They say she committed suicide but that doesn't make any sense. Abby would never do anything so dishonorable. It wasn't just her father, it's the way she was and I don't care what anyone says I just don't believe it, and I didn't have anyone else to tell so I wanted to tell you."

I hate it when every instinct in your body makes you want to put your arm around someone and every ounce of good sense says you mustn't do that, so instead I gave her a sympathetic smile and said, "You're going a bit too fast for me, but I don't have any place I have to go, so suppose you tell me the whole story. Take your time."

Jessica looked at me with a combination of relief and incredulity. Then she took a deep breath, frowned and said, "You really mean it?"

"I'm all yours," I said.

She relaxed visibly and began to talk in a more even tone. "I spoke of honor. Let me tell you what I mean."

I nodded encouragingly.

"In senior year Abby learned that the president of the National Honor Society got together with a friend every morning before classes to copy his math homework. We're not talking once in a while when he may not have had time to do it, but every morning."

"I imagine Abby verified this for herself." I was beginning to get a sense of another side of this young woman.

"Oh yes. The guys would sit in the basketball bleachers, so one morning Abby arranged to amble past so she could see what they were doing."

"Did she confront them?"

"No. She figured they would just deny it or tell her to buzz off. No, she went to the principal and demanded that he call a special meeting of the National Honor Society to discuss the meaning of honor."

"And did he?"

"Yes. Afterwards I'm sure he kicked himself, but Abby was going to be class valedictorian, after all, and she'd already won a National Merit Scholarship that had brought a lot of publicity to the school, so he didn't see how it could do any harm."

"I'm beginning to get an idea of how this must have played itself out. I suppose that at this special meeting Abby asked some abstract question like whether the members of the National Honor Society ought to display some sense of honor."

"That's it exactly. And of course nobody could very well dispute that."

"And then she publicly challenged the NHS president to deny that he copied homework every morning?"

"Yes. Everybody knew about it, and the guy knew that everybody knew, so he was pretty well cornered."

"I'll bet the principal was even more uncomfortable than he was."

"That's the way Abby described it to me. He had called the meeting, after all, but he found himself in a pickle."

"He couldn't very well condone cheating, but he didn't especially want to punish the NHS president."

"Right. So he sort of surrendered the discussion to Abby."

"Did she let him off the hook?"

"No way," Jessica said. "I think she just sat there with a look that said, 'So what are you going to do about this?'"

"And what did he do?"

"I have to hand it to him for thinking on his feet. Maybe that's a qualification for being a principal. Anyway, according to Abby, he looked very sternly at the NHS president and said, 'I'm assuming that we can count on this behavior to cease immediately.' The president looked him in the eye and said, 'Yes, sir.' Then the principal looked straight at Abby, said 'I think we've brought this matter to a satisfactory conclusion. Thank you for bringing it to my attention. Meeting adjourned.' And that was the end of it."

"And was that really the end?"

"Oh yes. Abby wasn't interested in getting the guy in trouble. It's just that she was personally offended by the state of affairs."

"By the incongruity between principle and action."

"I guess you could say that. Abby took questions of honor very personally."

"So you have doubts about her suicide."

"It's just not possible."

"Even though she was distraught over her father's death?"

"Especially that! Don't you see? It wasn't just Abby's sense of honor—it was her father's. She wouldn't do that to him, even if he were already dead. I know that doesn't make a lot of sense, but that's really the way Abby thought."

I stopped and tried to look at the situation from this altered perspective. "If Abby didn't commit suicide, have you thought about any alternatives?"

Jessica looked down again and shook her head. "I don't like to think about that," she said in a scarcely audible voice.

A large contingent of students began moving toward the exits and I imagined that afternoon classes were about to begin, but I didn't want to interrupt Jessica's story by consulting my watch. "Would you be willing to discuss it with me?" I asked.

She nodded reluctantly.

"I talked with Abby not long after her father's death. She took it pretty hard. After all, she really loved her father."

"It was more than that," Jessica said. "You might almost say she idolized him." The strange glow in Jessica's eyes made me wonder whether she didn't have a similar attitude toward Abby. "When she gave her junior recital—that was before her father got cancer—the hall was nearly full but it seemed as if she were performing for an audience of one."

"Well, if we rule out suicide, the only apparent alternatives are accident and murder. Have you ever visited The Cloister?"

"Just for Abby's recital. It was at night and I didn't get a chance to see much of the campus."

"Abby never invited you to visit her there?"

"No, except for the recital. After we went to college, we seemed to drift apart. I suspected that her father may have had something to do with my being invited to hear her play. He and I always got along really well."

I wondered about Jessica's relationship with her own father, but decided it wasn't my place to pursue the question. "Let me tell you a little about the place where Abby died," I said. "In order to get to the top of Jewitt Tower you have to walk up six flights of steps with a handrail and wire mesh always protecting you from falling into the central well. Even so, there are people who feel too uncomfortable to make the climb. Once you finally reach the top, you can look down into the open space, but the railing comes chest high and there's more wire mesh beneath the guard rail."

Jessica seemed to be following my description intently, so I continued. "Now I can understand that someone might have accidently slipped and fallen down a flight of stairs, but that isn't what happened to Abby. Her body was found on the stone floor at the base of the tower. It's really hard to imagine how someone could die by accident in that way."

Jessica looked as if she had been visualizing the scene in her mind. She didn't speak when I finished but simply nodded. "Are you sure you want me to go on?" I asked.

Jessica bit her lip and nodded.

"I haven't even thought about the possibility of murder until this moment. So far as I know, there was no mention of drugging, of concussion before the fall, or anything that would have rendered Abby unconscious. So a murderer would have to have lifted Abby—presumably unwillingly—over a four-foot barrier. I'm not saying it's impossible, but it would be physically demanding."

"But that's what you think happened?"

"I don't know. I understand your reluctance to accept suicide, but I have to say that murder doesn't sound any more convincing."

"So you don't believe me." Jessica's look suggested that she had suspected this would be the result all along, and now I was just proving her worst fears to be correct.

"I'm not saying that, Jessica. You've certainly raised strong doubts. I'm going to have to give this some more thought and perhaps ask some questions. Is that okay?"

"Thanks, Professor Crochet. At least you've listened to me."

"I'm not going to let this drop, Jessica. I'd like to know what happened to Abby, too."

Jessica leaned over and squeezed my hand. Then she scooted out of the room. I guess I was glad that one student out of that class had given expression to her feelings, but I'd been expecting feelings about music, not murder.

Chapter 6

THE FOLLOWING DAY, A TUESDAY, found me back at The Cloister. To learn more about Abby, I thought, what better place to begin than with her roommate, Wendy Atwater? As chance would have it, Wendy was my last pupil on Tuesdays and she had no objections to talking with me. A rather slender young woman with a long thin face and straight blonde hair that some might have described as stringy, Wendy wore the tall boots then in fashion and the long trench coat made popular by Katherine Ross in "The Graduate."

The Cloister dormitory complex seemed to have been modeled on Hampton Court, or one of the other great British manor houses. The U-shaped structure had four-story brick gabled wings extending from a central six-story tower topped with a stone facade. Additional turrets rested atop alternate gables, giving the whole affair an aura of ornate impregnability.

At the front desk Wendy introduced me to the house mother, who smiled and asked me to sign out when I left. As we walked up the stairs Wendy said, "Mrs. Merriweather is really nice. Not like some of the others. One of my classmates says her housemother is a real gorgol."

"I think that's meant to be 'gorgon.'"

"Whatever."

Wendy led me up to the room she had shared with Abby. The original symmetry of identical beds, desks, dressers and closets was set jarringly askew by the decor. Above Wendy's desk hung a bulletin board fairly bursting with photos, announcements, ticket stubs, a college calendar and a *Peanuts* cartoon. The wall over her bed bore posters of Rod Stewart and Michael Jackson as well as the famous Beatles Abbey Road photo. By contrast, Abby's side of the room was virtually bare save for a travel poster from British Railways over the bed.

Noting my glance Wendy said, "The College didn't have anyone else to share the room so I've been here alone. With no next of kin to claim Abby's belongings, the RA told me to just store the stuff in her closet until they figured out what to do with it. I guess the administration has more important things to worry about, because nobody's given me any further instructions."

"But you left the travel poster."

"I liked it, and if you take that away the room looks too weird."

I sat on the edge of what had been Abby's bed, bare except for a simple patterned bedspread. Wendy tried, without much success, to disguise the fact that she hadn't bothered to make her own bed. She turned her desk chair to face me and sat down.

"I appreciate your taking the time to talk with me," I began.

"I don't mind," Wendy said. "I really don't like to study much, if you know what I mean."

"I'm curious about Abby," I said. "I accepted the police verdict of suicide, as I guess pretty much everyone else has, but recently one of Abby's old friends has made me question that account."

Wendy looked at me quizzically. I got the impression that she was unaccustomed to thinking rapidly. She picked up an eraser from her desk and twiddled it idly in her fingers. "No, I'm sure it was suicide," she said at last.

"You mean the shock of her father's death?"

"That was no shock. He had cancer, for God's sake. She'd had months to prepare herself for his death, you know what I mean?"

"But still."

"No. Abby just had a thing about death."

"A thing?"

"Yeah. With her boyfriend."

"Her boyfriend?" I became aware that I was beginning to sound a little like the village idiot, and tried to recover. "I wasn't aware that Abby had a boyfriend."

"She never saw him. They met when she spent her junior year in England—she was a double major in music and English."

"I suppose that explains the poster."

"Right. Anyway, they wrote letters back and forth all the time. Abby spent more time typing letters than she did writing English essays, and she wrote an awful lot of English essays."

"You mentioned a special interest in death."

"Oh yeah. They used to write poems about death to each other. It seemed pretty sick to me, but whatever turns you on, you know what I mean?"

"I don't suppose I could take a look at the poems," I said.

"Nah. The police took all that stuff away. One of the officers glanced at the poetry and muttered something about a death wish."

"That's too bad," I said.

"Well," Wendy hesitated, as if uncertain whether to trust me.

"I'm not representing anyone, Wendy. I'm just curious about what happened to one of my students."

"I guess it won't hurt anything to tell you. One weekend when Abby was home visiting her father, I sort of snooped through her things and found the folder where she kept all her poems."

"And?"

"Well, there was one I thought was sort of pretty—weird, but still pretty, you know what I mean?"

"So you copied it?"

"Yeah. You're not going to tell anybody?"

"I wouldn't think of it. Do you think I could borrow it?"

"You can have it. I don't even know why I kept it. I mean, she's dead now, you know what I mean?" Wendy opened the bottom drawer of her desk and after rummaging around through various papers came up with a photocopied sheet.

"You may change your mind. I promise to return this to you," I said as she passed me the poem. *"Death, I await thy sweet release,"* read the first line. It occurred to me that there was more I might learn from Wendy so I asked, "What was Abby like as a roommate?"

Wendy fiddled some more with her eraser then said, "Abby wasn't my first roommate. I had a good roommate for two years before she transferred to Boston University. I had a different roommate last year but at the end of the year I had to request a change. She kept repeating the same phrases over and over and it drove me nuts, you know what I mean?"

I smiled and said, "So what about Abby?"

"Abby wasn't really a bad roommate," Wendy said. "She just gave you the impression that she'd memorized a manual called Roommate 101."

"How so?"

"Well, she'd asked if I wanted to order a pizza—I mean, who says no to a pizza? But I noticed that she never ate very much. And she never wanted to stay up late and talk, or confide in me about her boyfriend. I only knew his name because of the return address on the envelopes. She'd ask how I did on a test she knew I had coming up, but I don't think she really cared. It was just what she thought you did to be a good roommate."

I wondered whether Abby was more interested in causes than in people. I thanked Wendy for her help, promised again to return the poem, and took my leave.

Chapter 7

THAT EVENING, WHEN I SHOWED the poem to Sheri, she said, "You know, this sounds a lot like the lyrics we sang in 'An Evening of Amatory Madrigals,'" referring to a concert I had conducted with the Madrigal Singers at Chihuahua State. "You remember," she continued. "I thought it was so funny that you couldn't bring yourself to utter the word 'orgasm' in front of college students. I mean, did you really think we didn't know about sex? Hold on, I'll get the program."

As Sheri disappeared into the bedroom I thought about the concert. Elizabethan poets used the conceit associating death with sexual climax to put together a virtual Renaissance 'Joy of Sex.' Sheri returned with a copy of the Chihuahua State College program in which I had included the text of each madrigal we performed.

As we looked over the lyrics together I recalled the giggles that had ensued when we began rehearsing these piece, whose titles included "Susanna Fair Sometime Assaulted Was" (William Byrd), "Cruel, You Pull Away Too Soon" (John Morley), and "I Fall and Then I Rise Again" (Michael East).

"Here the young woman proposes masturbation instead of intercourse, in order to protect her virginity," Sheri said and intoned the lines in a fake British accent.

And if I grant to that which you request,
My chastity shall then deflowered be,
Which is so dear to me that I detest
My life, if it berefted be from me.
And rather would I die of mine accord
Ten thousand times, than once offend our Lord.

"And here's a request for simultaneous orgasm," I said, and imitated her intonation.

Phyllis the bright, when frankly she desired
Thyrsis, her sweet heart, to have expired;

Sweet, thus fell she a-crying,
Die, for I am a-dying.

"Is this a plea for fellatio?" Sheri asked.

If this you do to kill me,
Say, cruel nymph, why kiss not you then still me?
So shall you ease my crying,
And I could never wish a sweeter dying.

"It doesn't always work out as planned," I said. "Here's a reference to impotence, although I guess to be politically correct you'd have to say 'male erectile dysfunction.'"

I swore I would yet still she said I should not
Do what I would, and yet for all I could not.

"Here's one where the girl is driving the guy nuts with slow masturbation," Sheri said.

Alas, right out come slay me,
Do not thus still from time to time delay me.

"One of John Dowland's loveliest madrigals, 'Come Against, Sweet Love,' if you understand the word 'die' properly, is another plea for simultaneous orgasm.

To see, to hear, to touch, to kiss, to die
With thee in sweetest sympathy.

"Here's another request for fellatio to assist a second effort," Sheri said.

Dear love, be not unkind to thy beloved,
Who lies a-dying,
In mournful crying,
With a kiss revive me, O be thou moved.

"That seems to have been a popular theme," I said. "Here's another on the same topic."

She with a cruel frown
Oppressed my trembling heart with deadly swoon,
Yet pitying my pain
Restored with a kiss my life again.
Thus let me daily be of life deprived,
So I be daily thus revived.

"And yet, without knowing the key metaphor," Sheri said, "you'd think that all these poets were obsessed with death."

"Whereas actually they were just obsessed with sex."

"Much healthier obsession, if you ask me," Sheri said, and gave me a kiss. "So let's look more closely at the dead girl's lyrics."

I lay Abby's poem on the table and we read it together.

Death, I await thy sweet release,
This joyful agony's swift surcease,
Too long have I delayed this dying,
Now for thy relief I'm crying.

Will thy mighty sword suffice
To bring about my quick demise,
Or will my joyous end demand
Thy firm inexorable hand?

Whether by sword or hand thou take me,
Death, I pray, do not forsake me.

"Shouldn't that be 'takest' in the penultimate line?" Sheri asked.

"The verb has to be subjunctive after 'whether.'"

"Can't say I remember the second person familiar present subjective."

"Ring it up to poetic license for the sake of the rhyme," I said.

"One way or another, I can imagine what this dude in England must have made of it."

"But if you read it without the metaphor, you can see why the police might have attributed a death wish to young Abby."

"I read it with the metaphor, and I confess that all this steamy poetry is turning me on. Will you consent to slay me?"

"With my mighty sword?"

"Else I must die by my own hand," Sheri said as she led me into the bedroom.

Chapter 8

Two days later I was back at The Cloister. Natalie Porter, my last student before lunch, hung around after her lesson and asked whether she could talk with me. I asked if she wanted to have lunch together at her dorm but she said she'd rather find a place where we could talk more privately than at an eight-person table. I offered to buy her lunch at The Buttery, the campus snack shop, and she looked pleased.

In her bell bottoms, striped blouse and loafers, Natalie looked pretty much like any of the other students. Some might have described her as a bit chubby, but she seemed at ease in her body and I had no right to judge.

Springtime at The Cloister brought memories of my annual visits to this most beautiful of all college campuses when the Amherst College Glee Club joined forces with the Cloister Chorale for the Doberman Memorial Concert. A wealthy alumna had endowed the college with a fund permitting the choral director to engage a pick-up orchestra each year to perform major choral works by Haydn, Mozart and, in my sophomore year, the Bruckner E Minor Mass. The combination of great music, an excellent choir, and the verdant campus—one year we came out of a rehearsal to see a rainbow arching over the college pond—proved completely seductive to an impressionable nineteen-year-old. Now, at least for one year, I could come here every week.

Though I would never again sing in the Doberman Memorial Concert, Boston offered other vocal opportunities. Just after Christmas a friend had asked whether I would sing tenor in a solo quartet performance of the Brahms Liebeslieder Waltzes, and in an access of conceit I agreed. The evening of the first rehearsal found us in the music room of an archetypal college professor's house, replete with chamber organ, harpsichord, clavichord, treble viol, par-desssus (descant) viol, viola da gamba, dulcimer, Rauschpfeife, Celtic harp, glockenspiel, crumhorn, and a Zeitter & Winkelmann (Dutch) grand piano. The owner of all these instruments performed on them with varying degrees of skill, ranging from the viols, on which he was said to be rather accomplished, to the grand piano, on which he was not. On this occasion our host functioned as one duo-pianist upon the grand piano, with results discomfiting to all. The other duo-pianist tried to keep him on the beat (he tended to lose it) but with limited success. It might have been more practical to transpose his part for viols. In the event, the piano made an interesting sparring partner for the text, turning gentle brooks into treacherous rapids. Cider and cookies after rehearsal were never more welcome.

The Buttery formed an annex to the administration building, with bright yellow drapes, old-fashioned ceiling fans, Formica-topped square tables and heart-backed metal chairs. Natalie and I got our plates from the short-order cook—no waitress service here—and found a table next to a window overlooking the pond.

"I hear you've been asking about Abby," Natalie said after taking a few bites of her club sandwich and evidently finding it satisfactory.

"Do you music majors maintain a permanent grapevine?" I asked.

Natalie grinned at me and said, "Pretty much."

"You knew her well?" I asked.

"We weren't all that close in high school," Natalie said, "but she became my best friend here."

I wondered whether Abby would have said the same about Natalie. I didn't know that much about Abby yet, but she seemed to have something in common with Claude Debussy, the subject of my scholarly studies, who tended to keep his friends quite separate from one another. On one occasion, discountenanced by some breach in his protective web, Debussy begged one of his friends not to tell another that they had dined together.

"So what can you tell me about Abby?" I asked.

"Abby always seemed to be waging one campaign after another."

I thought about Jessica's National Honor Society story and asked, "What was her latest target?"

Natalie reddened a bit, as if not having foreseen how this conversation might go. "I know you're a professor and all," she said, "but you seem sort of disconnected from the permanent faculty."

"I guess that describes it pretty well."

"So you're not going to feel compelled to repeat what I tell you?"

"Not if it doesn't pose a threat to anyone's physical well-being," I said.

Natalie looked relieved. "All right. I might as well level with you. I'm not exactly here by choice."

"No?"

"I wanted to go to Huntington with Jessica—she mentioned talking with you." I nodded. "But Daddy wouldn't hear of it. He has pretty high expectations." I nodded again. "So he pulled a few strings and here I am."

"You're doing fine in my tutorial," I said, "but can I infer that The Cloister may present challenges in other areas?"

"You 'infer' correctly," Natalie said and smiled, as if pleased with the use of an unaccustomed locution.

"That's too bad," I said. "Among other things, college is supposed to be fun."

Natalie gave a sigh and said, "It's not much fun when you have three papers due the same day, and even though you gave yourself plenty of time you could still finish only two of them."

"So what did you do?"

"There's this company that will supply essays for a fee. You're sure you're not going to report me?"

"Cross my heart," I said.

"I had to do a paper on Virginia Woolf and I just couldn't write it in time so I bought one of theirs. Got an A- on the paper, too."

"Don't the professors spot purchased essays?"

"That's the beauty of it," Natalie said with some enthusiasm. "You supply the company with a sample of your writing and they give you a paper that sounds as if you'd written it."

"Pretty ingenious," I said, "but what does this have to do with Abby?"

"When I told Abby about it she was appalled. She didn't blame me, really, except to say that she would have been happy to help me if I'd only come to her. Mostly she just thought it was wrong that such a situation should exist. She said that the college should provide a tutorial service so that students who get stuck in a bind wouldn't have to fall victim to such people."

41

"That sounds like Abby," I said. "So did she launch a campaign to start an assistance program?"

"No. She decided to go after SIP itself."

"SIP?"

"Sisterhood Is Powerful. I think even the name offended her. She talked about their having perverted the language of feminism."

"What did she do?"

"The outfit lists only a post office box, in order to protect itself, but Abby somehow managed to follow a student from the post office to the company's office in town where she confronted the owners."

"Really!"

"Yeah. She said they were two former members of The Cloister crew team—great big women that she nicknamed Tweedle Dum and Tweedle Dee."

"What happened?"

"She told them to cease and desist or she was going to write an exposé and publish it in the student paper."

"How did they take that?"

"They just laughed at her and threw her out of the office. As I said, they were pretty big and it was two against one."

"And all this took place in the fall?"

"Right. I don't know whether Abby had a chance to finish the article before she died."

"You mentioned that you'd known Abby in high school," I said. "What was she like then?"

Natalie hesitated a moment and then asked, "Do you think we could have some dessert?"

"A woman after my own heart," I said. "I saw some inviting blueberry pie on the way in. Would that do?"

"You read my mind," Natalie said.

I walked to the counter and came back with two servings of pie.

"Yums," Natalie said after tasting the first bite. After a few more bites she looked at me and said, "I'm not sure I should be telling you this. Say only good about the dead, my grandmother used to say."

"Abby did something bad? I asked.

"No, just the opposite. In a way Abby was too good."

"How do you mean?"

"Abby's father used to be big in Moral Re-Armament."

"Isn't that some kind of right-wing organization?"

"Not the way Abby described it. Evidently they played an important part in re-establishing normal diplomatic relations between France and Germany after the Second World War."

"I see."

"Abby once gave a speech about MRA at an assembly. They believe in correcting wrong throughout the world by acting on the four absolutes: honesty, purity, unselfishness and love."

"So what was the problem?" I asked.

"Abby would go around asking people, 'do you believe in absolute love?' I mean, what are you going to say? It got a little creepy."

"Might have been even worse if she'd asked about absolute purity! Was Abby involved in Moral Re-Armament?"

"Not as such, but when we were in junior high MRA spun off another group called Up With People."

"I think I've heard of that. Didn't they give concerts or something?"

"That's right."

"Did Abby perform with them?"

"Not while we were in high school, but when she went to England last year she sang with a group there."

"Do you think that's where she met her boyfriend?"

"Abby doesn't have a boyfriend." Natalie looked confused and maybe a bit crestfallen to have been left out of the loop.

"Perhaps I'm mistaken," I said. Natalie's earlier phrase about making things right in the world fit in with what I understood of Abby's involvement with Sisterhood Is Powerful.

We chatted a bit longer and then I headed back to the music building to meet my afternoon contingent of music majors.

Chapter 9

"LET ME GET THIS STRAIGHT," Sheri said as we talked after dinner. "This essay service would take samples of a student's writing and then tailor an essay to match her style."

"That's my understanding."

"But where did the essays come from in the first place?"

"That's the inspired part of the operation. Evidently the people who set it up realized that while the Seven Sister schools—Radcliffe, Smith, Mount Holyoke, Vassar, The Cloister, and the rest—each claim to be distinctive, in actuality they all offer pretty much the same curriculum and draw from a common pool of authors."

"I'm with you so far."

"According to Natalie, they employ what she called 'bounty hunters' in each of the schools to seek out any paper receiving a grade of A. You can see how it might work—a student would express admiration over another student's paper, ask to read it, copy the thing, and forward it on to the central office."

"Which is right there in Waban?"

"Yes. The bounty hunters get a generous fee for their labors so there's lots of incentive to locate A-level essays."

"Then what?"

"The central office gradually accumulates quite a repertory of essays on all the topics likely to be required at sister schools. For example, Natalie needed a paper on Virginia Woolf. That's bound to be a pretty popular topic at women's colleges."

"Every college wouldn't have every topic, but among them you could probably find what you were looking for."

"That's the idea. Evidently the only rule was that a paper could never go back to its place of origin, or be used more than once at any other college, since that might give the game away."

"But even so, wouldn't it require a lot of labor to re-edit and retype the essays? I should think that would make the service pretty expensive."

"True. It costs a lot more than companies that just provide canned essays. But students at the Seven Sisters tend to be pretty well off, and from the students' perspective, the style-fitting feature makes the scheme pretty much fool-proof."

"I've got just two questions."

"Shoot."

"Why are you getting mixed up in this?"

The sudden change of subject took me aback and I fumbled for an explanation. "I suppose because nobody else is."

"You were perfectly willing to accept Abby's suicide."

"Yes."

"But now that you think it may not be suicide, you feel compelled to turn detective."

"The more I learn about Abby, the more it seems we have in common. There's a part of me that objects when things aren't right."

"I think I understand that. You don't take personal offense at the existence of poverty in Boston, for example, because there's not a lot you personally can do about it, but if one of your students is murdered— and I'm assuming that's the conclusion you've come to—it offends you that no one else seems to care."

"I think that sums it up pretty well."

"But if the essays and checks are sent to a post office box, and the outfit hides in some undisclosed office space, how are you going to find them?"

"I thought I'd retrace Abby's steps. Somebody has to pick up the mail every day. It shouldn't require professional training to watch the post office box and follow whoever opens it."

"Sounds like a plan."

"What's the second question?"

"Would you like to go to a movie?"

"Oh Sheri, I'd love to, but I really have to finish the chapter I'm working on."

Sheri had seemed actively engaged in our conversation but now she turned her body away from me and said, "You're no fun anymore."

"Well, the way the academic world is set up, you have to write to succeed."

"I know the phrase: 'publish or perish.' If you ask me, it bears a sinister resemblance to another phrase: 'He who dies with the most toys wins.' Life is more than just amassing an impressive *curriculum vitae*, Axel."

"That's what the Latin means—how you run your life."

"But why run? What's wrong with enjoying life? Relationships are more important than accomplishments."

"Try telling that to a tenure committee. And where would culture be without accomplishments?"

"Axel, I hate to be negative, but who's really going to read these books you spend so much time writing?"

That stung. No one in academia challenged the validity of academic toil, but I guess the inherent value of scholarship might not be self-evident to someone on the outside. I searched for a suitable response. "I don't have any delusions of grandeur, but I like to think that I'm making a modest contribution."

"Do what you want. I'm going out."

And she did.

Chapter 10

"I've solved Abby's murder, Professor Crochet," announced Penny Lapworth when she arrived for her tutorial the following Tuesday.

"What's this about murder?" I asked.

"Oh don't be coy, Professor Crochet," she said. "Everybody knows you're trying to find out who murdered Abby Fox."

"Really?"

"You can't expect to keep secrets around here." Not from Penny, at any rate.

"Let's say for the sake of argument that you were right. Why would anyone want to murder Abby?"

"Because of the mid-terms. She died just before mid-term exams."

"I'm really not following this, Penny. Now either you present your ideas in an orderly fashion or I'm going to ask you to walk in the door again and pretend this conversation never happened."

Penny didn't look as if she believed me for a minute, but she did pause to gather her thoughts. "All right. You know about the 80% rule."

"No, you've lost me already."

"The Cloister has a rule that if a student has an 80% average or better in a course, she doesn't have to take the exams. The rule applies both to mid-terms and finals."

"I understand that part, but I don't see what it has to do with Abby."

"There are two girls in her English course that have to get A's in order to get into med school."

"You're talking about their final marks?"

"No," Penny said impatiently. "Their mid-term marks. The med schools send out acceptances before Christmas and The Cloister holds its final exams after Christmas, so they have to rely on mid-terms."

"Okay. Keep going."

"Now the professor in this course marks strictly on the curve. You understand the curve?"

"Don't patronize me, Penny."

"Sorry, but I never know what you're going to misunderstand."

"He gives an A to the top 10% of students."

"20%. And it's a she."

"Okay. 20%. So where is this all leading?"

"Well, Abby has the highest mark in the class."

That didn't surprise me, so I simply nodded for Penny to go on.

"But she didn't believe in the 80% rule. She thought that everybody should be treated alike."

That also sounded like Abby. "This is all very interesting, well, maybe not all that interesting, but what does it have to do with your rather dramatic announcement?"

"You can understand that getting into med school is a very big deal for some students."

"I suppose so."

"So do the math. If Abby doesn't take the mid-term, and of course the way things turned out she couldn't, these students, who have a B+ average at best, get an A on the exam and that can make the difference in their whole future."

"Is that what happened?"

"Almost. One girl got into her first choice of med school and the other had to settle for her back-up."

"'Whereas if Abby had taken the exam ...'"

"She gets an A, the other students get B's, and good-bye med school."

"So you're saying that these students killed Abby?"

"Seems pretty obvious now that I've laid it all out, doesn't it?"

"And I suppose you've investigated their alibis for the night of Abby's death?"

"No, you're the detective. I'm just telling you how it had to have happened."

"Penny, I am not a detective. I think you're letting your imagination run away with you. To begin with, university admissions depend on more than just grade point averages."

Penny looked crestfallen. "I suppose you could say I'm living proof," she said.

"How do you mean?"

"I'm a legacy. I mean, we can't all be as smart as Abby Fox."

"A legacy?"

"My mother and grandmother both went to The Cloister and mom's the head of the Cambridge branch of The Cloister Alumnae Association. That's how I got in."

"Be that as it may, I think you see the point. I hope you haven't gone about accusing these young women."

"No, I saved the news for you. I thought you'd be excited."

Sounds emerged faintly from piano practice rooms. Beginner scales, novice exercises, and the occasional accomplished sonata brought to mind Debussy's "Doctor Gradus ad Parnassum," reputedly an evocation of students practicing in the Paris Conservatoire.

My conversation with Penny didn't seem to be getting anywhere so I tried leading the discussion in a different direction. "I get the impression that you wish you and Abby could have been closer."

Penny looked at the floor. "I just wanted her to be my friend."

"And that didn't work?"

"No. For instance, last spring Professor Falgarwood held an afternoon gathering at his house for all the music majors."

"Did he let you listen to a recording of him performing on the Sweelinck organ?"

"How did you know?"

"Just a wild guess."

"Anyway, he asked us to pair off for a game of musical chairs."

"Isn't that a bit quaint?"

"Well, I guess you could call Professor Falgarwood a bit quaint. Anyway, I was really hoping Abby would choose me."

"But she didn't."

"No. She calculated that with an odd number of people one person wouldn't be needed to partner, so she helped refill the punch bowl instead."

"Perhaps Abby just didn't care for parlor games."

"No. I think she just liked to be helpful."

"What else can you tell me about your relationship with Abby?"

"Well, for my twenty-first birthday I organized a big party, and when I told Abby about it she sounded really enthusiastic. Of course, she didn't actually promise to come."

"But you hoped she would."

From the look of disappointment on Penny's face, the event might just as well have occurred the day before. "She probably had something important that prevented her from coming."

"No doubt," I said. It didn't seem as if Abby had much patience for the Penny's of the world. "Why don't we put the sleuthing aside for the time being and see if you can sing the twelve-tone row you wrote?"

Penny shrugged her shoulders. I don't think she accepted my reservations for a minute, but I was still the teacher.

Chapter 11

I REMAINED AT THE CLOISTER after classes at the behest of the chairman, who had extended an invitation to dine at his house. In the absence of a real office to call my own, I went to the music library to do some work. On the way I heard some students chattering excitedly about a recital to be given that evening by a visiting violinist. We seen our share of musical stars during my graduate school days at Cornell. One season, Van Cliburn had to postpone a concert due to illness. The rescheduled concert came just ten days after a recital by Artur Rubenstein, an unusual juxtaposition that permitted a direct comparison of the two performers. Rubenstein had included Chopin's Polonaise Héroïque within his program and gave it an exalted, almost reverential, rendition. Van Cliburn played the same piece as an encore, striking the opening octaves almost before being fully seated on the piano bench and then tossing the piece off as simply a vehicle for displaying his formidable technique.

I guess musical performance stirs the soul of an aficionado the same way that a brilliant athletic accomplishment inspires cheers in a crowd of followers. One time in Boston I ran into a musician friend and we compared notes on concerts we had attended. A peculiar woman of indeterminate age, dressed all in black with a fur around her neck, interrupted us and went on for fifteen minutes to describe, in a heavy Austrian accent, how much it meant to her to hear people talking about music in the midst of this dunghill (a term that came up half a dozen times in the course of her monologue) and what an absolute passion she had for music, which provided the sustenance of her life, the only thing that enabled her to continue, day after day, living, as she did, in a dunghill.

Newton Falgarwood exerted sufficient influence among the rich and the powerful at The Cloister to raise several hundred thousand dollars to build a Sweelinck organ, named for the Dutch composer who died in 1621. Of course to be truly authentic the instrument had to be tuned in mean-tone temperament which rendered it inappropriate to later works. Only Falgarwood could have conceived—and then actually realized—a gigantic pipe organ on which you couldn't play the works of J.S. Bach!

Professor Falgarwood, for whom music worth studying ended in the early 17th century, made an exception for Mozart, whose piano concertos he taught according to a meticulous classification system whereby students would mark the scores with abbreviations. To satisfy the professor's requirements students were expected to write PTT (pre-tutti trill), PRA (playful rondo anticipation) and FIR (filled-in rest) in appropriate spots, and in case they missed any, the chairman had created rubber stamps to fill in omitted labels such as CKSR (change of key in sonata recapitulation) or EOMF (embellishment of the original melodic figure).

I arrived at Professor Falgarwood's residence at the appointed hour and was admitted by his partner Jean. We entered a living room decorated with dark drapes and heavy furniture centering on two grand pianos arranged in the *soixante-neuf* position. (Were they expected to propagate baby grands?) By contrast the kitchen, where we ate supper, was all white, with windows on two walls looking out at a grove of trees.

Trees, as it turned out, formed the principal topic of conversation, both Jean and Newton so devoted to the welfare of The Cloister's arboreal population that after a particularly heavy snowfall they had gone out to release each branch of its burden, lest it succumb beneath the weight. Over dinner they expressed indignation over the college's announced intention of cutting down half a dozen trees in order to expand a parking lot. I had never before witnessed such volatility in a conversation whose participants *agreed* with each other. Passions rose to such a point that Jean said, "I think it's time for an M.I."

"An M.I. Just the thing," said Falgarwood, who led us into the living room.

An M.I., as I soon learned, meant a musical interlude, and my presence permitted a performance that the two had clearly been anticipating, as they pulled out two copies of Bach's Trio Sonatas for organ. Jean sat at one grand piano to play the alto line, in octaves. Falgarwood, seated on the left at the other grand piano, performed the pedal part while I was expected to play the soprano line, always in octaves. I have never heard a more grotesque performance of Bach.

At the end of the evening, as Jean withdrew to the kitchen and Falgarwood led me to the door, the chairman put his hand on my arm and said, "You understand that the terms of your engagement call on you to enhance the musicianship of our music majors, not to meddle in affairs that, strictly speaking, are none of your concern. The Cloister abhors negative publicity." Before I had a chance to reply, he graciously bade me good evening and shut the door.

Chapter 12

THE NEXT DAY, AFTER ANOTHER hour vainly endeavoring to engage my stone-faced students at Huntington University, I took the trolley to Harvard Square for a meeting with representatives from G. K. Hall. In the course of transforming my dissertation into book form I had noticed that this Boston publisher had issued monographs not only on Poe, Baudelaire, Verlaine and Mallarmé, who fell within my purview of literary figures who had influenced Debussy, but on virtually every writer you could name. Why not a comparable series on composers, I wondered? And who better to write the volume on Debussy than Axel Crochet, bearded musicologist? A telephone call led to a letter which led to this meeting at the Pewter Pot.

One might argue that with so many authentic early colonial buildings in the Boston area it would be superfluous to add an ersatz replica. And it was easy to make fun of the fake beams in the ceiling, the wooden window shutters and the waitresses outfitted in long skirts and mob caps. But the restaurant's muffins proved to be a popular alternative to the prevailing doughnuts and the Cambridge community had embraced the enterprise as its own.

The carpeted floor muffled the sounds of conversation and reduced the normal restaurant noises of clattering plates and jangling silverware. Even the cloth napkins contributed to the peaceful acoustical setting.

The two representatives sent by the publisher, an earnest young man and an effusive young woman, were waiting at a table when I arrived. After we had exchanged pleasantries and placed our orders, I began to speak about my vision of Claude Debussy as the true father of twentieth-century music and my desire to explicate this thesis with detailed musical analyses and carefully-presented technical arguments. The earnest young man and the effusive young woman exchanged glances.

"While we respect your lofty academic ambitions," he said, "we hope you will be able to balance these goals with the practical concerns of a commercial venture."

"More sex?" I asked. The effusive young woman looked slightly flustered. "Concentrate on the historical warp and let the analysis woof for itself?" I asked. The earnest young man looked slightly confused.

"Debussy's best friend, Pierre Louÿs, once described spending an afternoon in the company of naked ladies, referring to the contemporary craze for *tableaux vivants*," I said.

"Naked is good," said the earnest young man.

"In 1903 Debussy abandoned his wife and fled with his mistress to the Isle of Jersey, an escapade he commemorated in a piano piece in which his usual reticence gave way to outright rapture," I said.

"Rapture is good," said the effusive young woman.

"In 1908 Debussy married the mother of his three-year-old daughter Chouchou ("little bastard"), for whom Debussy composed his Kitchen Cupboard Suite, with titles based on familiar children's songs: Dr. Blossom Ate a Possum; Rimbaud's Lullaby; The Smog Is Lifting; Serenade of the Streetwalker; The Little Absinthe Drinker; and the familiar Let 'Em Eat Cakewalk."

"What about chapter titles?" asked the effusive young woman.

"I was thinking along the lines of 'One Cadence Is Not Enough,' 'Valley of the Subdominants,' and 'Bitonality and Bisexuality,'" I said.

"I think we understand each other," the earnest young man said as he pushed a contract across the table for me to sign. We finished our muffins amid smiles of mutual satisfaction.

When I returned to the apartment that evening I found Sheri's response to this triumph a trifle disappointing. "Two books at the same time!" she said. "You've got to be kidding."

"One of them is nearly finished," I said in my defense.

"You know, I'm really concerned for you, Axel," Sheri said. "You and your endless to-do lists. You go through each activity as fast as you can in order to check it off and get to the next."

"Lists have always been my defense against Parkinson's Law."

"What's that?"

"'Work expands to fill the time allotted to it.' If you have all morning to dust the piano, piano-dusting will take all morning."

"So you figure that by cramming in as much stuff as you possibly can you can hold this Parkinson person at bay?"

"Something like that."

"What about valuing process more than product so you can actually enjoy your life?"

"Well ..."

"The course you're on—always hurrying to get the next thing done—could be seen as a race to the grave. Surely you don't believe that the person who dies first wins?"

I had to admit that Sheri had a point. Then I thought of American Musicological Society meetings I'd attended where scholars who had failed to land the Ivy League positions they coveted tried to justify their existence before colleagues who had actually made it. "I submitted an article," they would begin pathetically, as it finally dawned on them that the academic world cared not a whit that they might be good fathers or husbands or soccer coaches or church deacons, or that they might have advanced a few more steps in the direction of inner peace. But I had trouble explaining all this to Sheri. We did not make love that evening.

Chapter 13

PENNY LAPWORTH WAS WAITING FOR me when I arrived at The Cloister the next morning. "You've got to listen to this, Professor Crochet. This time I really know why Abby was murdered."

I sighed and let her into the room I used for tutorials. "Penny, I have only few minutes before I see my first student."

"This won't take long, but it's sort of complicated."

"I suppose you'll continue pestering me until I listen, so I might as well hear it now."

My show of reluctance seemed to have been wasted because Penny plunged ahead as if I had been breathless with anticipation. "It's because of racism."

"This sounds even more far-fetched than the mid-term theory."

"No, really. Listen. Last spring Abby waged a campaign against racism at The Cloister. She pointed out that we have scarcely any students of African-American persuasion."

"Surely she didn't put it like that, but I do see your point. The Cloister isn't completely lily-white, but comes pretty close."

"So she was pushing the admissions office to change its policy."

"You don't think they really had an anti-black policy?"

"It's more subtle than that. Can you follow some more math?"

I stifled a groan and said, "I suppose so."

"Okay. Now any girl with top grades, glowing recommendations, and a decent community service record is going to get accepted into The Cloister regardless of race, right?"

"That makes sense."

"But all the Seven Sisters schools are competing for the same students. So if you want any particular quality—a viola player, a field hockey star, or, in this case, a black student—you're going to have to lower your academic requirements."

"It sounds kind of cynical, but I see your point."

"But you can't draft all the viola players, field hockey stars or black students you'd like, because that would lower the overall academic standard."

"I'm not sure I agree with you, but let's say you're right."

"Then put it this way—you can only admit so many academically second-tier students before the whole college becomes second tier."

"And this means that ..."

"There's intense competition among interest groups for second-tier students."

"I guess that makes sense."

"And what's the largest, most vocal interest group of second-tier students?"

"I can't guess."

"Me!"

"You?"

"Legacy students. You know. Girls whose mothers and grandmothers attended The Cloister. You try to reduce that quota and all hell is going to break loose."

"So this is where Abby comes in?"

"You bet. She hadn't gotten anywhere with the former administration but the new president was touched by Abby's idealism and agreed to let her speak to the Admissions Committee when they met in the fall to determine quotas for the coming year."

This fit with what I knew of President Clearwater, whose announced intention of bringing a breath of change to this tradition-bound institution probably included a rebalancing of its racial composition. "And let me guess—Abby died just before this meeting was to take place."

"You got it."

"And you think that the head of The Cloister Legacy Association, or whatever it's called, murdered Abby?"

"She wouldn't do it herself—she'd get someone else to do it. Someone like my mother, for example."

"Your mother?"

"I don't know where she was that night. Do you?"

"Penny, this is ridiculous."

"It would only be ridiculous if Abby were still alive. But someone killed her, and this makes more sense than any other explanation. I mean, do you have a better solution?"

"No, but ..."

"So this one will have to do until you find one. Do you plan to ask my mother for an alibi?"

"Penny, you keep forgetting that I have nothing to do with the police."

"Of course not; the police think it was a suicide. It's up to you to prove them wrong."

"That may or not be true, but I can assure you that asking your mother for an alibi is not going to improve the situation."

"Whoops. Here's your first student. I'd better leave." And off she went, full of misplaced self-assurance.

Despite annoyances like Penny Lapworth or the stubbornly unresponsive Huntington students, I found this year infinitely preferable to last. In the fall I found that I'd been drafted into the army of the unemployed. Now the Massachusetts bureaucracy cannot hope to compete with, say, the Paris bureaucracy. The French have developed the art of delay to the point that you almost believe the endless shuttling from one office to the next is actually getting you closer to your destination. This, of course, is sheer deception. The French term is *leger-de-main*, lightness of hand, in other words the clerk can shuffle papers faster than you eye can follow. But the Massachusetts bureaucracy made up in sheer inertia what it lacked in elegance.

A clerk would walk twenty feet to a bin, pull out an 8 x 11 sheet, walk twenty feet back to the counter, adjust his stool, pull out a pencil, sharpen it, line it up next to the card, and finally read the name on the sheet in a high-pitched voice. Receiving no response (after awhile people would get impatient and leave), he would climb down off the stool, walk twenty feet to the bin, withdraw another sheet, return to the counter, climb back up on the stool and light a cigarette. Halfway through the cigarette he would motion to a security guard who would amble over to the counter. (The place crawled with security guards.) The two would chat for awhile. The clerk would finish his cigarette then call the name on the second sheet. It was my name. I would scuttle up to the desk, answer a few questions, carry the card to the end of a very long line, and when I finally reached the front, I would be given a time and told to reappear a week later.

Eventually I was granted an interview, after which a secretary presented me with a magic card, filled with pin holes, covered with rainbows and mushrooms decorating a mandala, which emitted a soft purple glow. "Give this card to the Tooth Fairy who lives under the Yum-Yum Tree at the end of Counter 3," she told me. I was strongly tempted to take a bite from the side marked "Eat Me," but was deterred by the boldfaced instructions: "Do Not Hold, Rape, Fondle or Masticate."

The Tooth Fairy smiled as she rolled my card into a cylinder, covered it with Vaseline and pushed it gently into the folds of the waiting cashbox. Then the heavens parted and a golden light encircled me. "It's coming down on you," she murmured. Nine seconds later the cashbox clicked, blinked, moaned softly, and delivered three checks, drawn on the Left Bank of the Charles. "Come back with your card next week and we'll do it again," the Fairy winked. Actually, I'm fantasizing. Unemployment wasn't nearly this much fun.

One day I received a call asking if there were a musicologist in the house. Yes, I replied. Good, said the voice, which belonged to the chairman of the music department at what I will call Open Admissions University.

"One of our teachers has had a nervous breakdown and we need someone to take her classes for the rest of the term, teaching first year theory, ear training, keyboard technique, and field hockey. Are you interested?"

"Well, I don't know," I answered. "I have this thing going with a Tooth Fairy downtown but I'll think it over."

A few days later I appeared in coat and tie for my interview. "Say something for us in music theory," one of them demanded.

"*The purpose of an analysis (or a composition) is to reconstruct (or construct) a musical structure. We bother to reify "analysis" (and "composition") and "analytical methods" ("compositional methods" or "techniques") because of the conviction, reinforced by confirming practice, that, beginning from the simplest levels of intersubjective auditory experience, pieces are constructible most favorably up to a certain point though hierarchical functional paths that point through increasingly divergent, coherently subdivided paths, up, finally, to the singular stem: the individual piece,*" I said, quoting from *Perspectives of New Music*, my favorite cure for insomnia.

"What did he say?" whispered the voice teacher (voice teachers don't speak music theory). "I'm not sure, but I think it had something to do with I-IV-V-I," answered a multilingual musicologist.

"I think Mr. Crochet's qualifications are in order," said the chairman. "Let's go right to the Ultimate Questions. Do you prefer peanut butter smooth or crunchy?"

"Crunchy."

"Do you eat ice cream cones with jimmies or without?"

"With."

"Do you believe in the Infinite Perfectibility of Fifths, the Unredeemable Sinfulness of the Tritone, the Resolution of all Dissonances, and the Light at the End of the Tunnel?"

"I do."

"Do you promise to Observe all Rests, Raise all Leading Tones, Renounce Cross Relations, Avoid Deceptive Cadences, and forbear to use the first note in the row until all the other eleven have been exhausted, now and forever, Mass Transit Gloria Mundi?"

"I do."

"Then I proclaim you a member of the Glorious Company of True Deceivers, and entitle you to perform the miracle of transsubdomination, whereby the ignorance which spills from your lips will become truth in the notebooks of generations of students to come."

"Huzzah!" cried the multitude, as they shook my hand with the secret grip and the last rays of the sun cast freckled hexachords on the wall.

Or so I imagined it. The reality was much less colorful. Before long I settled into the routine of teaching four courses. In "Second Year Elements" students came in for individual half-hour piano lessons once a week starting at 8:00 a.m. The first students seldom showed up so I had a chance to read at least the front page of The New York Times. The others had ingenious explanations of why they hadn't practiced since their last lesson. I wish I could say I made this up, but I have neither the audacity nor the imagination for it.

- The piano broke when she was moving it from one room of the house to another, and the piano technician couldn't come before the middle of next month, but she had been thinking about all the things I said last time. (Shades of Professor Harold Hill's "think system" in *The Music Man*.)

- Everything you learn helps everything else, right, so that hours I spent on my new jazz composition are helping me even though it took all my practice time this week.

- This has been an emotionally disturbing week. (Amen)

- I forgot. (I think I liked this one best of all.)

The First Year Theory class suffered under the disadvantage of a succession of temporary substitutes preceding me, the more or less permanent substitute. My first act in office was to give a diagnostic test to see what they knew. Out of a possible twenty musical skills (writing key signatures, identifying intervals, hearing triads, etc.), each worth one point on the test, the class of two dozen students scored a *total* of 36 points. In the three weeks that followed, the class's aggregate score rose 200%, but unevenly, so that some students could demonstrate fifteen skills while others still had none. Once a week some student I had never seen before would turn up to announce that he had just gotten out of the hospital, or detox, or whatever, and demand to know what he needed to do to get an A in the course.

The First Year Elements class consisted of five regulars and a bunch of people who never came at all. The class protested vigorously when I told them that they had to practice. "We all work," they said, "and we don't have pianos at home and the school closes at five." We arranged a compromise whereby I would holler at them for not practicing and they would ignore me.

The Sightsinging and Eartraining class was theoretically an adjunct to First Year Theory, but in practice the two classes were mutually exclusive. Half the class just looked at me, smiled, and shook its collective head when I asked it to sightsing; the other half never showed up at all.

One of the students asked me the purpose of the music department. I had to confess that I didn't know, but would try to find out. "Are they trying to turn out performers?" she asked.

"Not likely, since no one practices," I said.

"Well, if they can't play an instrument," she persisted, "they must be scholars."

"But they don't know anything about music, so they can't be scholars."

"Then they must be teachers," she said, and I had to agree.

Chapter 14

THE WABAN POST OFFICE WAS a fifties-modern structure with waist-high red brick followed by white-painted wood and glass. Plate glass windows on the front wall afforded a complete view of the interior: a counter on the left, an array of mailboxes on the right, arranged to offer postal workers easy access from behind. The left wall contained bulletin boards with public announcements, forthcoming stamps and wanted criminals; the right wall held a large framed quilt above a plaque describing it as the product of a community-wide project celebrating the town's centennial. A chest-high table in the middle of the room offered space for addressing envelopes and a small calendar (assisted by a large clock over the mailboxes) for the benefit of those who had difficulty keeping track of the time. Not a chair in the room: evidently post office policy discouraged loitering.

The first time I visited the post office, thinking I could simply keep an eye on the mailbox whose number Natalie Porter had provided, I went through the motions of addressing and stamping a letter, reading the criminal announcements and admiring the centennial quilt for fifteen minutes without spotting any SIP personnel, although I was surprised to see a large number of students from The Cloister. When I noticed Wendy Atwater among their number, I approached her.

"What's everyone doing at the post office?" I asked. "Don't students receive mail at their dorms?"

"Yeah, they deliver mail there, but all the stuff goes into a big basket on the table in the front hall."

"I would think that was more convenient than coming over here."

"But less private. A lot of the girls don't want their dorm-mates seeing where their personal mail is coming from, if you know what I mean."

That may have explained the exclamations of delight and occasional high-pitched giggles I heard as young women opened the contents of their cubbyholes, more likely to be *billets doux* than bills. Of course the presence of all those undergraduates also made my job more difficult. I hadn't spent more than fifteen minutes in the post office lobby before a clerk asked me to state my business, although he didn't express himself quite that way.

"Hey, Mac!" he barked.

"Are you addressing me?"

"What are you doing here?"

"This is a public building."

"That may be, but it's intended for post office business, not a place to pick up girls."

"Sir, many of these young women are my students."

"Yeah, Mac. I saw you talking with one of them. What, are you trying to expand the field?'

"I resent your implication."

"Be that as it may, the United States government isn't running a dating service here."

"But I ..."

"Beat it, Mac."

I briefly considered obtaining a pair of binoculars to watch the mailbox from outside the building but decided it would make me even more conspicuous. How did private eyes get away with surreptitious surveillance?

On my second visit I hit upon the clever stratagem of actually renting a post office box, a process I succeeded in extending to considerable length by posing the kinds of questions more appropriate to someone twice my age confused by early dementia. The clerk probably thought I was a nut, but the exercise gave me a legitimate excuse for being in the building. Still no one from SIP.

On my third visit I spotted several pieces of mail through the clear plastic door of the SIP box, and by means of an elaborate charade—checking and rechecking my own mailbox, looking at the time, searching for coins in my wallet, going outside pretending to feed the parking meter, returning to check the mailbox again—succeeded in observing a young woman open the SIP mailbox, remove its contents, and leave the post office.

At this point I made a critical error. In retrospect I ought to have remained in my reluctant role as amateur sleuth and allowed the young woman to lead me unawares to her destination. Instead, overeager at discovering a clue, I accosted her on the street, identified myself as a member of the college faculty and demanded she take me to the office on pain of being reported to the college administration. In the short run, at least, the plan succeeded and she took me down a side street to a building of office suites and up one flight of stairs to an unmarked door, where she gave a series of knocks in a pre-arranged pattern and was admitted.

The room, designed for utility more than hospitality, had no comfortable chairs for waiting customers, no artwork on the wall, no plush rugs or attractive window treatments, no side tables covered with magazines. One entire wall was lined with filing cabinets in a forbidding gun-metal gray. Tables on an adjoining wall held half a dozen typewriters, a number of apparently college-age young women making the balls of the IBM Selectrics whir. The opposite wall had windows and a door evidently leading to an inner office. Young women at other tables were marking up typed manuscripts and comparing them with other documents. At my entrance all activity ceased and my unwilling guide announced, "It wasn't my fault; he made me let him in."

Before long the door of the inner office opened and out strode two large women: Tweedle Dum and Tweedle Dee, I surmised, both in blue jeans, one wearing a blue Cloister Crew sweatshirt, the other a crimson Harvard sweatshirt, one with light brown hair cropped quite short, the other with darker brown hair tied back in a pony tail. "This office is not open to the public," one said in a voice evidently accustomed to giving orders.

"Perhaps we could talk privately," I suggested.

"Do you have a banana in your ear?" asked the other. "She said get out."

"I thought we might discuss a certain red, bushy-tailed carnivore," I said.

The first woman kept coming forward but her companion understood the reference to Abby Fox and grudgingly directed me to the back office.

We entered the small space. No one offered me a seat so I delivered my message standing. "The two of you were seen entering Jewitt Tower on the night of Abby's death," I began. This wasn't true, at least not to my knowledge, but they had no way of knowing that.

The woman in the Cloister Crew sweatshirt threatened to call the police if I didn't leave at once.

"That's not a bad suggestion," I said. "I imagine the police will probably be interested in the operation you're running here as well as reopening the case of Abby's death."

Certain that this would stop the pair dead in their tracks, I was surprised to see the woman in the Harvard sweatshirt reach over to tap on the window to the main office. Several young women appeared and escorted me out the front entrance. This hadn't gone quite as I'd planned.

Two days later, when I returned to The Cloister, I discovered a message from the music department chairman requesting that I meet with him at the conclusion of the day. What was this about? After seeing my students—happily Penny Lapworth wasn't among them—I proceeded to the chairman's office.

Newton Falgarwood's office displayed the seemingly obligatory framed parchment of Gregorian chant but no filing cabinets and no work table covered with photocopied manuscripts. Falgarwood actually studied and thought about music, but wrote strangely about it. The same labeling technique that he insisted on in student "analyses" pervaded his academic studies, but he had a tendency to seize on details in widely separated works and then link them with the same dogged determination, insane cleverness and ultimate futility with which a paranoiac knits together a bizarre picture of the world. The hospitality of the evening we had spent together had entirely disappeared and the absence of a smile made his strange hair style appear downright threatening.

"Sit down, Crochet," he began. No Axel this time. He began to pace back and forth as if uncertain how to begin. "Sexual harassment is a serious charge in any context," he said at last, "but nowhere more so than in a women's college." I began to protest but he silenced me with a hand gesture. "I have to say that I opposed your engagement from the start. It seems to me that employing young unmarried male professors to teach nubile undergraduate women is just asking for trouble. I was overruled by those bedazzled by your credentials. Now, however, it appears that I was correct in my misgivings. I understand that a young man like yourself might not be immune to feminine charm, but I would have thought that by this point in your career you would have learned to exercise a certain measure of self-control. What do you have to say for yourself?"

"Can you at least give me the name of the complainant?" I asked. Falgarwood did. I'd never heard of her. "That's not even one of my students," I said.

"It's not enough to become enamored of one of the young ladies in your charge," Falgarwood said, "but to harass a general member of the student body strikes me as the behavior of someone utterly lacking in discretion."

"I never even talk to students other than music majors," I protested.

"Then it seems all the more unlikely that the complaint would be frivolous," he said.

"I never ..."

"I'm sure you understand the venerable Latin phrase *in loco parentis*. I may be old-fashioned but I believe that the parents who entrust their daughters to our care at The Cloister assume 'in the place of a parent' to mean a good parent and not an incestuous one."

"Now really ..."

"When I offered you a word to the wise the other evening, I assumed that that would be the end of it. I never dreamt that your perverted interest in that poor Fox child, one might even use the word 'necrophilia' ..."

"May I say something?"

"I assumed that my advice would have set you back on the right track, but you persisted in your folly."

"That's not fair."

"I believe I've done the best I could, and I will be able to look back at my handling of this situation with a clear conscience."

"But ..."

"No, don't thank me. I was only carrying out my responsibilities to the best of my abilities with my conscience as my guide."

"Thank you?"

"Needless to say, if you had entertained any hopes of obtaining a permanent position here at The Cloister you must abandon them."

"Is this an official reprimand, going into my record?" I asked.

"I'm afraid it is. You will, of course, be permitted to finish out the remaining few weeks of your appointment."

Falgarwood clearly had no interest in listening to my protestations but I waited to see whether he had anything else to say. Only a curt nod indicated that the chairman wished to terminate the interview.

As I left the music building I caught sight of Natalie Porter headed in the direction of the dormitory. I caught up with her and asked whether I might take a look at her copy of the pictorial directory of students (referred to demeaningly in men's colleges as the 'pig book'). As we walked I described my misadventure at the SIP headquarters, omitting all reference to my uncomfortable interview with the chairman.

"So you actually found the place," she said. "I'm impressed."

"But it didn't get me anywhere," I said. "They seemed immune to threats."

"That's what Abby said."

When we reached Natalie's room she produced the student directory and I had no difficulty locating the name of the student I had allegedly harassed. I guess I should not have been surprised to see the face of the young woman whom I had followed to the SIP office. Sexual harassment charges are easy to lay but difficult to refute.

On the long ride from Woodland to Boston I reflected on Sheri's words and decided she had a point. My insistence on investigating Abby's death, without training or official standing, had led only to disappointment. I didn't think Newton Falgarwood would broadcast a groundless sexual harassment charge, but one could never be sure. I found Sheri's arguments for relationship vs. accomplishment troubling. Ultimately I didn't think one had to choose between one and the other, but it struck me that if you gave your partner only the time left over after you'd met all your responsibilities, you weren't likely to have much of a relationship. The key probably lay in scheduling couple time like anything else, and I planned to tell her this, but when I got to the apartment there was no Sheri, no suitcases, and no note.

Chapter 15

TWO DAYS LATER, WITH NOTHING to draw me homeward after my lessons at The Cloister, I had a milkshake at The Buttery and tried to retrace Abby's steps on her last evening of life. Abby climbed to the top of Jewitt Tower every evening to lock the door to the carillon, so I did the same, noting that this part of the tower, being open to the public, offered no impediments to her murderers. (Somehow the idea of raising an unwilling conscious victim over an elevated railing made the notion of a single assassin seem unlikely.) Would the two heavy-set women I had encountered in the SIP office have readily made this climb, I wondered? Then I reflected that the Cloister crew team quite likely trained on these very stairs.

Having reached the top of the public area, I tried to imagine a place of concealment. The practice keyboard lay in an open gallery just to the side of the tower's central shaft and didn't afford much cover. The only place I could think of to hide was in the narrow space behind the practice carillon. From that vantage point one couldn't be seen by anyone heading toward the door leading to the final spiral staircase.

I eased behind the practice keyboard. In the dust I could make out footprints. Whoever swept the tower floors hadn't penetrated to this obscure corner. And spider webs. I really hated spider webs. I took a deep breath and crept on. The footprints bore an unusual design: an Escher-like pattern of fish swimming in opposite directions. Must have been some kind of running shoe, I imagined. I'd noticed a sports shop in the village. Perhaps I could learn more there. I walked down the six flights of stairs and across the campus to the village.

"GOOD SPORT, W.H. Good, Proprietor," read the sign of the small sports boutique on Waban's main street. A bell tinkled as I opened the door. Racks of clothes extended on both sides of a passageway to the sales counter. In Boston this counter would have been placed nearer the entrance to discourage thieves from grabbing garments and running out of the store.

Past the clothing one could see wall shelves with a wide variety of sporting equipment ranging from skis and poles, apparently left over from winter, to fishing gear and hiking boots. An area of open wall displayed posters and photos of various sporting figures.

Behind the counter stood a sandy-haired figure whom I took to be W. H. Good himself, a supposition confirmed by the thin brass label pinned to his shirt pocket. I wondered how anyone could actually sell sports equipment while wearing a bow tie, but maybe it worked for him; who knew?

Noticing the blown-up photograph of spring skiing at Tuckerman Ravine on Mt. Washington, I asked the proprietor whether he had ever skied there. "Yes," he said, "but that was many years ago."

"I've climbed the Tuckerman Trail in summer," I said, "but I've never gotten up the nerve to hike up there in winter."

"Every year some damn fool injures or kills himself skiing over the headwall," he said, "but you can have a good time if you take proper safety precautions."

"Still, I think I'll stick to regular ski areas," I said.

"So what brings you here? You don't seem to be too interested in the merchandise."

"I was hoping that you could tell me something about a sports shoe." I described the design of the footprint I'd seen in Jewitt Tower.

"Oh, yes. Nike made that shoe a few years ago. Didn't sell many. They've been doing a lot better with what they call the "waffle trainer" that Bill Bowerman designed for them last year. You'll see the latest models over there on the shelf."

"So the fish design didn't catch on?"

"Can't say it did. Of course the college bought up quite a few of them for the crew team. I guess they thought it would give them a better grip on wet surfaces."

"Did it work?"

"I never received any complaints so maybe they did."

Having seen a photograph of Roger Bannister celebrating his achievement, two decades earlier, running the first sub-four-minute mile, I asked Mr. Good whether he had run track.

"That was a long time ago. I used to run the 800. Set a high school record that lasted for a couple of years." A smile took years off his face and he seemed to disappear briefly into the glory days of a bygone era. Then the tinkle of the bell indicating another customer brought him abruptly back to the present and he excused himself.

Chapter 16

ACCORDING TO THE LARGE CLOCK mounted on a pole outside the sports boutique I just had time to get to the Step Sing at Memorial Chapel. Natalie Porter had urged me to attend, and since I'd missed the Junior Show I figured I owed her one.

The campus glowed with the comforting light of dozens of artfully placed lamps, which illuminated the leaves above them and cast beams on the pathways below. No student at The Cloister need fear the dark.

I'd forgotten the sheer size of Memorial Chapel, with its Tiffany glass at the north and south entrances, the tower rising from the middle of the building, and the broad main entrance with its wrought iron gates. On the steps leading up to the doorway stood what must have been more than a hundred undergraduates, all dressed in purple, each holding a songbook. Natalie had told me that in the old days the students knew all the college songs by heart. Now the students needed an *aide-mémoire* as they followed the direction of the song-mistress standing on a wooden platform at the base of the steps. I recognized some of my music major students among their number.

When the purple-clad group had finished their program and begun to file off the steps, to be replaced by a similar cohort arrayed in red, organized cheers arose from the multitude of students in front of the steps. I had difficulty understanding the words but I gathered from the tone that the cheers formed a kind of affectionate heckling of those who had just performed.

I cast my eyes around the crowd, noticing in particular the few spectators not dressed in one of the four official colors. Recognizing Jessica Lansdowne, one of my students from Huntington, I edged my way over to her side. She glanced up and said, "Hi, Professor Crochet. I wondered whether you might be here."

"Hi, Jessica. What brings you to The Cloister?"

"Natalie invited me. She said I might find the event amusing but I think she's also happy with the results of the work they've put into preparing this program."

"Has she sung yet?"

"No—they're yellow. That's the last group to sing."

"Could I talk with you for a few minutes?"

"Sure thing." Others around us were already showing signs of annoyance with our conversation so we moved a bit apart from the crowd where we could still hear the singing but enjoy a bit of privacy.

"I've read and marked your papers but haven't talked with you since our conversation two weeks ago."

Jessica looked down thoughtfully. "I hope I haven't gotten you involved in a hornet's nest."

"You've been talking with Natalie," I said. Jessica nodded. "Well, I think you were right. Abby didn't commit suicide." I told her what I'd discovered and the conclusions I had drawn. "Abby seems to have led a more complicated life than I had appreciated. The National Honor Society story you told me was evidently just the tip of the iceberg."

"Mmh." Jessica seemed to be a bit uncomfortable with what I was saying but I didn't understand why and so kept on going.

"I know that her late father was an army officer and all, but that doesn't fully explain her involvement with all these moralistic campaigns. I keep wondering why such an attractive young woman seemed to avoid personal relationships, or at least the kind of relationships I see among other students here."

Jessica looked at me hard and I could see that she wanted to say something. I waited. "I like you, Professor Crochet, and the way you've treated a difficult situation at Huntington makes me think you're a pretty straight shooter."

"I do my best."

"If I tell you something in confidence can you promise not to share it with anyone at all?"

"Yes."

Jessica took a long breath and let it out again. "Okay, here goes. Abby was sexually abused as a child."

"You mean recently?"

"No, I mean just after her mother died."

"But she would have been around five."

"People think that sexual abuse begins only at puberty but that's not necessarily true."

I didn't know whether Jessica was speaking from personal experience now but it was her story to tell, so I let her tell it, and simply nodded.

"She didn't tell me all the details, and it's been a few years since we had this conversation, but as I recall, after Abby's mother died, her father sold their large house and he and Abby moved into someplace easier for a single parent to maintain. There was something about a gap in closing dates and for awhile the two of them lived with Abby's uncle and his wife."

"And that's when it happened?"

"Yes. Her father hadn't yet retired at that point, her aunt worked, her uncle was either retired or unemployed, I don't remember which, but he had plenty of opportunities."

Cheers from the sidelines marked the end of the red group's performance. We looked up and saw a company of students dressed in green take their places on the steps.

"How long did this go on?"

"Several months, I believe."

"And Abby never told anyone?"

"Not until she and her father had moved into their new house."

"Then what?"

"She told her father everything that had happened."

"And he believed her?"

"Happily, yes. That's the worst thing for an abused child—to get up the courage to tell an adult and then not be believed."

Again I suspected that Jessica had had first-hand experience in what she was telling me, but it was not for me to pry so I simply asked, "What happened?"

"Abby's father was very close to his brother. I suppose he was tempted to simply break relations, but instead he confronted him, and he confessed, and he told him if this ever happened again he would be sure that he went to jail, and if he survived jail—evidently pedophiles don't do well among prison populations—he would personally kill him."

I managed to sort out the rapidly changing pronouns. "As you look back at this story, what do you think happened to Abby?"

Jessica paused for a moment and I could see her trying to separate the larger picture from the details of narrative. "I think she drew closer to her father—she knew that she could trust him to protect her in the future, even if he hadn't done so while they were at the uncle's house."

"But further from everybody else?"

Jessica nodded. I could sense that that "everybody else" probably included her. "You know how girls sometimes exchange charm bracelets or bits of jewellery marked BFF?"

"Best Friends Forever?

"Right. I don't think Abby ever did that with anyone. She made friends, sure, but never with the complete openness of a BFF."

I thought about Wendy's remarks on Roommate 101 and nodded. "You asked me to learn about the details of Abby's death, but you've helped me better understand the details of her life. Unfortunately, it seems to be just those details that helped contribute to her death."

Jessica didn't say anything but just put her arms around me and gave me a hug. At that moment I looked across the crowd and saw Newton Falgarwood glancing in my direction and frowning.

Jessica and I remained to hear the yellow group, which included Natalie, Wendy, and Penny, the seniors among my music major tutees. When the Step-Sing ended, Jessica went to join her friend and I took the long trip home to my solitary apartment.

Chapter 17

I ARRIVED AT THE CLOISTER on the first Thursday in May, my last day at the college. The students would have a week of preparation time before exams, some of which would be spent in their dorm rooms or the library, but certainly some time sunbathing on the lawns as warm weather interfered with the best of intentions. Then came two weeks of exams, but since my tutorials involved no testing, my responsibilities ended here.

Penny Lapworth's face glowed with excitement when she greeted me. "It's because of secrets," she announced. "Abby knew things she wasn't supposed to know."

"Penny," I said, "I've already figured it out," but there was no hope of stopping this juggernaut. How had this young woman become so confident in getting her own way? Did others invariably melt before her ebullience or the cuteness of her slightly upturned nose? Or had she inherited this way of talking from a similarly-inclined parent? In my musing I nearly lost track of her argument.

"You probably know that The Cloister has a strict policy against students being married to professors."

I didn't know, but it sounded like just the kind of policy that The Cloister would have in place, and goodness knows The Cloister liked to enforce its policies strictly. Or was my thinking being distorted by my chagrin at being called on the carpet by Falgarwood?

Penny merrily chattered on. "If a secret marriage ever came to light, the girl would get expelled, which might not be all that bad because once she'd been accepted at The Cloister she could probably get in pretty much anywhere, but her husband might have a hard time finding another job."

Tell me about it, I thought to myself. During my second and, as it turned out, final year at Chihuahua State I'd written letters to every college and university in the country that had a music department, excepting only fanatical religious schools, in my search for employment beyond the stinking desert of southern California. All in vain, though occasionally I'd get a letter from some department chairman expressing enthusiasm over my credentials followed by regret at his inability to offer me a job.

I had moved to Boston on a whim, as a city that "gave off good vibes," the very phrase indicating the extent to which I had "gone native" during my California sojourn. Safely back on the East Coast I had managed to obtain several temporary positions but nothing in the tenure track.

Penny, oblivious to my meandering thoughts, rushed ahead with her explanation. "I've heard rumors of just such a marriage going on right now. Of course, they're extremely secretive about it. Can you imagine what it must be like for her, sneaking off to a house when all of her classmates are going back to their dorms? It might not be so bad for him—after all, professors are supposed to live in houses, but imagine that whenever they met in public he'd have to pretend not to know her—his own wife!"

"Penny ..." Once more I tried unsuccessfully to interrupt this torrent of fantasy.

"Suppose Abby threatened to expose them. That would certainly give the man sufficient motive to get her out of the way to protect his job."

"Penny, murder is serious business. You don't just kill someone because you think she might be a threat."

"In the ghetto people get killed just for looking at someone the wrong way, or showing disrespect."

"The Cloister is hardly a ghetto."

"You'd be surprised," Penny said. "You have no idea how cliquey it can get in the dorms."

"There's never been a murder on campus," I said.

"There has now," Penny said. "Or suppose Abby had a crush on a professor. He might be afraid for the consequences and get her out of the way to protect his career."

I decided this had gone far enough. Too far, in fact. "Penny, I already know who killed Abby. I found their footprints. She was threatening to expose an essay service."

Penny gave me an astonished look. "And you didn't tell me! I thought we were a team."

What had this young woman been imagining?

"I'm really disappointed," Penny said, and rushed from the room without giving a second thought to her scheduled final tutorial.

My morning classes ended with Natalie Porter. I'd enjoyed her reliably cheerful disposition through the year, and told her so as we concluded our last lesson. I thanked her for supplying the information that allowed me to learn how Abby had died, although I couldn't see any way that the culprits would ever be brought to justice.

"Who have you told about this?" Natalie asked, with a note of concern in her voice.

I explained how, in exasperation, I had tried to halt the flow of Penny's endless theorizing by letting her know that the search had been concluded.

"Didn't you know?" Natalie asked. "Penny's a bounty hunter!"

"I can't see how that makes a lot of difference at this point," I said. "As things have worked out, I will probably never return to this campus again, much to my regret."

Natalie seemed unmollified. "Watch your back, Professor Crochet," she warned as she took her leave.

During my afternoon tutorials a piece of unfinished business continued to call for attention at the back of my mind. At the end of my last lesson with Wendy Atwater, I asked whether we might take one more look at Abby's belongings, stashed at the back of her closet.

"Suits me," Wendy said. "I don't have anything else to do."

As we crossed the campus I marveled that familiarity had in no way diminished my delight at being able to live my life, however briefly, in such beautiful surroundings. Just as my daily walk through the Boston Public Garden never failed to produce some new detail for my delectation, so each traverse across the campus produced some tiny reminder of the privilege I felt to be a temporary part of this lovely, albeit peculiar, community.

Wendy hauled out the few boxes that remained of Abby's belongings. "Did you want to look at her clothes, too?" she asked.

"No," I said. "I think I'll find what I'm looking for here." I emptied one of the cartons onto Abby's bed: ribbon-bound letters, probably from the British boyfriend; make-up containers; pens, pencils, erasers, and bottles of White-Out; emery boards, bracelets. Evidently whoever had gathered Abby's belongings for storage—most likely Wendy—hadn't made any attempt to separate the transient from the treasured. They weren't her things after all. (An unspoken "if you know what I mean" entered my mind unbidden.)

Then I spotted it, an object that had escaped my attention on my first inspection because I hadn't known what to look for. Now I recognized it: a post office box key like the one I had in my pocket. I thanked Wendy for her indulgence, getting a "Whatever" in response, and hurried across the campus to the Waban Post Office.

"I won't be needing this any longer," I said to the clerk as I turned in my key and waited for the return of my deposit.

"You didn't get an awful lot of mail, young man," the clerk observed as he crossed my name off a file card.

Fortunately the post office, more concerned with its own convenience than with the privacy of its patrons, still maintained the old system whereby the number of each mailbox appeared stamped into the flat surface of the metal key. I located Abby's box, opened the door of the compartment, and withdrew its contents, a single manila envelope.

I took the envelope over to the work counter in the middle of the room, opened it, and pulled out half a dozen typewritten sheets. Abby really had completed her exposé of Sisterhood Is Powerful. How that title must have rankled! Everything Natalie had told me, everything I had discovered for myself, and more: Abby would have made a fine investigative reporter had she lived.

I hesitated for only a moment before asking the clerk for a fresh envelope, filling it with the product of Abby's labors, addressing it to the editor-in-chief of the student newspaper, and presenting it to the clerk for proper postage. I toyed briefly with the idea of making another copy to send to President Clearwater. Then I recalled Newton Falgarwood's words, "The Cloister abhors negative publicity."

No wonder the administration had been content to let Abby's death remain a suicide. A student taking her own life is naturally regrettable, but she must have been unbalanced to begin with—mark it down to a momentary lapse by the admissions department. Send a tasteful bouquet and a note of regret to the next of kin, if any, and be done with it.

A murder investigation, on the other hand, would constitute a public relations catastrophe: police detectives snooping around the campus, the unsavory stench of violent death hovering over it. Even if the local police department could be browbeaten into maintaining silence, nothing would prevent newspaper, and worse, television reporters from making lurid speculations. There must be many readers and viewers in the Boston area who would take pleasure in the predicament of a negative pall falling upon this enclave of privilege. Let *Schadenfreude* reign supreme.

No, as far as The Cloister was concerned, it really was suicide. It had to be suicide, and nothing that an untitled bearded musicologist could say or do would alter that convenient truth.

Chapter 18

ON THE BUS FROM WABAN village to the Woodland T station I thought about Sheri. It had been a week since her departure from the apartment. I wasn't concerned for her safety—she had, after all, packed her suitcases—but I felt uneasy that I had so badly misjudged the state of things between us. Sheri had expressed her dissatisfaction with my involvement with Abby's death and my misplaced priorities, from her perspective, regarding work and leisure, or accomplishment and relationship, as she put it. But I hadn't looked upon our disagreements as fights or her arguments in support of her position as ultimatums. Had I completely misread the situation?

I esteemed Sheri's sense of adventure and independence. In order to be with me she had left her home and friends, several of whom had counseled her against her involvement not just with a man several years older than she but an Easterner to boot. I admired her determination to start a career in an unfamiliar city and celebrated her success at landing an editorial position with a Boston publishing house. To be sure, for the moment she was only an assistant editor but that rank seemed appropriate for someone with no previous experience.

In valuing Sheri's independence had I perhaps underestimated her need for interaction with me? I found Sheri to be a great companion but we had never really discussed what she sought in our relationship.

The bus arrived at the station and I made my way downstairs to the subway platform. Some of the M.T.A. rail vehicles stood well above the tracks, and you mounted a set of stairs to enter them. So they were trolleys, right? Much of the time they ran underground. So that made them subways, right? The Riverside branch of the Green Line ran both underground and above ground and sometimes you mounted stairs, as in Boston, and sometimes the train arrived at platform level, as here at the Woodland station. Rather than waste time debating nomenclature, Bostonians simply referred to the entire rail system as "the T."

I leaned out over the tracks looking for the train. Nothing in sight. In the middle of the platform the crowd became denser as passengers arrived from the parking lot or from one of the several buses whose lines emanated from this station. Some kid with a transistor radio held to his ear created a mild din at the opposite end of the platform. Alone at my end I had no complaints about the sound.

I leaned over the tracks again and saw the familiar square-fronted train approach, its small dual headlights glowing and its pantograph drawing power from the overhead electric lines. At this end of the platform the train was still travelling at a pretty fair clip, but it would slow to a stop by the time the lead car reached the far end.

With my attention focused on the arriving train I don't know what provoked me to turn around; perhaps my peripheral vision extended farther than I realized. Approaching me I saw two large figures: Tweedle Dum and Tweedle Dee. As they neared they raised their hands to shoulder height in front of them, the universal "back off" gesture. Well, they wouldn't have to worry about me any further. I didn't expect to see either the Cloister or the SIP offices again. Much as I regretted Abby's death, I was glad to put the whole sorry business behind me. Newton Falgarwood, with his distrust of unmarried young men; Olive Earle, with her supposed knowledge of young women and their need for stability; Penny Lapworth, with her harebrained theories: I would be relieved never to have to deal with any of them again.

As the two women grew closer I realized my mistake. They weren't trying to signal their displeasure with me; they intended to push me off the platform into the path of the oncoming train. If I continued to reflect on the situation I would soon be dead. Had there been only one of them I might have been able to dodge to one side or the other, but they had effectively closed any avenue for escape. As they increased their pace to a run I instinctively fell to the ground, pressed my arms against my head and prepared to be rolled off the platform.

This appeared to be the single action for which the two assailants had not prepared. Expecting some kind of response on my part, they had evidently calculated that their considerable momentum would easily overcome any defense that I might mount. Lacking the anticipated resistance of my puny but stationary body, and tripping over the prone object at their feet, the pair had flown over me and off the platform on a fatal collision course with the arriving train. Turning my head, as I desperately resisted being swept after them, I thought I caught a glimpse of a swimming-fish pattern on the bottom of one sole.

Chapter 19

"I THINK WE MAY WANT to rethink this whole thing," I said.

Sheri looked dismayed. "You mean you want me to go away again?"

"No—just the opposite. I want to change things so that you won't want to."

After spending several hours with transit personnel, paramedics, Woodland police officers and eventually even a state trooper, I was deemed medically fit and legally free to go on my way. Arriving home I found that Sheri had prepared dinner, arranged flowers on the table, and generally settled in again.

Sheri had wanted to hear about everything that had taken place while she had been away, and I told her.

"So both of the SIP women died at the scene?" Sheri asked.

"The one closer to the train was killed immediately. The other one died en route to the hospital."

"I don't think anyone ever really *deserves* to die," Sheri said. "Certainly Abby didn't deserve to die. And you don't deserve to die. But it always hurts me to see people getting their values so mixed up that they value material profit over human life."

"I'm sorry they died," I said. "But I'm not sorry to have proven that Abby never committed suicide. It may not mean much, after the fact, but I like to imagine that I gave her back a small measure of honor."

"You're being ironic," Sheri said.

"No, I'm serious."

"After all this, you can still use the word 'honor' without seeing the irony?"

"I guess I'm missing it."

"You idealized this Abby girl, Axel. The person whose honor you've saved isn't real."

"That doesn't seem fair."

"No? Okay, let's take it from the top. First that Huntington student ..."

"Jessica."

"That's right, Jessica. She tells you how back in high school Abby embarrassed the principal, and really herself, by insisting on putting an abstract principle above any concern for people."

"Well ..."

"Then Natalie tells you how Abby falls in love with the four absolutes of Moral Re-Armament—what a name to attract the daughter of a military officer. Probably one way she could make up to her father for not being a boy—but she uses them to browbeat her fellow students."

"I don't think she saw it that way."

"Then instead of having a real sexual relationship she engages in a long-distance literary-sexual relationship with some guy in England. The poets meant the conceit linking orgasm and death to be fun, Axel, not a substitute for actual intimacy."

"But ..."

"Then comes her fatal attraction to the Sisterhood. Now I'm not for a minute trying to justify that high-priced cheating syndicate, but look at the naïveté of this student waltzing into a business office and insisting that they stop what they're doing because it offends her principles. Abby seems colossally out of touch with reality. And I haven't even mentioned that pathetic Penny creature who had such an obvious crush on Abby and was snubbed."

"I've never looked at it that way."

"Of course not. In a sense you're as bad as she was, falling for an abstract vision of a damsel in distress—a dead damsel, I have to point out—then recklessly following her footsteps until you nearly got killed yourself. Don't misunderstand, Axel, I'm not angry. In a way your innocent heroics are almost touching, but I am upset. I nearly lost you!"

"I guess when you put it that way there is a certain quixotic quality to all this."

"But don't you see? Don Quixote was a literary creation. Cervantes himself never faced death beneath the wheels of a subway train."

I had to laugh.

"Okay, I know—a glaring anachronism—but you know what I mean. Now I don't want you to think I'm unsympathetic to Abby Fox.

I can imagine that if the most important person in my life were taken away when I was very young, I might well conclude that people are unreliable and I could only trust principles. It doesn't sound as if her father, with his devotion to Moral Re-Armament, ever set her straight from that error. If Abby had been better connected to people instead of principles, she might still be alive."

"I sense there's a connection to us behind all this."

"Go ahead; I've talked enough."

"It goes back to accomplishment (an abstraction) versus relationship (a personal reality)."

"That's a nice way to put it."

"Well, you need have no fears. If I'd ever had any illusions about Abby Fox, you've managed quite handily to dispel them. I really am all yours—no fantasy."

"That's good to hear. And despite everything, I do hope the student paper publishes Abby's exposé," Sheri said.

"I think there's a very strong chance. Natalie Porter described the editor as someone who would like nothing better than to take on The Cloister over the issue of freedom of expression."

"So will people eventually figure out that Abby was murdered?"

"As long as Penny Lapworth is around, I don't think you have to worry about that."

"Do you think they'll listen to her?"

"They will now. I'd be surprised if she hasn't already gone up to the tower to examine the footprints."

"But you're done with the story?"

"I'm done. And I'm glad you're back."

"I couldn't just leave you and not give us a chance to try to work things out," Sheri had said when I arrived home. Now we were working things out.

"I came to some conclusions while you were away," I said as we sat together on the sofa after dinner.

"Tell me," Sheri said, and snuggled against my shoulder.

"Work never ends."

"Boy, I'll say," Sheri said. "What else?"

"What I mean is that you could work twenty-four hours a day and never finish. But that's not necessarily a bad thing."

"Working twenty-four hours a day?"

"No—treating work as a process, the way you suggested. You put in the hours every day—maybe a lot fewer than I've been doing, but enough—and accomplishments come along as a matter of course."

"What about deadlines?" Sheri asked.

"That's where I need to be more realistic. I'm thinking that it might be a good idea to seek your advice before I set a deadline. But I'm getting this all backwards."

"How do you mean?"

"Love and friendship, as abstract concepts, exist outside of time. But as practical realities, love and friendship require time to sustain them."

"You mean the way that you either put the effort into relationships with old friends—letters, telephone calls, Christmas cards, visits, whatever—or else they fade away and die."

"And if that's true for friendship it must be doubly true for partnership. I confess I've taken you for granted, but I love you and I want to spend more time with you," I said.

"And I with you. I appreciate it that you've taken my ideas seriously."

"Well, I have to admit that what you said makes a fair amount of sense."

"There's something else."

"What would that be?"

"While we were apart, I missed your body. I think those amatory madrigals may have had something to do with it."

Without any conscious decision we found ourselves drifting into the bedroom. As we crossed the threshold Sheri kissed my ear and murmured, "Die, for I am a-dying."

"Prime numbers are what is left when you have taken all the patterns away. I think prime numbers are like life. They are very logical but you could never work out the rules, even if you spent all your time thinking about them."

— Mark Haddon (*The Curious Incident of the Dog in the Night-time*)

PRIME SUSPECT

Chapter 1

979853562951413 WERE WOULD BE ONE WAY to begin this story. "**Prof's Legions Seek Message from E.T.**," a headline in Magnolia University's student newspaper, *The Reynolds Rap*, would be another. Less easy to capture in words would be the look that appears on a girl's face the morning after she's become engaged. I had seen that look on the face of Sheila McCormack, one of my classmates in French Romanticism. Now Sheila was dead.

My name is Axel Crochet, musicologist, or if you like, music historian. In 1990, thanks to a grant from the American Council of Learned Societies, I took a leave from my troubled career as a professor and spent a year as a student at Magnolia University in North Carolina. I had already learned enough French to write a book on Debussy's songs. Now I enjoyed an opportunity to obtain a proper foundation, studying French literature, culture, composition, linguistics and phonetics. Magnolia conferred on me the title of Visiting Scholar and gave me a small office; the chairman of the French Department, Marcel Trente, introduced me to his colleagues somewhat disdainfully as "a kind of super-freshman." I suppose at age thirty-two I might have seemed old to be a student, but I completed six courses in the fall term, with five more in the spring term, now halfway over.

Monongahela University, my academic home, seemed relieved to get rid of me for a year. Since coming to Monongahela from California I had tried every teaching style I could think of as an alternative to lecturing and had failed at every one. The laid-back students at Chihuahua State College in California tolerated my experiments with amusement. They had no intention of doing any work but persisted in asking questions about my ideas of educational reform until I saw through their ploy. The students at Monongahela displayed no such interest. They had spent years mastering the status quo and resented any attempts on my part to alter the rules. My department chairman had rather pointedly suggested that in addition to studying French during my leave of absence I might do well to rethink my approach to teaching.

Somehow I didn't think that Professor Plowright's course on French Romanticism would provide the model I needed. Gordon Plowright, a short, dapper, grey-haired man, never appeared in public without a jacket and the cravat favored by 19th-century dandies. Plowright prided himself on teaching without notes or a lesson plan. As a result we caught glimpses of one grand vision after another without ever getting down to a close analysis of a text.

We spent an entire week being about to get to a one-page poem by Lamartine without ever actually arriving there, and Lamartine was only the first poet in our anthology. I got the impression that the good professor didn't really want to talk about poetry, although he had a great deal to say about *about* poetry. Prof. Plowright possessed an immense command of nineteenth-century literature, so vast that he seemed incapable of answering even the simplest question in less than ten minutes, and often his classes could be dull, dull, dull. In lecture after lecture the good professor managed to ramble along avenues of abstraction without ever coming to the arcade of the actual.

I was sitting at a work table in the reference section of the library when a voice behind me interrupted my reverie. "Excuse me, Professor Crochet," said Beth Carruthers, one of my classmates. "Can you spare a moment?"

"Of course," I said. Beth sat in front of me in Prof. Plowright's classroom, beside Sheila McCormick. In recent days the two young women had exchanged giggling whispers more appropriate to schoolchildren than university graduate students. Sheila had the rugged good looks of an Oregonian backpacker. When she had entered the classroom a few mornings earlier, bearing a beatific smile, Beth had been its recipient, although anyone in the room must have noticed that special glow.

Beth herself was an uncommonly pretty girl. The bevy of southern belles in the class (most of the graduate students in French seemed to be female) occasionally led me to wonder whether the South had somehow captured a disproportionate fraction of the gene pool for pulchritude. I led her to the small office that the university had assigned me on the third floor of the library and invited her to sit down.

Beth glanced around at the few objects with which I had attempted to personalize my cubbyhole—a poster for the New York City Marathon, an abstract sculpture of an owl, a framed Vasarely print. "What's that?" she asked, pointing at a small wooden box covered with a black-and-white photograph of cat tails in the snow.

"It's one of my treasures," I said, opening the box. "A present from my thesis advisor, Ted Morris." I showed her the fossil inside the container then opened a small sheet of paper inscribed in a familiar hand and read the words aloud:

"Nature is a temple
Her quick pillars send forth oracular words now and again
Old words; meanings lap in them.
A while ago brachiopods lived at Monkey Run Road, Ithaca R.D. 2
More recently Axel Crochet worked harder than would have seemed
natural
He sent forth some new words
Ted Morris isn't about to forget that." This was the first time I had read the words aloud, and it brought back memories of my weekly meetings with a remarkable teacher.

"The beginning sounds like Baudelaire," Beth said.

"Good for you," I said. "Baudelaire created a number of the poems that Debussy set to music; I wrote about the poetry and the music in my doctoral dissertation."

"That's a lovely present. I can see why you treasure it. Your thesis advisor is a lot more concise than Prof. Plowright. Wasn't that the most boring class you ever attended?" she began.

"I don't know," I said. "I think the Lamartine lecture provided some pretty stiff competition?" She laughed, and then her face became more serious as she approached the real reason for wanting to talk with me. She seemed reluctant to begin. "You're upset about Sheila's death," I prompted. "Have you known her a long time?"

"We met freshman year and we've been best friends ever since," Beth said. "You really get to know someone when you've been her roommate for four years. But we were more than roommates. I know it's a cliché but we used to tell each other that we were soul mates. We shared books, exchanged clothes—it's almost as if we had been sisters. When it came time to go to graduate school, we decided to stay at Magnolia, partly so we could still be together. "

"And now your 'sister' was going to get married."

"How did you know about that?"

"I saw it on her face the day that she must have announced the news to you."

"She was so excited to be getting married, and I felt confused: I was happy for her but also sad to be losing her."

"And now it seems you've lost her for good. A hit-and-run accident, the student paper said."

"It isn't fair," Beth said. "Sheila's life ending just when she was so excited about her life ahead? I've had a tough time focusing on assignments with her gone."

Her eyes began to fill with tears again and I tried to think of a way to help this young woman with her grief. "The two of you probably made a pretty good study group."

"I'll say!" Beth's face brightened a bit. "Sheila was good at remembering names and facts, while I could usually see the overall themes of a subject. And it wasn't just studying for tests. We were each other's editors when it came to writing papers. I learned a lot from Sheila, and she used to say she'd learned a lot from me." Her attention seemed to wander, as if she were recalling their most recent session. Then she looked back at me and said, "But that's what I wanted to ask you."

"What's that?"

"My computer is being repaired and since I had an essay due Sheila lent me her PC. Now I'm not sure what to do with it."

"I suppose you could give it to her parents or her fiancé."

A strange look came over Beth's face. "You mean you don't know?"

"Know what?"

"Sheila was engaged to Randy Preston."

"Preston. Wasn't he the runner that died last week?"

"Captain of the cross-country team," Beth said with a mixture of pride and regret. "It's so sad! They might have been characters out of one of those melancholy French novels we've been reading."

"Didn't the student paper say that he died of a heart attack?"

"Yes. I thought it was pretty strange for a runner, but the article talked about James Fixx dying young, and he was a marathoner and everything."

"But Fixx died at fifty-two. Randy couldn't have been more than twenty-three or so."

"Right. Just like that football player who died in Texas," Beth said.

"But that was a combination of dehydration and heat exhaustion—the coach insisted in holding a practice in full equipment when it was too hot to be out at all."

"What are you saying?"

"I don't know. It's just hard to believe that two young people could die within a week of each other, and not two random people but two kids engaged to be married."

"A car accident and a heart attack don't seem to be related," Beth said. "And Randy's father also died young of a heart attack, although not as young as this."

"All the same." The story didn't make sense but I wasn't sure how I could help. "About that computer. Can't you give it to Sheila's parents?"

"They live out west. They've already made arrangements for Sheila's body to be transported home for a funeral service, but they asked me to deal with her things. They said I could keep any of her clothes that I wanted, and that I should mail them any small personal objects, but otherwise it was up to me. The computer seems awkward to ship, and I'm sure they already have one at home."

"Do you think I could take a look at the computer?" I asked.

"I don't know what good that would do, but I have it in my apartment. Why don't you come over this evening?"

Beth left the library and I set about the task of looking up references for a class presentation I was scheduled to give two days hence. As I turned a corner in the stacks, I surprised two undergraduates locked in embrace who hastily disentangled themselves and scampered off in a confusion of giggles. After finishing my work I locked up my notes in the office, walked down the long spiral staircase in the center of the library, and headed towards my apartment.

The Magnolia University campus had to be one of the prettiest I'd ever seen, with Georgian architecture arranged in graceful patterns, tree-lined paths and great expanses of lawn which recent rains had turned an almost preternatural shade of green. The sight of students playing Frisbee reminded me of my own graduate school days, not so long ago, when a friend and I would relieve the strain of transcribing neumes for our paleography course by tossing a Frisbee. With practice we could eventually send the disk nearly the entire length of the Arts Quad. I never got into the game of Ultimate Frisbee, but I loved the sensation of sending the disk on long flight.

As I walked by the edge of the green the wind caught the Frisbee and sent it out of reach of its intended recipient, on a trajectory that brought it in my direction. I took a few quick steps, caught the Frisbee on the fly, and then sent it sliding on a low path to the most distant player. The boy who had planned to catch it whistled appreciatively.

"Didn't know you could throw a Frisbee that far, Axel." The words came from Todd, one of the students in the Alternative Curriculum, a student-run program that I'd been helping to advise since the Christmas break. He and Marla, another student in the program, continued past me on their bicycles before I could frame a suitable response.

In California I had published an article about my teaching experiments there. Since then my ideas on teaching had changed considerably but members of the Alternative Curriculum, discovering the article, took me for a radical, and when they found I was actually on campus, invited me to join the program. It didn't occur to me at the time that I might not fit in as well as they hoped. It wasn't just the mild irritation of having teenagers call me by my first name. It was their tacit insistence that I accept their academic and intellectual standards as my own. Todd had been one of the first to detect the discrepancy between my published words and my current thinking, and he treated me with more than a little bit of suspicion. The insolent expression on his face made it clear that his words had not been intended as a compliment.

Then, as often happened at Magnolia in the spring, a light rain suddenly began to fall, sending the Frisbee players to seek shelter and spurring me into an easy jog to my apartment in the university housing complex at the edge of campus.

Chapter 2

BETH'S APARTMENT, IN THE SAME building as mine, seemed like a time capsule from a bygone era: Peter Max posters on the wall, macramé hangings, elaborate decorative candles, mobiles in which shining metal spheres formed a miniature solar system, even bricks-and-boards bookshelves. I noticed a few concessions to the present: albums by the Mahavishnu Orchestra, Santana, Spanky & Our Gang and The Fifth Dimension appeared in compact disc form; the apartment had several comfortable chairs and a sofa but no sign of beanbag furniture or slingback chairs. Beth saw me eyeing a poster for The Mama and the Papas and offered an explanation.

"My dad saved most of his stuff from when he lived in California in the early Seventies. When I turned fourteen my parents said I could decorate my room any way I wanted, and when I discovered all these things in the attic I decided they were just what I needed. The following year my dad died unexpectedly during a routine operation; I've held on to this stuff both because I like it and sort of as a way of preserving his memory."

"Do you know anything about that era?" I asked.

"I don't care for the drug culture, but I like the belief in community and helping other people."

"That puts you in the minority."

"How do you mean?"

"There's a polling firm that's been administering essentially the same questionnaire to college freshmen for the past forty years. In the Sixties, 75% of college freshmen put a high priority on discovering themselves and helping others, while only 25% wanted to make a great deal of money. Now it's exactly the other way around."

"In that case I guess you could say I'm old-fashioned."

"My own decorating tends toward the modern, but I agree with you in admiring the idealism of the Sixties."

Beth pointed to the PC sitting on a desk made by placing a wooden door across two filing cabinets. "This is Sheila's computer. I only used it to write my essay. I'd feel uncomfortable looking at her files."

"I can understand your reluctance to invade your friend's privacy, even if she's no longer around to object. Suppose we do this together. If what we find seems too personal we can back off."

"Okay." Beth still sounded a bit uncertain.

I turned the computer on. "No password," I observed. "That makes things easier." Sheila's files were organized into a series of MS-DOS directories. I started WordPerfect running and saw that Sheila had a fairly orderly mind, at least when it came to her computer. She had sub-directories for each academic subject. "You don't have an Internet connection here, do you?"

"No. I couldn't afford the monthly connection fees. If it's important, I use the computer in the library."

I continued running through Sheila directories. "It looks as if we're in luck. She seems to have copied and stored all her e-mail messages, so we don't have to locate her Internet service provider." Sheila's tidy habits extended to the organization of her electronic mail into files for family, friends, activities, and so forth.

It seemed reasonable to start with the file labeled "Randy," but Sheila seemed to have been something of a cyber-packrat: the file contained dozens of messages. "It may take a while to sort through all of this," I told Beth.

"Are the messages filed chronologically?" she asked.

"It looks that way."

"Then why don't we start with a month ago and see if that tells us anything?"

"Sounds like a plan," I said. A search of the first several messages suggested that Sheila and Randy had used their computers in place of a telephone. Among the entries for the first few days I found half a dozen brief messages discussing what movie they planned to attend the following weekend. As we continued reading the messages a pattern seemed to emerge. On some message-less nights Sheila and Randy evidently studied together. Other nights a flurry of short messages would go back and forth between their residences. They had apparently decided to save their personal conversations for occasions when they could talk directly, for the electronic messages were limited to abbreviated greetings like LVU and TT.

"Tah tah?" I asked Beth.

"More likely 'till tomorrow,'" she said.

We continued plowing through the messages without finding anything out of the ordinary until we hit one dated three days before Sheila's death.

"*Hi, Ran,*" the text read. "*The funniest thing happened when I turned on my computer. A number flashed on the screen. 979853562951413. Any ideas?*"

"*No clue,*" came the response. "*I didn't think you did math on your computer.*"

"*I don't do math at all if I can help it. Yuck!*"

"*It's too long for a telephone number, and if it's just junk mail, why would anyone send it in code? Does it really matter?*"

"*I dunno. I just don't like the idea of somebody putting something on my computer without my knowing about it. It isn't even an e-mail message.*"

"*If it bothers you, let's talk about it some more when we get together.*"

Beth and I continued perusing the messages up to the most recent without finding another reference to the mysterious number.

"Do you think this number has anything to do with … you know?" Beth asked.

This wasn't the first time a woman in need had called on me for assistance, and I had to confess a certain weakness for offering aid when I could. I had my hands full with French courses and the Alternative Curriculum. But I was a scholar and this number represented a fact, although one whose significance I didn't understand. It also represented a challenge. I'd always liked puzzles and this seemed intriguing: no rules or limits. But let's be honest. If just anybody had posed the problem, I might have been able to resist. But I'd felt attracted to Beth since the first time I'd seen her in class. I would have had difficulty refusing her a favor. I wrote the digits down carefully.

"Have you ever done any climbing in the mountains?" I asked.

"Some."

"You know the tension you feel when you don't know where you're going to go next and your relief when you find a place to put a foot or a hand?" Beth smiled and nodded. "Well, it looks as if we have a handhold."

I looked at my watch and said, "I promised a friend in the phonetics class that I'd attend a concert this evening. He plays in the orchestra. Would you be interested in joining me?"

Beth looked pleased at the invitation but cast an eye to the books on her desk and declined. "If you ask me out another time," she said with a smile, "I'll probably say yes."

"Sounds good to me," I said.

"Thanks for coming over," Beth said, and gave me a brief hug. "I feel better."

"I haven't done anything yet," I said.

"I have great confidence in you," she said.

Chapter 3

I HAD THE IMPRESSION THAT Beth would have liked a longer visit, and I was already regretting my promise to attend a program of student performers playing concerto movements with the Magnolia University Symphony Orchestra. As it turned out I would have been better off spending time with Beth. An unforeseen effect of listening to big pieces played by young performers is that all the seams show. The Tchaikovsky first piano concerto, for example, can be an exciting work, and a professional pianist is able to conceal what the student cannot: the piece contains lovely themes and impressive passagework but it also has an appalling amount of padding. The orchestra wasn't much help in this respect. When the woodwinds took over the second theme, it sounded for all the world like the Guckenheimer Sauerkraut Band.

The Liszt first piano concerto was even worse. The entire brass section sounded like refugees from the Magnolia marching band. Since the entire movement derives from a single seven-note motive (comprising only three different pitches) you would think that the brass should have had plenty of opportunities to perfect their entrances. In this performance the movement consisted of an endless succession of Dum dum dum dum da da dum BLAT!

Next morning, my ears still ringing with unintended dissonance, I headed Professor Nelson's Proust class. The trouble with reading Proust is that you start remembering physical sensations, like the taste of the doughnut I enjoyed at the Student Union this morning, a taste which equaled and surpassed that of any doughnut I had enjoyed elsewhere, offering a melting texture covered with a thick sugary glaze, a taste whose superiority to that of mundane store-bought doughnuts approached the transcendence of Amtrak French Toast over the kind you make yourself; and the sensation of tasting this luscious delicacy of a doughnut suddenly unlocked the involuntary memory of a similar sensation experienced in the past, namely the doughnut that I had enjoyed at the Student Union two mornings earlier, an experience fully as rich as that of this morning, and yet the memory of which was perhaps even more poignantly eloquent than the initial sensation, since the enjoyment of the doughnut at the time, though fine indeed, diminished as the stomach gradually filled, while the memory which one retained of the sensation most often arose when the stomach was empty, say an hour before dinner, when the absence of an available doughnut (the Student Union doughnuts were baked on the premises each morning and were exhausted by ravenous readers of Proust within a few hours) only served to heighten the vivid recollection of the desired sensation and led one to write sentences that threatened to go on and on with no end in sight until at last the mind reluctantly accepted the impossibility of the situation at hand and, sublimating the primary desire within the sole acceptable substitute, trundled off to the kitchen to make a peanut butter and jelly sandwich.

Prof. Nelson strode back and forth at the front of the classroom as if treading the boards of a stage grown familiar after hundreds of performances, stopping now and again to jot an important point on the blackboard. By exposing the underlying structure, Nelson made the huge novel seem less daunting. Today he took up the theme of snobbery, which runs throughout the novel, distinguishing between social and intellectual snobbery. Nelson concluded with a beautiful phrase: "snobisme insondable et partout—édifices d'inclusion et d'exclusion." (Unfathomable, ubiquitous snobbery—a social fabric designed to include and to exclude).

Nelson's teaching style seemed preferable as a model to that of any of his colleagues, or indeed to any models I had essayed thus far in my career. In my earliest classes as a college professor, rejecting the lecture method as antediluvian, I imitated the best of my teachers from graduate school and embraced the ideas I had read about radical educational reform. My students back home at Monongahela University would have none of it. They had spent the better part of their lives mastering the existing educational system—not liking it, mind you, but understanding its structure of predictable rewards for predictable performance—and had little enthusiasm for Prof. Crochet's alternative methods.

I was reflecting on the widely varying teaching styles I had observed here as I left the French building after my Proust class and headed to the math building for an appointment with Professor Loomis.

Chapter 4

ONE COULDN'T GUESS WHETHER PETER Loomis had preserved a preference for the crew cut from the era when it was still in vogue or whether he had recently adopted the style as a method of disguising hair loss but, along with his horn-rimmed glasses, it gave him a youthfully earnest appearance which went with his evident enthusiasm for talking about mathematics with anyone who would listen. Unlike other mathematics professors I had met, he seemed quite prepared to address you at whatever level of sophistication you could muster, rather than looking down on you for not having studied the more arcane aspects of his subject.

He smiled when he looked at the fifteen-digit number that I had copied from Sheila's computer. When I looked perplexed he explained, "You're the third person to show me this number in the last ten days."

"I don't understand," I said.

"A Miss McCormack and a Mr. Preston brought me this same number and asked what it meant."

"What did you tell them?"

"I explained that I had no idea what it meant, but that I found it interesting because it was a prime."

"You mean a number divisible only by itself or one?"

"You seem to have remembered something from high school."

"You could tell that just by looking at it?"

"By no means," Loomis chuckled. "If I could do that I'd be a wealthy man."

"How do you mean? Are prime numbers really that important?"

"They are nowadays. Have you ever heard of public-access cryptography?"

"I know what cryptography is but I don't know about public access."

"This may take a few minutes to explain. Are you game?"

"Certainly, but I'm afraid my math skills aren't very strong."

"Then let me try to simplify it for you. Suppose I want to send you an important parcel in the most secure manner possible. I could put it in a box and lock it, but imagine that I have no safe way to send you the key to the lock. Solution: I'd put my open lock in the box, keep the key and send the box to you. You'd replace it with your own open lock, keep the key and then use my lock to lock the box and send it back to me, so that no one could tamper with the lock that would eventually hold the important parcel. I'd use my key to open it, put in the parcel, lock the box with your lock and send it back to you. Your key opens it and you have the parcel."

"Isn't that an awfully inefficient way to do it?"

"Certainly." The professor's eyes twinkled. "Nobody's going to send a chest back and forth three times. But you can imagine doing the same thing electronically."

"Ah, I see. You and I don't have to have the same key."

"You've got it. Do you understand why encoding information is a fairly hot topic?"

"You mean sending messages between spies?"

"Oh my, it goes much further than that. Now that information can be communicated so easily between computers, there's a need to conceal its meaning should it fall into the wrong hands. Think about health records or bank documents or corporate information. Old methods of keeping it secret are too cumbersome?"

"Why's that?"

"Traditional methods of encryption require the people at each end to have the same deciphering tool, along with, say, some agreement on which code is used on which day. In public-access cryptography, the encryption key is publicized but each person has a private deciphering key."

"But what does that have to do with prime numbers?"

"It's easy to multiply two prime numbers together, but once you have the product, if it's large enough, it would take a supercomputer to figure out the two factors. Public-access cryptography depends on making public large numbers that nobody can factor."

"So how did you know that the number I brought you was prime?"

"I looked it up in a table of primes when Miss McCormack brought it to me, and recognized it when you showed it to me. By the way, that's a particularly nice prime: it consists of the first fifteen digits of pi in reverse order."

I looked at the number again and thought about the few digits of pi that I'd memorized back in high school: 3.14159265358. "Sure enough. It works."

"Here are a few of my favorite primes." Prof. Loomis took a sheet of paper from his desk and copied numbers onto the blackboard. There was no class present but I guessed pedagogical habits were hard to break. "This is one of my favorite palindromic primes—it reads the same forwards and backwards:
17000000000000071

And here's a beautiful repunit prime:

1111111111111111111

Here is a lovely 39 digit prime:

737373737373737373737373737373737373737

And here is another amazing prime: 73,939,133. When you strip numbers away one at a time from the right side, every number obtained is prime. Wow!

73939133
7393913
739391
73939
7393
739
73
7

I'd never thought about numbers as being particularly beautiful, but it was hard not to be impressed by the patterns. I thanked Prof. Loomis and walked toward the Alternative Curriculum Center, my mind still reeling with the idea of large primes. With a warm sun shining on magnolia trees just about to blossom, this would have been a fine day to empty one's mind and live in the moment. Of course, at the Alternative Curriculum, that seemed to be all they ever did.

Chapter 5

THE ALTERNATIVE CURRICULUM DIDN'T RESEMBLE any other department at Magnolia University. One of the assistant deans had taken the program under his wing and finagled space for it in a one-story building scheduled to be replaced in the not-too-distant future by a high-rise parking garage. The program tended to attract students who might otherwise have dropped out of the university, a point which the assistant dean had stressed in defending the AC against traditionalists who could see only a dangerous erosion of academic standards in a student-run program.

A few kids were sitting around on cast-off sofas and chairs as I entered the main room of the centre. An oversize painted rainbow extended from the bottom of one wall, stretched across the entire length of the neighboring wall, with a brief foray onto the ceiling, then reached the floor again on a third wall. Around me I heard the muted jangle of heavy metal leaking from headphones, the AC having democratically decided to ban open radios after an historic battle over the choice of channels threatened to split the group irrevocably. No such ban existed on smoking, and the air stank with the odor of stale cigarettes, with just a trace of marijuana, presumably enjoyed in the absence of faculty members. The university had to draw the line somewhere. As a non-smoker I endured the foul air as best I could, knowing that my attendance here was only temporary.

"Did you hear what happened this morning?" Matt asked. So far as I knew, none of the kids at the AC had last names. Matt, an agreeable lad with but a single ring in his ear, wore a T-shirt bearing an unprintable slogan over the obligatory blue jeans. "Gloria's key got stuck in the lock. If it hadn't been for Cam, I don't know what we would have done." Cam, happy, round-faced, round-bodied, and nearly empty-headed, lived more or less full time at the centre, evidently surviving on order-in pizza. Most of the students took at least a few regular university courses, but Cam seemed to consider the AC a perfect home and showed little interest in leaving it, certainly not for academic reasons.

I saw a slender figure in blue jeans and a leather jacket cross the back of the room and disappear down the corridor. "Who's that?" I asked Matt.

"Oh, that's Jeff. He doesn't talk much but you don't want to cross him."

"I thought I'd seen him on campus."

"He's the projectionist for the Clearwater Film Society."

"Maybe that's it."

"Were you there two nights ago?" Marla joined the conversation. She would have been an attractive girl even without the long, straight hair that seemed a throwback to the days when girls kept ironing boards out not for their clothes but for their hair. "The film broke during *Cat Ballou* right at the point when Jane Fonda was undressing. A lot of guys in the audience started whistling and booing. Jeff came on the P.A. system and told them that if they didn't stop, he was going to set the rest of the film on fire." These students were even more credulous than I'd thought. Sixteen millimeter film, as Jeff surely knew, had a flame-resistant acetate base. Only the original thirty-five millimeter film had a flammable nitrate base, and that had been replaced in the Fifties.

Marla drew me aside to show me the paper she'd written on the English madrigal. I looked it over briefly and asked her which madrigals she'd particularly enjoyed. She gave me a puzzled look so I rephrased the question. "Which madrigals did you listen to in doing the assignment?"

"I didn't know I had to listen to them," she said. "I copied notes out of the encyclopedia and put them into my own words." There was a trace of defiance in her tone. I felt as if I were walking into quicksand.

"But this is a paper about music," I said. "If you were writing a paper about Shakespeare, wouldn't you expect to read one of the plays or a sonnet?"

"I can't understand Shakespeare," Marla said. "That's why I decided on the madrigal."

"But this is completely dishonest," I said. "What point is there in quoting somebody else's ideas on something you haven't experienced yourself?"

Marla's lip started to tremble; then she gave me a sly smile. "Are you trying to come on to me?" she asked.

"Don't be silly," I said.

"What's the matter? Don't you think I'm pretty?"

I could see I wasn't going to get anywhere with this conversation. I handed her back the paper. "Tell you what," I said. "Go over to the music library, ask for a recording of English madrigals, and see if you can link anything you've written with anything you hear. Then I'll read your paper."

"Okay," she said uncertainly, as if realizing too late that choosing a musical topic had been a major mistake.

Cam wandered into the room and Todd said, "Boy, it's a good thing you were here this morning. I don't know what we would have done otherwise."

I wondered whether the Alternative Curriculum fostered an alternative form of learning or just an alternative to learning, whether an excess of academic freedom had fried these kids' minds or if it was just the grass.

Gloria, a slight blond woman wearing large hoop earrings and a striped blouse over blue jeans and boots, called the meeting to order. Some people pulled chairs closer; others were content to sit on the floor. The participants didn't seem especially sleepy but you'd have had difficulty proving that they were awake.

"We have a problem," Gloria began. "The dean of Arts & Sciences wants to shut us down."

"Any special reason?" Todd asked.

"It seems to be just the usual stuff," Gloria said. "The Alternative Curriculum supposedly doesn't meet the high academic standards of the rest of the university."

"What about Dean Marshall?" asked Marla. "He's always looked out for us before."

"He's on leave this term," Gloria said.

"It looks as if our enemies have been waiting for their moment," Todd said. He cracked his knuckles as if to say that he'd prefer to crack a few heads.

"Doesn't the Faculty Senate have the final say?" asked Cam.

"That's what I wanted to talk to you about," said Gloria. "We can ask to make a presentation before the Senate to make our case."

"It might help if you all turned up in jackets and ties," I said.

"Aw come on, man," said Cam. "I don't even own a jacket." Todd looked at me as if I'd come from another planet.

"So we're supposed to show everybody how much we've learned at the AC?" Marla asked.

"That's the general idea," said Gloria.

"It looks to me like a no-win situation," said Matt. "If we try to imitate ordinary students and talk about our marks in the regular curriculum, they'll say we don't need the Alternative Curriculum at all. But if we show them the stuff that we're really interested in, they'll say that's not an 'appropriate field of study' for Magnolia."

"We could try to make a film showing what we actually do here," Marla said.

"That sounds too much like work," said Cam.

"Better not show the pot-smoking," said Todd.

"I didn't hear that," said Gloria.

"This program has been running, what, four or five years?" I asked.

"About that," said Gloria.

"So the registrar's office will have a list of participants," I said. "Take that to the Alumni Office, find half a dozen former AC members who have succeeded in more or less conventional ways—the Alumni Office always knows about Magnolia's most successful graduates—give them a call, and ask them to write a few lines saying how important the AC was to their experience at Magnolia."

"That might actually work," Gloria said. "Any volunteers to try Axel's idea?"

"I'll check at the Registrar's Office," Marla said. (Anything would be better than listening to madrigals.) "I should be able to get the list before our meeting on Friday."

"That might just work," said Todd. His tone seemed to imply that he would have thought of it himself if I hadn't rushed in to take over and rescue the students. The others had already started pushing their chairs away from the circle—they didn't like meetings any more than serious study. I left the building and headed to the library.

Chapter 6

THE UNTHINKING MAY REGARD A university research library as a building full of books. Anyone who has tried to work in a research library knows that the books on their own are virtually useless without a system for accessing them. The trouble is, large libraries don't appear all at once but develop gradually over time. You can always construct a larger building to house the books as the collection grows but what do you do when an antiquated cataloguing system proves to be unworkable? Few libraries enjoy a budget large enough to re-catalogue all the books, keeping up with current acquisitions being a sufficient challenge in itself. Thus the Magnolia University library had three non-compatible systems in place: the Harris system, named for the early university librarian who invented it; the Dewey Decimal System, mainstay of American public libraries since being issued by Melvil Dewey in 1876, and the Library of Congress system, particularly suited to the needs of research collections.

The record collection at the music library displayed an even greater variety of cataloguing systems. The very earliest acquisitions were simply numbered from 1 to 100. The next record librarian instituted a system of numbers and letters that went as follows: A1 to A26, then B1 to B26, and so on through the alphabet, returning to AA1 to AA26, sometimes written as 2A26. No one could explain why the break-back point kept coming at the number 26, but at least the system was consistent. In 1967 a third system came into effect, whereby records were catalogued by the number of the year in which they were acquired, hence 67-1 through 67-200. In 1969, for example, the library purchased the entire Nonesuch catalogue, and these records sat together on a shelf as 69-1 through 69-80 or so. Nobody thought it worth the trouble to renumber the old acquisitions, figuring that so long as you could find the records it didn't really matter where they were. (Students enrolled in music courses had to listen to records, tapes and cassettes for their assignments, and while I was a bit surprised one afternoon to see that one girl had completely filled a cubicle with her knitting, which continued apparently unhindered by the sounds coming through her earphones, the librarian assured me that she was not a music major.)

The main university library housed a complete run of the local newspaper. Anything before the current year was stored on microfilm but I was able to locate accounts of the deaths of Sheila McCormack and Randy Preston in actual paper issues. Neither event had generated much of a story. Sheila, evidently related to an Oregon branch of the Massachusetts McCormacks, had died instantly when struck by an automobile at the town's principal intersection. The writer of the article noted that two other vehicular accidents had occurred at the same spot within the past six months and mentioned the efforts by some members of the town council to install a better system for protecting pedestrians. The death of Randy Preston apparently merited even less coverage, the writer noting Preston's success in cross-country competitions and including the inevitable reference to the death of marathoner James Fixx. Preston's death evidently occurred somewhere on the Magnolia cross-country trails and though one of his teammates had run for emergency assistance when Preston fell, he had died in the ambulance en route to the hospital.

When I arrived at Magnolia in the fall, I had required assistance in discovering the cross-country route, a series of dirt roads running along, and occasionally through, the Magnolia golf course. "I'll run with you part of the way and show you where the four loops intersect," a girl had volunteered, before taking off into the woods at a killing pace. I managed to keep up until we got to the intersection. "This way takes you to the East Loop and that way takes you to the West Loop," she explained before disappearing roughly in the direction of the South Loop. I must have wandered around the course for three quarters of an hour, following first one loop then another. There were signs, all right, but they all said X-Country and pointed to another loop. Passing runners would try to set me straight: "You keep going on this road up the hill, then take the loop to the left and continue until you get to the clubhouse; it's quite a ways yet."

Later in the year the *Reynolds Rap* reported that the Magnolia cross-country team had remained undefeated at home for the past two seasons. Anyone reflecting that the team's success in contests at other venues had been satisfactory but unexceptional might imagine that the Magnolia cross-country course presented special obstacles to visiting teams—nothing really flagrant, mind you, nothing that would arouse the interest of the NCAA, but enough to make a difference of a few seconds here and a few seconds there.

The route proper began at the edge of the woods surrounding the golf course and alternately skirted and crossed the links in a dizzying pattern devised by some sadistic math professor. At a bend at the bottom of the first hill came the first of three mud slides. Those who unwittingly took the faster inside portion of the curve soon ended up upended. The correct strategy was to stick with the narrow stretch of gravel at the far side of the curve. (Those who managed to figure this out by the second mud slick were usually confounded by the third, which reversed the situation.) At the edge of the first traverse of the fairway lay a number of sinkholes overgrown with grass, capable of producing twisted ankles among unwary harriers and visiting musicologists.

Then up over a grassy bunker from which the knowing would bound to a point of safety just past a blind sand-trap and back to the woods across a wooden bridge which the elements had narrowed to a single plank-width at the far end. (The brook beneath was just deep enough to soak the feet, and the hopes, of the one or two runners who inevitably ended up there when the main pack of competitors encountered the crossing.) A fallen tree, negotiable from only one unlikely angle, presented the last physical obstacle before The Nexus, the junction of all four loops of the course, whose confusing white arrows led more than one enemy runner down the road to disqualification. (The more prudent waited for a Magnolia runner to lead the way.) It wasn't exactly a steeplechase, but it would do until something better came along.

If Randy Preston had suffered a heart attack in this labyrinthine system, it would have been difficult for an ambulance to reach him in time to save his life. I was determined to make one more inquiry before accepting the heart attack story, but just as I was about to leave the periodical room I heard the sound of laughter from a nearby table. Gordon Plowright could scarcely contain his mirth at something he was reading. I walked over to see what was so funny.

"Axel, you've got to read this," he said, pushing the latest issue of the *Reynolds Rap* into my view. "Football Scholars Take No Timeouts for Classes," read the headline.

"One of my colleagues mentioned that there might be something of interest in today's paper, but I had no idea it would be this," he said.

"What happened?"

"We all know that the university offers a few easy courses so that football players can stay in school, but the sociology department seems to have turned it into a regular art form."

"How's that?"

"One professor has 150 independent studies going on at the same time, covering virtually every course in the sociology major."

"So what's the problem?"

"The problem is that the football players he has enrolled don't do anything. They don't have to attend class, they read one book, if that, write one brief paper, and they've got a credit."

"Well, one easy course here or there doesn't make that much difference, does it?"

"You don't understand: there are students here who have never attended any classes at all—they've done their entire major with this one teacher."

I read a remark attributed to one of the football players. "He's the kind of teacher that, you know, he wants to help you out, not just pile a lot of stuff on you."

"Doesn't look as if there were any stuff at all," said Prof. Plowright.

"Here's another," I said. "'I didn't do nothing illegal or anything like that.'"

"No. As the song says, 'Nice work if you can get it.'"

"So what brought the story out in the open?"

"Evidently the quarterback was given an award as Scholar Athlete of the Year for his excellence in sociology. The chairman of the department couldn't recall ever teaching the fellow, and when he asked his colleagues who taught the required courses for the major, they hadn't had him either."

"He did the whole thing independently?"

"Right. So when the chairman asked the kid about the statistics course—that's the stiffest offering in the sociology major—he said he didn't have to learn any math, he just had to write a short paper saying what it looked like."

"And that was the course?"

"Evidently."

"You know, this isn't new."

"How do you mean?"

"It's right out of *Tom Sawyer.*" I recounted the story of the church that gave out ribbons of different colors for memorizing Bible verses. You earned a blue ribbon for two verses; ten blue tickets could be exchanged for a red one, ten red tickets for a yellow one, and for ten yellow tickets, the equivalent of memorizing two thousand verses, you were awarded a plainly bound Bible. Tom, having traded licorice, fish hooks, marbles, and other items for ribbons, came up to the front of the church with nine yellow tickets, nine red tickets, and ten blue ones, and demanded a Bible.

"I think I remember this," Plowright said. "The superintendent, in giving Tom the Bible, asks him, as someone whose exemplary memory has given him such a prodigious command of Scripture, to name two of the disciples."

"And Tom, looking sheepish, says 'David and Goliath.'"

"If it hadn't been for the Scholar Athlete award, this scam might have gone on for years."

"Talk about being a victim of one's own success!" I said.

"The team went undefeated this season, too," Plowright said.

"And those that don't turn pro will become sociologists."

Chapter 7

POLICE OFFICERS, AMONG OTHER SKILLS, learn to cultivate a "commanding voice," a resonant, authoritative tone calculated to encourage compliance. College professors receive no such training, but we do tend to speak with a tone of knowledgeable confidence, at least in our fields of expertise, which tends to make people assume that we know what we're talking about. I attribute to this tone, as well as to a mild bit of deceptiveness, my success in dealing with Francis Peabody, county coroner for the region surrounding Magnolia University.

The telephone book informed me that the county morgue would be found at the same address as the county sheriff's office, just down the street from the local police headquarters. I entered the building late in the afternoon, when most of the staff would have been counting the minutes until departure, and headed for the lower level. I maintained a brisk pace, kept my eyes straight ahead, and no one challenged me until just before I reached the door to the morgue itself. At that point a secretary gave me a questioning look. I gave her a big smile and a half-salute and kept on going, leaving her to wonder whether she shouldn't have recognized me.

The door to the morgue itself was unlocked so I walked in. Every part of the room was white or chrome, from the walls to the furnishings, so that you might almost have thought you were in a medical institution devoted to maintaining life rather than in a room from which all life had passed. A cabinet with glass doors containing small vials of chemicals, and tall measuring instruments mounted on wheels would not have been out of place in an operating room. Then I noticed the differences: the rows of white doors, about the same size as storage lockers in a bus terminal, behind which cadavers lay in waiting, and the sluiceways running along the sides of what I had first mistaken for operating tables. No patient would leave this room alive.

Francis Peabody looked up from his desk when he heard the door open, then stood and came toward me. He was a tall man with a long face, in the physical, not the metaphorical, sense. His narrow eyes looked through old-fashioned spectacles of the sort I'd seen only in historical villages but his mouth suggested a man who managed to find humor in life regardless of the lugubrious nature of his profession.

"I'm sorry not to have called ahead for an appointment," I said. "I'm Dr. Crochet." (No lies so far, even though no Ph.D. I knew ever actually used the honorific.)

"Good afternoon, Doctor," Peabody said, shaking my hand. "I don't believe I recognize the name."

"I'm from out of state. The Preston family …"

"Oh, yes. That runner. Strange case. I would like to have performed an autopsy, but the Prestons refused. Are you the family physician? Did the boy have a history of a heart condition?"

"None that I'm aware of, but I imagine that the family told you about his father's death, also of a heart attack. Are these the boy's things here?" I asked, gesturing to an open box containing a running outfit.

"Yes. We expect the family to be coming tomorrow for the body."

"Do you mind if I take a look? I'm something of a runner myself."

"Help yourself," he said. "But I don't think you'll find anything out of the ordinary. The shirt was loose-fitting, nothing that could have produced constriction." As Peabody went on with his recitation I picked up one of the running shoes, a well-worn Nike product showing mud stains from the Magnolia cross-country trails. Nothing out of the ordinary on the bottom. I pressed my fingers along the inner surface of the shoe, which felt about the same as my own running shoes. Then I examined its mate, without finding anything unusual until I pressed down on the inside heel and felt a tiny prick. Could Randy have somehow gotten a thorn into his shoe? Nothing visible. I lifted the detachable heel pad and looked at its lower surface. Part of the grey rubber had been cut away and in the resulting cavity lay a small capsule.

"What do you make of this?" I asked the coroner, holding out the heel pad for his inspection.

"That's strange," he said. "Never thought to look inside his shoes."

"There appears to be a tiny needle extending into the shoe proper.

Most likely it wouldn't have penetrated the surface until someone had been running on it for awhile. Hard to imagine that Preston would have put it there himself, though."

Peabody wasn't even there to hear the rest of my words. He strode to his desk holding the heel pad in his hand and was talking urgently into the telephone as I exited the morgue and made my way back to the street. I didn't know what kind of chemical Peabody would trace from the vial, but its presence alone was enough to convince me that Randy Preston's death had not been accidental.

I went back to my apartment to see what I could find for supper. I sometimes eat out, though I mostly avoided the university cafeterias after my experience with the Christmas Candlelight Buffet advertised in the student paper. "Graduate Center Dining Halls Invite You To An Annual Spectacular Holiday Feast." I went with Sharon, a young visiting professor in the history department. Nothing ever came of the date—I think she found me too short—but I won't forget the dinner.

"This must be quite a meal," I told her. "Look at that line!" The queue wound around the outer wall of the dining hall, then disappeared up a long flight of stairs, across a lobby and down another hall. Forty-five minutes later we arrived in the candle-lit dining hall.

"What's in the punch?" Sharon asked.

"I can't see in this candlelight—tastes like cloves."

"Cloves and Hawaiian punch." Our first warning. We still could have turned back, but we'd already invested forty-five minutes in the venture so we loaded our trays with bits of banquet and headed to our seats.

"This oyster stew is a bit watery," Sharon said.

"But fresh!"

"Are these little crackers the oysterettes?"

"Must be." I realized where I'd seen the meat before: at college we called it Mystery Meat. So it was really "Steamship Round of Beef carved to order." You learned something every day.

"But the potato is good."

"The peas and corn are a little weird, though."

"The best thing is the Bavarian Stollen."

Time passed, then I ventured to say, "Well, that sure was spectacular."

"And annual, too," Sharon said gamely. Then we exchanged

memories of high school dances where covering the baskets with crepe paper was supposed to make everyone think the gymnasium was a Winter Wonderland for the Senior Prom. Mediocre food isn't bad in moderation—we all managed to live through college, after all—but a whole banquet of it left one a bit bilious

The thought made me long for something healthy and I managed to find ingredients for a nice Salade Niçoise.

Chapter 8

AN HOUR LATER I WAS sitting across the coffee table from Beth in her apartment, just as the predicted thunderstorm hit. "You think Sheila's death wasn't an accident either?" Beth asked.

"What do you think?"

"I don't know. It's bad enough that my best friend is dead. Now you're suggesting that someone killed her intentionally."

"Does it seem more likely that somebody killed her fiancé and within days she died accidentally?"

"I just don't like thinking about it." The sky darkened further and Beth turned on another lamp.

"I know the idea is disagreeable," I said, "but you knew Sheila better than anyone else. Can you tell me more about her life?"

"I'm not sure what there is to tell. She was my roommate until this year when she got an apartment of her own. There wasn't any problem between us—she just wanted more privacy when she and Randy started getting serious."

"I see. What did she do when she wasn't in class or studying?"

"She spent a lot of time with Randy. She and I would play tennis occasionally. I can't think of anything special."

"Did she belong to any organizations, support any causes?"

"None that I can think of. Once a year she made contributions to Greenpeace and Amnesty International, that sort of thing, but she wasn't actively involved herself. Oh, and she volunteered for the SETI project." Thunder crashed several blocks away and a moment later the lights went out. Beth and I waited briefly for the electricity to return but when the darkness continued she made her way to the kitchen and came back with a couple of lighted candles.

"It looks as if you're prepared," I said.

"It freaked us out when we first came to Magnolia," Beth said. "The storms and the electricity going out all the time. The dorms have emergency lights so at least the hallways aren't totally in the dark. But when we moved to the University Apartments we learned to keep a supply of candles handy during storm season. Is this enough light for you or should I find some more candles?"

"I think this'll be okay. Your eyes get used to it after awhile."

"So what were we talking about?"

"You mentioned a SETI project."

"Oh yes. It's Professor Kilby's brainchild."

"Isn't he in the astronomy department?"

"I guess you could say that, but for most people at Magnolia Prof. Kilby *is* the astronomy department. He's one of the big movers and shakers on campus. Haven't you heard of the infrared observatory?"

"I'm afraid not."

"That's Kilby's biggest claim to fame. The project has gotten so big that graduate students come here just to work in the observatory, knowing that they'll have no trouble getting a job when they leave."

"What's he like as a teacher?"

Beth rolled her eyes. "I'm not sure you want to know."

"How do you mean?"

"Well, he has a reputation for really hating women. A few female students have dared stand up to him, but mostly the observatory is an all-male preserve."

"Doesn't he get in trouble for harassing women students?"

"Actually, I think he has a perverted notion of affirmative action: essentially he treats everybody badly."

"And he can get away with it because he brings in so much research money."

"That's university life for you. Say, can I get you something to drink?"

"Do you have any fruit juice?"

"I think there's some orange juice in the fridge."

"Suppose you mix that half and half with ginger ale."

"Gee, you're a cheap date." Beth went into the kitchen and returned a few minutes later with two glasses, hers evidently filled with some kind of cola. "Is this your first time in the South?" she asked.

"First I've been here for longer than a couple of days," I said. "It really is a different world."

"What's impresses you most?

"Well it's hard to miss the slower rhythms of the southern drawl, and from what I've encountered this year, southern hospitality is no myth."

"Even in a university town like Reynolds?"

"Sure thing. Last week I ordered blackberry cobbler at the local Backyard Burger, and learning that they were all out, I settled for cherry but said I'd be back some other time. The aged counterperson said, 'I'll look forward to that.' It completely blew me away."

"Yeah, the older people cling to the traditions."

"What about you? Were you a debutante?"

"I considered it, and my parents were prepared to pay the $2000 fee."

"That much?"

"You bet. Of course that would have given my daughter, if I ever have one, the right to 'come out,' too."

"But you decided against it?"

"If you had the choice between a debutante ball and a year of graduate study in Great Britain, which would you choose?"

"That would be an easy for me, but I'm neither female nor southern."

"Well, it wasn't that hard a choice for me, either. I'll bet the custom doesn't last another generation."

"You could be right, but from what I've seen of the force of tradition down here, I wouldn't want to wager on it." I realized that this girl was having more of an effect on me than I'd acknowledged, and tried to bring the conversation back to Sheila's computer. I knew I'd seen Kilby's name somewhere before Beth mentioned it.

"Is that the same Kilby that was mentioned in the article in the student paper? '**Professor seeks message from E.T.**' or something like that?"

"I know it sounds pretty dumb the way they told it, but when Sheila explained the project to me, it seemed to make sense."

"Tell me about it."

"Well you've heard of Carl Sagan. He's convinced that we could be receiving messages from other intelligent life forms if only we'd listen."

"I take it you mean listening for radio signals?"

"Right. So SETI has this bank of radio telescopes looking for signals."

"Have they picked anything up yet?"

"Well that's the problem. Space is full of all kinds of radio waves. The trick is to find out what's noise and what might be a message."

"So how does Sheila fit in with this?"

"Prof. Kilby's project takes the data from these monitors and sends it to people who volunteer their computers when they're not using them—at night, for instance—and they use the computers to hunt for patterns in the numbers."

"I still don't get it. Did Sheila have to take her computer to Prof. Kilby every night and pick it up again in the morning?"

"No, silly. It's all done electronically. I think she said something about installing a piece of software."

We chatted for a while longer, and when I made to head off to the library, Beth asked if I couldn't stay longer, but, charming as I found her, my duty to Proust won out, and I told her I'd see her in class the next morning.

"I'm still waiting for that invitation for a date," Beth said with a smile.

"You shouldn't have to wait much longer," I said.

Chapter 9

GETTING THROUGH PROUST IS HARD work. Prof. Nelson mentioned that he read *A la recherche du temps perdu* every second year. I considered that it would be a miracle if I could get through the *roman fleuve* even once. I set myself a nightly assignment of fifty pages, with a reward of seeing a film at the Clearwater Film Festival. But tonight, after reading my quota of page-long sentences in French, I headed not to the theatre but to the periodical section of the library. The too-coincidental deaths of Randy and Sheila continued to bother me, and one of Beth's remarks had set me thinking.

The periodical section was practically empty, in contrast to the morning crowd of students looking up sports results in out-of-town newspapers. Fluorescent lights behind translucent panels made the ceiling glow brightly. An assistant librarian walked across the room without giving me a second glance. Weekly publications sat piled on neatly-labeled wooden shelves; the most frequently-consulted journals were mounted on long bamboo sticks. I wondered if I was the only one to notice the irony of placing back issues of the *Reynolds Rap* alongside copies of *The London Times*, *Le Monde*, and *The Washington Post*.

In recent days the *Reynolds Rap* had become embroiled over a dispute between the Editorial Board, which supported the United Farm Workers, and the Advertising Board, which wanted to run a series of ads sponsored by the Gallo Company. Both sides invoked the principle of free speech and the Publications Board had threatened to suspend publication of the paper if the Gallo ads were not run. The case eventually went into arbitration. Meanwhile the Magnolia radio station refused to accept advertising from either Gallo or the UFW on the grounds that it received so many protest calls when it ran either ad that the switchboard broke down.

This supplanted the previous campus issue, the decision of the Clearwater Film Society to show "The Devil in Miss Jones," a porno flick, in order to make up a deficit in its treasury. Once again free speech was invoked, this time in answer to the administration's arguments that the showing of the film was not educational and would antagonize alumni, thus jeopardizing the current endowment campaign. The film society compromised by holding a symposium on pornography between shows, thereby turning the entire presentation into an educational event. One letter-writer suggested that a comparable symposium be held between halves of Magnolia football games, encounters rarely celebrated heretofore for their educational value.

I missed "The Devil in Miss Jones" but did make the mistake of attending the showing of "The Night of the Living Dead" on Halloween. From out of the Gothic depths of Magnolia's subjacent catacombs a horde of drunken ghouls emerged to fill the theater with bestial mutterings and drown the tinkle of beer bottles rolling down the aisle with frenzied guttural encouragement of the jumbled scenes of cannibalism portrayed on the screen which, far from being cathartic, only further roused their base appetites so that leaving the theater, and finding no suitable human objects for their madness, they noisily assaulted street signs and light poles to the disgust of passersby and pious musicologists.

The next day I learned that the place to be on Halloween was the university library. One fellow was studying his human sexuality text when a gorgeous Renaissance damsel sat down across from him and murmured, "In my day we didn't talk about it, we just practiced it." He offered her a refresher course but she modestly declined. Then in came a group of people with carefully-lettered garbage buckets over their heads, dressed as a six-pack of beer, complete with a plastic wrapper joining them together on which someone had written "When you say Budweiser, you've said a lot."

Eventually I turned up the article on Prof. Kilby's SETI project. I had wondered how individual personal computers could be linked. The article compared the network of computers to the array of radio telescopes employed to search for extra-terrestrial radio signals. According to the newspaper, participants were sent a software package which, when installed on their machines, allowed them to receive data via the Internet, process it, and send it back to the source. This took advantage of the computer's processing capabilities during off-hours when the owner wasn't using it. One phrase in particular caught my attention: "The SETI network constitutes a virtual supercomputer." I recalled Prof. Loomis' use of the same term and realized that it wasn't just my math skills that weren't up to this investigation; I needed the help of a computer geek. I looked at my watch and wondered whether it was too late to ask Beth to help me. Perhaps I was just happy to have an excuse to see her again.

As I left the periodical room I saw Todd working in the reference section. He looked up, saw the surprised expression on my face, and said, "What's the matter, Axel? Don't you think AC students can read?'

"Well, I …"

"Come on, admit it. You think we're basically a bunch of self-absorbed illiterates."

"I wouldn't say …"

"Just because we don't like grown-ups telling us exactly which courses we have to take to satisfy their major doesn't mean we aren't interested in education."

"I never said …"

"It seems to me you'd learn a lot more if you'd listen to students once in a while instead of just telling us what to think. Aw, what's the use?"

Todd went back to his work and I gave up trying to engage him in discussion. These Alternative Curriculum kids did seem stubborn once they'd formed an opinion. On the other hand, it had surprised me to see Todd in the library, so perhaps I had my own prejudices to deal with.

The rain had stopped as I headed across campus to the University Apartments but the sidewalks were still wet and the grass beside them looked suspiciously squishy. I passed and greeted Prof. Nelson, evidently returning home after the film. When I visited Magnolia the previous May, Nelson had put me up in his townhouse, a short walk from campus. He had shown me the specially-constructed desk in his bedroom enabling him to wake up at five in the morning and write for three hours in bed before going to teach his classes. Out of curiosity I had looked up Nelson's name in the library card catalogue and been astonished at the phenomenal number of entries. Nelson wrote, he told me, not for experts in the field but for intelligent undergraduates, and his books had been widely adopted for college courses in French literature.

During my time at Magnolia, Nelson never mentioned his colleagues in the department but on more than one occasion he spoke enthusiastically about a Magnolia football or basketball player, enrolled in one of his courses, who had offered Nelson tickets to the game so that he might appreciate someone whose athletic abilities surpassed his academic skills. I would have liked to be on such terms with my students. For that matter, I would have liked to be teaching at Magnolia instead of Monongahela.

Chapter 10

BETH ANSWERED IN A WARY voice when I knocked at her door, but when I identified myself she let me in and greeted me with a smile. I had to smile myself at the sight of her pink bathrobe and oversize furry slippers decorated with hamster faces. "You came back," she said. When I explained that it was about Sheila, Beth's face turned to a frown of disappointment and concern but she led me inside and sat beside me on the sofa. The sounds of Santana played softly in the background.

"I know this may sound crazy, but I think Sheila's death is related to her connection to the SETI project," I said.

"I hope you're not going to tell me she was killed by extra-terrestrials."

"No, but I think it had to do with her computer being linked to hundreds of others. The problem is, I don't know anything about computers, and if there really is a connection, I'm going to need help."

"Not from me, I hope. You need a computer geek."

"Right."

"I know just the person. Her name is Bridget Jeffries and her house is just on the next block. Let's go ask her."

"Won't this be too late?"

"Computer people live in a different time frame from the rest of us. This is just the beginning of their active period. Give me a couple of minutes to change my clothes." Beth returned wearing blue jeans, a Magnolia University tee-shirt, and apparently nothing else. It took an effort for me to focus on computers.

Outside the weather had cleared after the earlier storm, the stars were out, and a nearly full moon low on the horizon looked enormous. I'd heard various explanations for the effect, demonstrated to be purely psychological, the most convincing of which claimed that since danger, for our prehistoric ancestors, was more likely to come from in front than from above, our brains were programmed to exaggerate the size of objects in the horizontal plane. Whatever the scientific cause, the effect was dramatic and poetic.

On the brief walk Beth explained, in answer to my question, how a graduate student could afford to live in a house. Bridget's father, a successful computer entrepreneur, had crunched the numbers and decided it was a better investment, given the real estate situation in Reynolds, to buy his daughter a small house and sell it after her graduation than to pay for room and board at the university.

Our designated computer geek seemed to be accustomed to receiving nocturnal visitors. Bridget's sparsely furnished apartment contrasted with Beth's Sixties time-warp and her short hair and boyish figure stood in contrast to Beth's embodiment of the Southern belle. Beth introduced me as a Visiting Scholar from "up North" and Bridget as someone who knew computers inside out, and Bridget led us into the kitchen, evidently the center of activity for the house. Memos adorned the refrigerator door, cookbooks sat on a shelf beside the gas stove, and a bunch of papers rested beneath the telephone. Bridget cleared a few textbooks off the round table in the middle of the room and we sat down on unmatched chairs. Daddy had evidently bought the building but left Bridget to furnish it on a student's allowance.

"For some people computers are a hobby. For Bridget they're a combat sport. Tell Axel about your brothers," Beth prompted.

Bridget smiled and said, "I have two older brothers. When they weren't picking on me they ignored me. Guess that's par for the course. So when they went out I'd re-program their video games."

"Is that possible?" I asked.

"That's what hackers do," she said.

I explained the purpose of my visit. "This morning Prof. Loomis told me that if he knew how to factor large primes he'd be a wealthy man because he could divert other people's bank accounts into his own. He explained the mathematical part—it had to do with public-key encryption—but I don't understand how someone could hack into a bank in the first place."

"It's not so hard." Bridget seemed to enjoy the idea of a challenge. "First you find the name of a bank employee. That's not difficult in a town as small as this. Let's assume the bank uses a system like initial plus last name. You use that as your user-name. To get the password, you could run a program which goes through all combinations of English words and symbols until you hit one that lets you in."

"Wouldn't that take a long time?"

"Right. So a better method would be to pick a particular employee and learn all you can about him—it would be easy enough to obtain the names of his wife and children. People use passwords that they can remember, so they're likely to use a familiar name, perhaps with a symbol inserted somewhere in it. So you run a program that tries these family names with all combinations and placements of symbols. With any luck it wouldn't take you too long to find the password."

"Okay. So let's say I can get into the bank's computer system. Prof. Loomis says that the data is encrypted, and that you'd need a supercomputer to break the code."

"That's about right."

"But the student paper said that Prof. Kilby's SETI network was the equivalent of a supercomputer. If somebody could get into the network, couldn't they use it to factor the public key and crack the encryption?"

A smile crossed Bridget's face. "That's very clever," she said. "It never would have occurred to me."

"Then bear with me for a minute. Let's imagine that someone, let's call him the Hacker, has broken into the SETI network. Could he really read the e-mail of the participants?"

"Nobody would join the network if they thought that were true, but if you could hack into the network, you'd be able to do it."

"How does that work?"

"If the system uses Outlook, then breaking into the system would allow someone to read all the e-mail."

"But I don't understand what this has to do with Sheila and Randy," Beth said.

"They went to see Prof. Loomis because of some numbers that turned up on Sheila's machine." I said. "I'm guessing that of all the hundreds of computers in the network, Sheila's is the one that happened to discover the prime factors that made up the encryption key. Of course, as far as she was concerned, it was just a number."

"But if she and Randy discussed it by e-mail," Beth said, "the Hacker would have known about it."

"And decided they were a threat," Bridget said. "This isn't just a game, is it?"

"I think the Hacker killed them both, but there's no way to prove it."

"Do you have Sheila's PC?" Bridget asked. I nodded. "Bring it over to the Computer Center tomorrow afternoon. I may be able to find something in the program that linked it to the SETI network."

"I thought those programs were supposed to be inaccessible to the users," I said.

Bridget just raised a single eyebrow. It must have taken her hours of practice to master that trick, but I got the message. That's what hackers do.

When Beth and I returned to her apartment she invited me in and I accepted.

"Can I tell you something, Axel?" Beth asked.

"Sure thing."

She hesitated. "This is a little hard."

"Then breathe and take your time," I said.

Beth smiled and then continued. "Well, earlier when you knocked on the door, I was really glad to see you. Then you said it was about Sheila, and I felt disappointed that you hadn't really come to see me."

I waited until a quick flurry of feelings subsided, and said, "Oh Beth. I feel pleasure every time you come to sit in front of me in class, but never wanted to become involved with you because I'm only here for the year. Then tonight, when you came to the door in those silly slippers, and I thought about how comfortable I am in this Sixties hippy haven, I felt almost overwhelmed, and it took all my will power to keep the discussion focused on Sheila."

Beth leaned over to kiss me and I put my arms around her. "Maybe we can do both," she murmured.

Chapter 11

ON WEDNESDAY MORNING, ASSIGNED TO make an oral presentation in Prof. Trente's class, I rose early and headed to campus only to find my way blocked. Another storm had begun during the night and continued unabated until just before dawn. Steps had turned into waterfalls, sidewalks had become streams, and the road I had to cross looked more like a river. With the water level well above ankle level I had to adopt extreme measures. Removing my shoes and socks and rolling up my trousers to my knees, I tied my shoes together, carried them around my neck and waded across, holding my precious notes high above the water. I had no fear of catching cold: the steamy atmosphere banished all threat of chill.

As I entered the French building I found that some fellow cross-country runner had already expressed my thoughts in a bit of doggerel posted on the bulletin board:

Oh, to be in Reynolds
Now that spring is there,
And whoever runs in Reynolds
Had better be aware
That the friendly footpaths of autumn tide
Have turned into tributaries six feet wide
While the tender turf has become a slough
In Reynolds—and how!
Gone are the snows along with passing season?
Incessant rains surpass all power of reason,
As though the gods preferred the solipsism of Verlaine
And spurned Villon's hibernal quest—
Drizzle, shower, storm, then shower again—
That's the kind of day with which we're blessed,
Lest you think that after one such spray
The rain clouds had had their say.

And though the fields look safe enough at morn
All will be mud when noontide's rays adorn
This sloppy slank, this erstwhile lawn—
Pity the harrier, woebegone!
[With apologies to Robert Browning]

I entered the empty classroom and began to cover the blackboard with notes, names, dates and visual representations to support my presentation on the 13th-century motet in France. (I had volunteered to go first so that I could make maximum use of supplementary materials to shore up my shaky command of French.) Prof. Trente entered, saw what I was doing, and nodded. The students filed in, and I was reminded again of the absence of Sheila McCormack.

The class began and when Prof. Trente needed to indicate the orthography of some term he went to the blackboard and erased part of my outline as the rest of the students gasped. Then more and more of the outline disappeared beneath his eraser as the class wriggled in discomfort and sympathy for their visiting colleague. Finally he looked at the title, "Les grandes étapes dans le développement du motet français du 13e siècle," and then looked at me and said, "Oh, is this yours?" I commented that he had seen me writing on the board when he came in. "Oh," he said, "I just didn't make the connection."

Each student had to give a short report on a subject of his or her choice: the search for the Holy Grail; medieval tapestry; Catherine de Medicis. Since one can scarcely speak in French for only three minutes on any subject of interest, particularly when one has spent a week doing research on it, the reports ran closer to six to eight minutes. For some reason this upset Prof. Trente, who intentionally scheduled the reports in the final three minutes of the period so that they inevitably ran over the class hour. This tendency toward arbitrariness, insensitivity, and occasionally even ruthlessness produced a certain antipathy on the part of some faculty members toward the man's chairmanship. After denying tenure to one assistant professor (married with family, eleven years of teaching experience), Trente had the nerve to suggest that the French House at Oberlin was looking for a housemaster at a modest stipend.

"He'd probably let you postpone it till next time," Beth whispered to me from the desk beside mine.

"Nah; he'd probably do the same thing again," I said. She used her hand to stifle a giggle.

I made my way to the front of the class to give my presentation, suddenly bereft of pedagogical supports. "He rode all unarmed and he rode all alone," I thought to myself. Nope. Wrong country; wrong century. What was there about Beth that made me think of Lochinvar? Perhaps I really did have a thing for damsels in distress. The other students looked at me expectantly. I decided to fling caution to the winds and wing it. I liked 13th-century motets, liked the slightly alien sound of modal harmony, liked the way three different texts—some sacred, some secular, some Latin, some French—could be combined in the same piece. The class responded to my enthusiasm and I saw their attitude of sympathy turn into genuine interest. What had started out as scary turned out to be fun. Their applause at the end of my short talk meant as much to me as the applause at the end of a piano recital that had taken me half a year to prepare. For years I'd rejected lecturing as a teaching style, but this brief experience suggested I might actually be good at it.

I celebrated with a trip to the Student Union where I managed to snag the last remaining sugar doughnut, then headed to the library to start a composition for Mme Cointreau.

Chapter 12

THE UNIVERSITY COMPUTER CENTER OCCUPIED a subterranean enclave beneath the elegant Alumni Hall. Were its sunless rooms behind thick concrete walls a matter of physical security, or did a university considered to be a citadel of liberal learning feel embarrassed by the necessity of housing the wizards of cyberspace? The cumbersome quarters only contributed to computer science students' reputation as hypogeal beings whose esoteric expertise belonged to the "night of the living dead."

I wasn't sure where to look for Bridget when I entered the main room but apparently the intrusion of an outsider sent an invisible message, *"Not one of us,"* to the several dozen students working at computer terminals. I saw Todd sitting at a console near the entrance.

"You look a little out of your element, Axel," he said. "I thought French and music were your fields."

"I'm meeting a friend."

"Don't you think you're a bit old for the girls here?"

"It's not like that." Why did I always feel on the defensive around this guy? Fortunately Bridget appeared at that moment and led me to her console, directing me to roll up a chair.

"I take it this is the first time you've been here," Bridget said, noticing my disoriented stare. Identical modules supported by bird-like feet each contained a monitor, a roll-out drawer for a keyboard and a work area, cunningly arranged to cram the maximum number of units into the available space. The complex configuration of computer consoles, illuminated by a simple pattern of flat ceiling panels, seemed to turn the human figures into mere robotic units in some sci-fi fantasy. I guess if you worked here awhile you took it for granted. I tore my gaze away from the hypermodern tessellation and directed my attention to the subject at hand.

"I've examined Sheila's computer," Bridget told me, indicating the small PC sitting beside her own machine on the desk. She typed in a few instructions and numbers appeared on the screen. "Here's the record of each time her machine was accessed for the SETI network. As you can see, the times are all between 1 a.m. and 6 a.m.—I guess they figure normal people won't be using their computers then."

"Does the SETI data get stored on each individual computer?"

"It looks to me as if they've installed a program that deletes the data once a month. Otherwise people would start to complain that the project was taking up too much of their computer space. We have a lot of capacity on the machines here in the center but in a network like the SETI project you pretty much have to figure on the lowest common denominator."

"So what happens if one computer in the network finds a message from outer space?"

Bridget smiled. "You're not going to get a message on any of these machines. The whole point of the project is to process raw data looking for patterns. If any kind of regularity appears, that set of data goes to a central computer and they start trying to decipher it."

"How can you tell if there's a pattern?"

"The numbers they're looking at represent background noise in the universe—just a bunch of random digits. Any kind of message will look quite a bit different."

"The screen you've displayed just gives a list of dates. What do the actual numbers look like?" Bridget pressed a few keys and a series of figures appeared. I must have looked perplexed because Bridget asked me what was wrong. "None of these look at all like the number that Sheila mentioned in her e-mail to Randy. Aren't there any other numbers in the machine?"

Bridget opened a screen that showed the organization of the computer. "Was Sheila interested in mathematics?" she asked.

"Not as far as I know. What makes you ask?"

"There's a file here called 'Mersenne.'"

"What's that—a French wine?"

"No, a French mathematician. He was particularly interested in prime numbers."

Prof. Loomis' brief lesson popped into my mind. "That might be it. What's in the folder?"

Bridget opened the folder to display a vast number of files. "Do you really want me to go through all of these?" she asked.

"If they're arranged by date, why don't you start with the last one," I suggested.

Bridget opened the file and a number flashed onto the screen: 979853562951413. "That's it!" I said.

"I thought you weren't a math person? How can you recognize that number?" Bridget asked.

"It begins with 9 and ends in 13. My birthday is September 13th."

"So you're not sure about all the numbers in between."

"No, but if you don't believe me, we can check it against Sheila's e-mail."

"I'll take your word for it. But where did all these files come from?"

"I was hoping you could tell me that. You're sure this isn't part of the SETI project?"

"No way. That number is much too long, and the SETI people aren't going to set up a file folder called 'Mersenne.' Somebody has a sense of humor."

"Is there some way to find out where the number came from?"

"That's going to require hacking into the records of Sheila's ISP?"

"Is that legal?"

Bridget gave me a look of disdain. "I thought you said this was a matter of life and death."

"Well, yes."

"Then all right. Come back here at midnight and I'll tell you what I find."

"Midnight? Aren't the campus buildings locked after ten?"

"All except this one."

I thanked her and promised to return on time. Todd beckoned to me as I approached the entrance and I stopped at his work station.

"You'd better not get her in trouble, Axel," he said.

"What are you talking about?"

"We look after our own," he said with a hint of menace in his voice.

"Todd, what it is with you? Do you really dislike me that much?"

"I just think you should stick with what you're here for and stop trying to be 'one of the kids.' It's embarrassing to watch."

"I'm not trying to be anything," I said and then stopped. I didn't know where my poking around was going to lead and I certainly didn't see any reason why I had to account for my actions to this pimply teenager.

"Hmph," he said and turned back to his computer.

I left the Computer Center and calculated that I had time for a short run before dinner. In contrast to Monongahela, where I'd still be wearing a sweatshirt over a running jersey, here I'd already been able to run bare-chested. The South kept finding new ways to charm me.

Chapter 13

By the middle of the evening I'd managed to complete a brief composition for Mme Cointreau's conversation and composition class the next day, the exercises for Prof. Wicks' phonetics class, and most of the daily installment of Proust. I looked at my watch, realized that I'd missed the Clearwater film for the evening and vowed to push on to the end. But the elusiveness of the young girls with bicycles that Marcel encounters at a seaside resort, combined with the vagueness of Proust's semi-impenetrable prose, produced an irresistible desire to spend time with an actual female person, and at length I closed my books and walked over to Beth's apartment.

Beth had just washed her hair so her previous evening outfit of bathrobe and silly slippers was now set off by a giant white turban. "I was going to talk to you tomorrow in class, but I'm glad you came over," she said. We walked into the living room and sat on the sofa. The gentle rhythms of "Guantanamera" sounded through the loudspeakers. "My brother's best friend works on the police force so I asked him to see if he could find out anything about Sheila and Randy."

"I take it he got some information?"

"It's not exactly good news. The police have decided that Sheila's death was an accident." Beth reached up to rearrange her towel turban.

"The paper described it as a hit-and-run, but you'd think with a girl getting struck by a car at the busiest intersection in town, someone would have noticed the license plate."

"Someone did, and they even located the car. It was abandoned in a field not far from campus."

"Whose car was it?"

"It belonged to some little old lady who didn't even know that her car was missing, but evidently she was pleased with all the attention."

"What do the police make of it?" I asked.

"Well, evidently there was a lot of liquor spilled in the car and a bottle nearby. They're describing it as a joy ride."

"Not much joy for Sheila."

"If they ever find the driver there'll be manslaughter charges but it sounds as if there wasn't any evidence in the car, other than the alcohol, so they're still treating it as an accident."

"What about Randy?"

"Oh, that's considered a murder, all right, thanks to the stuff you found in his running shoe, but you can't take fingerprints from a running shoe, and after they made routine calls to local druggists, they're more or less back at square one."

"Couldn't they identify the poison?"

"That wasn't a problem, but I'm afraid I couldn't even pronounce the name."

"Poisons and primes. This guy seems to know a lot." The music had moved to The Byrds singing "Turn, Turn, Turn." I wondered whether Beth knew she was listening to words right out of Ecclesiastes but decided not to change the subject.

"Did Bridget help you find anything on Sheila's PC?" she asked. I recounted the conversation I'd had with Bridget in the Computer Center and mentioned that the Hacker had apparently created a folder called Mersenne. "You're kidding!"

"Don't tell me you've heard of Mersenne."

"You're going to laugh, but that was the name of our cat."

"Why on earth ...?"

"My dad taught math at the Stanford. I think he was a bit disappointed when I didn't inherit his gifts, but at least I know about prime numbers."

"So what's the connection with Mersenne?"

"He was a 17th-century French monk who came up with the idea that 2^n-1 was a prime."

"Let's see. 2^2-1 is 3, that's a prime. 2^3-1 is 7, that's another prime. 2^4-1 is 15. Wait a minute; 15 isn't a prime."

"No. It doesn't work for every number. Mersenne proposed a list of numbers for which the formula would work. The list was wrong, but at the time there was no way to check it for the big numbers. But nowadays if you find a number of the form 2^n-1 that works, they call it a Mersenne prime."

"You mean people are still looking for them?"

"Sure. You remember what Prof. Loomis told you. Finding primes is big business. Often there's a big celebration when a new one is discovered."

"You're putting me on," I said.

"No, really. You've commented on what you call my memorabilia from Dad." I looked again at the Peter Max poster beside my head. "Here's something else I saved." Beth went to her desk and took an envelope from the drawer. I could see the postmark through the clear plastic envelope in which she'd protected it.

"This was the University of Chicago's way of celebrating their discovery."

"This is hard to believe."

"So what was in the folder in Sheila's computer?"

"That was apparently where the Hacker kept the winning numbers. But I still don't get it. If all it takes is a computer to generate a prime number, why did the Hacker have to hijack the entire SETI network?"

"Don't you see? He wasn't trying to produce prime numbers; he was trying to find prime factors."

"What's the difference?"

"You knew right off that 15 wasn't a prime, right?"

"Sure. 15 is made up of 3 times 5."

"And 3 and 5 are both primes."

"Right."

"Okay. Now suppose you have a big number." Beth pulled a calculator out of a desk drawer. "Say you had 2881. Is that a prime?"

"No clue."

"No. It turns out to be 67 times 43."

"You didn't have any trouble discovering that."

"That's because I created the number myself by multiplying 67 and

43. But if you have a really large number, it's very difficult to find its prime factors."

Prof. Loomis's explanation started making more sense. "I think I get it," I said. "To crack a really large number you'd need a supercomputer."

"Or a network of computers all hooked together. That's why the Hacker hijacked the SETI group."

"And out of all the computers in the network, Sheila had the misfortune of being the winner."

"And Randy had the misfortune of being the only person she told about the number on her screen."

"So they both had to die."

"But why did they have to die?" Beth asked. "As far as Sheila was concerned, that number appearing on her computer was just a petty annoyance. You read the message she sent Randy?"

"I agree, but the Hacker probably didn't look at it that way. I imagine he was afraid that whoever got that number would go to Professor Kilby to ask what it meant. Was this the message from E.T. that everyone had been waiting for?"

"And even if Kilby didn't spot it as a prime number—as Prof. Loomis explained, that's not easy to do—he would recognize it as something out of place. Remember—the SETI project was looking for patterns, not for primes, and that number didn't have any particular pattern to it."

"So Kilby might conclude that someone had taken over the network."

"But wasn't Bridget able to find out who was controlling the network?"

"She said she had to hack into Sheila's ISP." I looked at my watch. "In fact, I'm supposed to go over to the Computer Center to see if she's found anything."

Beth looked disappointed to see me go. I promised her that when we worked this out we could talk about something more romantic than prime numbers. She smiled, kissed me, and sent me on my way.

Chapter 14

THE CAMPUS OF MAGNOLIA UNIVERSITY at night was one of the darkest places I'd ever visited. The antique streetlamps, spaced far apart, seemed to have been designed more for atmosphere than for security. I counted myself lucky to have visited the Computer Center by day, for I would have had a difficult time locating it in the midnight gloom. As it was I stumbled on the stairs leading down to the side entrance that Bridget had instructed me to use.

For all that, it might as well have been mid-day once I got inside, judging from the feverish activity of the nocturnal inhabitants of the place. I found my way to Bridget's cubicle and she seemed pleased to show off her progress.

"I've managed to sort out the signals to and from Sheila's computer. None of this would matter if the computer were being used by itself, but when computers are tied together things get a little complicated. There's the SETI network that Sheila joined and then there's this other traffic back and forth between her computer and a computer that seems to be located in Malaysia."

"That must be the Hacker."

"It looks that way."

"Does this mean that he's broken into every computer in the SETI network? How could he do that?"

"Let's assume he hacked into SETI directly. That would give him access to all the machines in the network. Then it would just be a matter of mailing out a worm that would introduce the factoring software on each computer."

"That would be the 'Mersenne' file we found."

"Right."

"But wouldn't the SETI people know what had happened?"

"Not necessarily. There are probably close to a thousand computers in the network. They'd still be sending SETI data back and forth, hunting for patterns. The SETI software takes a bit of time to crunch the numbers, and the computers are all sending back negative reports in any case. That is, unless you've heard about any new messages from E.T."

"But Malaysia! How could the Hacker know that Sheila had found out about the prime factor? If he had to monitor the e-mail from a thousand computers, it would take forever."

"He doesn't do it personally. He sends all the e-mail messages from computers on the network through a program that looks for certain keywords. The Hacker isn't interested in the personal lives of his unwitting participants. He trusts the program to let him know if anything pertinent turns up."

"So the computer program would have alerted him that Sheila knew about the number, and then he would have scanned her e-mail in greater detail to learn about Randy."

"That's the way I see it."

"But how could someone in Malaysia arrange to have two people in North Carolina murdered?"

"You said there could be a lot of money involved in this. Wherever there's a lot of money, you have to figure organized crime."

"So you think the Hacker could just be someone working for a larger operation?"

"It certainly seems possible."

"How did you track him to Malaysia?"

Bridget turned to Sheila's computer and typed in a command. Hundreds of lines of software instructions filled the screen. "Here's the program that … uh-oh."

"What is it?"

"I didn't think he was this clever."

"What's happened?"

"The Hacker must know about us. There's a tripwire built into this code. When I called it up on the screen, it sent the Hacker a signal that someone was trying to discover the source."

A crash of thunder seemed to make the building shudder and the lights flickered briefly. I must have jumped because Bridget said, "There's nothing to worry about. The auxiliary power system kicks in automatically if anything happens to the electricity outside."

"But I don't think that's our main problem. Look what happened to Sheila and Randy. How long do you think it would take the Hacker to send his hit men after us?"

Bridget frowned for a moment and then said, "As long as we're here in the center there's no way to identify us personally, but I'm still finding this a bit scary. Maybe we should get out of here. Would you mind walking me back to my house?"

"Not at all. This place doesn't feel very safe any more."

The thunderstorm had settled into a steady spring rain by the time we walked up the steps toward the street. Bridget grabbed an umbrella from a rack near the door and we huddled together as we walked down the dark street.

"Where do we go from here?" I asked.

"My house is just down the next street."

"No, I meant, what do we do about the murders?"

"I don't know. I was happy to help you when it looked like a simple hacking job, but I don't want to end up in a coffin."

"I don't want that either." When we arrived at Bridget's apartment I said, "I really appreciate your help." Bridget just smiled and entered the front door. I heard the bolt snap into place and figured she was safe for the night.

Chapter 15

MME COINTREAU, ONE OF TWO native speakers in the Magnolia French
Department, embodied the Gallic passion for bureaucratic procedures.
On the first day of her course in conversation and composition the two
of us carried out the following exchange (*en français, bien entendu*):

Mme C (having counted the class several times against her roll-
book and failing to establish a one-to-one correspondence): "And you,
Monsieur?"

A: "I talked to you on the telephone in June …

Mme C: "Have you taken French 100?"

A: "No, but you gave me permission …"

Mme C: "Well then, I withdraw the permission. You can't take
French 127 without French 100!"

A (in desperation, blowing my cover): "But don't you remember?
I'm what they call a Visiting Scholar here."

Mme C: "Ei yi yi, *un professeur!*" (The whole class stared and I
felt like Alice in the Wonderland flower garden, trying to prove that
she wasn't a weed, only to have one of the flowers panic and start
crying "Serpent! Serpent!" I took an empty seat and hoped I looked less
conspicuous than I felt.)

Our class assignments involved writing responses to letters from
famous French authors (Gautier, Proust, Napoléon), reviewing grammar,
and retranslating English translations of Baudelaire, Rimbaud, *et al*
back into French, and then being dismayed by the originals. It took
me several weeks to learn how my classmates managed to keep up
with their assignments and preserve their sanity: some simply didn't
do them. A number of students, just back from a year in France, could
do at sight exercises that I required hours to prepare.

I entered the French building and took my place in the classroom.
For once my inadequacies in French would remain unexposed as Mme
Cointreau delivered her only lecture of the course. As she stalked about

the room, dressed in a white blouse with subtle pinstripes, a black-and-white skirt with zigzag patterns and close-cropped jet-black hair that would presumably be maintained at that same shade until the day she died, I couldn't help reflecting that if she took off the bright red-orange scarf she'd fit perfectly in Leon Nelson's monochromatic apartment.

"French schoolchildren study the history of their country for twelve full years," she began. "Both the nature of the subject and the duration of the study have an effect on impressionable young minds. They hear first about their ancestors, *les Gaulois*, a race of tall, powerful men with blond hair and blue eyes, united from various tribes into a nation in 52 B.C. by Vercingétorix, France's first hero, who mounted a shining white horse and led these brave warriors into battle against the barbaric Roman invaders under that swine Julius Caesar." I watched as my classmates scribbled names and dates into their notebooks.

"Wide-eyed, *les enfants français* look at their teacher and ask, 'And Vercingétorix won!' Well, no. Julius Caesar, the miserable brute, conquered his army, took him prisoner, dragged him to Rome and fed him to the lions. And their faces fall, the first of an endless succession of shattered hopes."

"In the Middle Ages," Mme Cointreau went on, "the Hundred Years War concludes with Jeanne d'Arc, the young heroine of *la douce France*, who presents herself to the puppet king Charles VII at Chinon, demands an army, and leads it into thrilling battle against the British, who capture her and burn her at the stake. Sigh."

I see a few frowns on my classmates' faces. "At the end of the eighteenth century a young Mafioso named Napoléon comes to France from Sicily, seizes power, raises an enormous army, excites the French imagination with new hope and threatens to conquer Europe until he is brought low at Waterloo, a victory for the English yet another defeat for the French. In 1870 the Franco-Prussian War ends with the subjugation and invasion of France. In World War I France is invaded again. In World War II France is occupied."

"In effect," Mme Cointreau comes to her conclusion, "the history of France is a history of military defeats." You can imagine the effect that twelve years of this must have on the minds of French schoolchildren simply by comparing it with the way American history was presented to us. No wonder the French take such pride in their language, their literature and their art. When Victor Hugo died in 1885 he was accorded the kind of national obsequies that other countries reserve for their generals. And with good reason: look what happened to the generals.

A disheartening presentation, perhaps, but I found it a relief from Mme Cointreau's usual teaching style, which involved testing us on the exact memorization of French dialogues taken from a book she had co-authored. Sheila had been a whiz at these assignments, and I suspected that she had employed Randy to coach her as she committed the endless succession of phrases to memory. Much as I tried to concentrate on French composition and conversation, my mind kept returning to this missing classmate, a woman I scarcely knew but who was the closest friend of a woman with whom I had become very close. Proust, primes, poison—the teasing alliteration reminded me of the disparate elements in a puzzle that the police didn't even regard as a problem. Were it not for my allegiance, and affection, toward Beth, I would have been happy just to set the puzzle down. The sagas never tell about rescuing knights who fail.

Chapter 16

THURSDAY AFTERNOON BROUGHT ME TO Prof. Wick's course in phonetics. Carlton Wick, a sandy-haired young man with oversized glasses and an earnest, open expression, looked more like a scuba diver (his passion) than a university instructor (his profession). Unlike many academics, he displayed an infectious enthusiasm for his field of study without ever harboring the slightest hope that anyone else might share his interest. He understood that had it not been obligatory for French majors, his course would never attract sufficient enrolment to remain in the catalogue, but that knowledge seemed to stimulate him to make the course as interesting as possible.

It had taken me a long time to realize that the *o* in *encore* should be pronounced like the *u* in *nut* and not like any *o* that we use in English. When I mentioned this to Prof. Wick one day after class he told me the story of his daughter, studying French in her elementary school. Her instructor had some peculiar notions about French pronunciation and Prof. Wick was distressed when he heard his daughter counting *un, deux, trois, quatre, cinq, six, sept, huit, nerf, dix.*

"No, dear," he corrected, "that's *neuf.*"

"Teacher says *nerf,*" replied his daughter.

"Listen to your father, dear," her mother intervened. "He has a Ph.D. in phonetics."

"Teacher says *nerf,*" the child maintained.

"Let's try it again," said her father.

"... *huit, nerf, dix.*"

"Do you have any children?" Prof. Wick inquired. I shook my head. "There's always something. Last Saturday, during my daughter's violin class, a boy interrupted the lesson to confess that he might have done something he ought not to do. 'And what might that be?' inquired the teacher. Turns out the child had dropped his violin into the alcove fountain. The teacher walked over to the fountain, retrieved the one-sixteenth size instrument, and then gently explained why it would be better to keep violins out of the fountain. Meanwhile sixteen young fiddlers played the D major scale in sixteen different keys."

Today the class focused on the French *u*, which happily gave me no problems since it was the same as German umlaut *u* that I'd learned back in high school. After class I chatted with Prof. Wick, who was at about the same stage as I in his academic career, and we talked about the relative pleasures and pressures of being a college professor as compared with a college student. He noted that within a single calendar year I was experiencing both roles. "Of course, this is nothing compared with the pressure on high school kids," he said.

"How's that?"

"This is the season for college acceptances. My oldest son is aiming for Berkeley."

"Think he'll get in?"

"He has a good chance. But California seems so far away. I hate to imagine the air fares when he comes home for holidays."

"There's a remedy for that. Did you read the student paper last week?"

"I must have missed it."

"The latest twist is for parents to pay tuition with a credit card tied to air miles. Apparently it works out that a year's tuition can pretty much cover the cost of travel."

"I'll keep that in mind. But I'm not sure how much confidence I want to place in credit cards."

"How do you mean?"

"Last month my statement showed two entries that didn't make any sense to me. It was a couple of hundred dollars each time—not catastrophic, but not something I can afford to overlook."

"Did you call the bank?"

"That's the strange part. The people at First National looked at my credit card account and said that the charges were legitimate. But I haven't had my credit card stolen or anything. I didn't know that kind of thing was possible."

I had difficulty concealing my excitement. If this was the Hacker's work it represented the first link I'd seen between the theoretical possibility of cracking an encryption system and the application of that knowledge to commit theft. I didn't want to talk about it until I had more to go on, so I asked Prof. Wick to keep me posted and decided to head downtown to the First National bank to get more information.

Wick's description of his daughter's violin class called to mind the annual orchestral extravaganza at the Magnolia University Chapel: an uncut performance of Handel's *Messiah*—all three and a half hours of it. The three performances always sold out in advance, so at least 3600 people got to hear the timeless oratorio. Unwilling to pay the outlandish ticket price, but curious about any annual event at Magnolia (the Christmas banquet had made an unforgettable impression), I stopped in at the chapel after the Friday night movie just to see how things were going.

The two-hundred voice chorus was just completing "Their sound is gone out into all lands" and the bass soloist lurched into "Why do the nations rage?" He was a fairly light bass and tended to disappear on the low notes, but the symphony orchestra, which the megalomaniac choirmaster had been insulting all week, played superbly (mostly by ignoring the hysterical hand-waving of the conductor and keeping a careful eye on the concertmaster).

A young musicologist on the staff had had the thankless task of introducing ornaments here and there to make the gargantuan ensemble sound more "authentic." A couple more ditties and it was time for the Hallelujah Chorus, the audience taking its customary seventh-inning stretch with another hour of music yet to go. This year they had evidently chosen the little-known 1812 version of *Messiah* in which Handel added trumpets and timpani to the orchestra, which I had to admit created a magnificent noise against the outsize chorus. At the "King of Kings" section trombones and tubas joined the trumpets and they set off cannons by remote control on the lawn outside. At the reprise of "For ever and ever" all the chimes started ringing at once and fireworks whizzed high above the chapel tower: it was marvelous.

Then an aging soprano, dressed in black voile with deep décolletage and a mangy boa, began to caterwaul, "I know that my Redeemer liveth" in a god-awful swoop, and I quietly fled.

Chapter 17

WHEN I WAS IN GRADE school banks looked like fortresses from the outside, evidently to give customers a sense of security in contemplating their precious savings carefully preserved behind solid walls. The Reynolds branch of the First National Bank looked more like an automobile showroom than a fortress, with vast sheets of glass offering a clear view of everything taking place in the lobby. Perhaps a more sophisticated generation of customers understood that the unseen vault was virtually impregnable. Or perhaps the design reflected the reversal in the banking system: now customers mostly owed the banks money, in the form of mortgages and credit cards, rather than the other way around.

I wasn't sure how to handle this. This bank, for all the openness of its architecture, was unlikely to give much information to a non-account-holder. Then I remembered what Bridget had told me about how easily one could obtain information about people. Quite possibly Wick had made his complaints by telephone rather than in person. I hoped that my phonetics teacher wouldn't mind if I borrowed his identity briefly and when the receptionist asked why I wanted to see the assistant manager I gave her Carlton Wick's name and cited irregularities with my credit card billing as the reason for my visit.

Jason Wellsby, the assistant manager, wore the perpetual frown of someone whose problems just never go away. He made a half-hearted attempt at a smile as I entered the tiny cubicle that he probably referred to as his office but as soon as I sat down his face furled again, with frown marks extending from his eyebrows right up to the top of his balding crown.

"Ah yes, Mr. Wick. I believe we've spoken on the phone." I was in luck so far; evidently the assistant manager had never actually laid eyes on Carlton Wick, but was he really so tone deaf not to distinguish a Yankee from a Carolina native? Then I remembered Wick mentioning that he had taught at the University of Delaware before coming to Magnolia. Evidently he was no more a native than I. "I understand that certain entries in your VISA statement didn't make sense." I suspected that Jason Wellsby was subjected to pressures from above as well as below. I had known men in his situation who would have directly accused the customer of making an error, if not of trying to defraud the bank. On the other hand, perhaps this was just the low-key southern style.

"I've double checked all my receipts," I ventured, "and I have no record of the two items I mentioned. Is it possible for someone else to use my card without my knowledge?"

Now Wellsby began to look even more uncomfortable. "I'd have to say no and yes." I waited for him to continue. "When you make a purchase using your credit card, the merchant transmits information about the card number and the amount of the purchase to us. We pay the merchant and then bill you in your monthly statement."

"I take it this information is transmitted by computer, like e-mail?"

"That's right."

"Doesn't that mean that a person who somehow hacked into the bank's computer would have access to all the credit card accounts?"

"That's the beauty of our security system." For the first time Wellsby actually showed a sign of enthusiasm. "The data is all encrypted. So even in the unlikely event that someone could break into the computer—and I should emphasize that that eventuality is extremely improbable— there'd be no way to make use of the data."

"So the information is encrypted at the source and sent to whatever bank administers the credit card."

"That's right. Each bank has a unique ID and public key encryption certificate." Wellsby was beginning to sound a lot like the brochure I had seen on display in the lobby.

"But I take it there's another side to your answer."

Wellsby's face returned to its default frown. "I know it's theoretically impossible, but we've had several complaints like yours in the past month. The head office has promised to send a computer expert to look at the situation but so far ..."

A large, angry woman entering the office prevented the assistant manager from finishing his sentence. The flowered print of her dress must have contained half a dozen different hues but her face carried an unambiguous shade of red. "Who are you?" she demanded of me, and not waiting for an answer she turned on the hapless Wellsby and exclaimed "What's come over you? Sharing proprietary information. And with someone who isn't even one of our depositors." Over her shoulder I caught a glimpse of the receptionist's face. The woman turned to her and said, in a less angry but still firm tone, "You did the right thing, Julie." Evidently the receptionist knew the clientele better than the assistant manager but rather than confronting me directly had taken her suspicions to the top.

I could see no way that further conversation would aid my case so I prepared to duck out of the office. The manager turned around. "You sit right down here. I'm not through with you!" She was significantly bigger than I and probably stronger too. I sat. "I'll talk to you later," she said to Wellsby. "Now as for you," she turned to me, "do you realize that impersonating an account-holder is a Federal offense?" I strongly doubted this but her tone of conviction raised the possibility that it might actually be true. In any event, I didn't feel motivated to argue the case. "Who do you think you are, waltzing in here asking a lot of question? And, more to the point, who are you actually? I'd like to see some identification, and I mean right now." As a rule I don't like to dramatize my life but it wasn't hard to imagine what the *Reynolds Rap* would do with this story. "Yankee Prof Expelled in Bank Bust," or worse.

When Julie appeared a moment later to pass a message to the bank manager I decided I probably wouldn't get another chance and bolted for the door. "Wait a minute!" shouted the irate woman. "Where do you think you're going? Stop that man!" I broke into a run and managed to get out of the building before the sleepy security guard caught on. I hoped that my foolish play-acting wasn't going to make life more difficult for the genuine Carlton Wick, but the encounter gave me an idea that I wanted to share with Bridget.

In the middle of the afternoon students and faculty members assembled in the university chapel for a memorial service for Randy Preston. His father, evidently a state senator, arrived in a black limousine preceded by several motorcycle policemen. I recognized Todd and Jeff from the Alternative Curriculum and a few other students from my French classes. I took a seat next to Beth shortly before the service began.

The university chaplain was in rare form. I'd never seen a man so in love with his own voice, and so enamored of the microphone that offered him possibilities of dynamic variation undreamed of by ministers of old. "As we read in Isaiah," he intoned, "those who hope in the Lord will renew their strength. They will soar on wings like eagles; they will run and not grow weary, they will walk and not be faint." The chaplain's rendition carried us high into the oratorical stratosphere for the eagles, then a pregnant pause after "not," followed by a "weary" that positively ached with lassitude. His voice marched in military cadence toward "walk," then virtually disappeared by the time it reached "faint."

I suppose I shouldn't have been surprised that the chaplain would make reference to Randy's engagement to Sheila, and I guess I might have expected that he would describe the young man as "a bridegroom coming forth from his pavilion, like a champion rejoicing to run his course." But when he took on the role of Randy's fiancée, his voice rising in dulcet tones to an unsuspected higher register, and quoted from Genesis, "Why did you run off secretly and deceive me? Why didn't you tell me, so I could send you away with joy and singing to the music of tambourines and harps?"—then I started to become suspicious. Sure enough, a moment later the chaplain, reflecting on the unpredictability of life, quoted Genesis again: "My days are swifter than a runner; they fly away without a glimpse of joy."

I whispered to Beth, "He doesn't have a clue who Randy is. Someone told him Randy was a runner and he put together a sermon by finding every reference to running in the Bible Concordance."

"You're kidding!" she said.

"Just listen," I said.

Sure enough, the chaplain went on to speculate on Randy's life in heaven, this time quoting Proverbs: "When you walk, your steps will not be hampered; when you run, you will not stumble."

"Oh no," Beth whispered. "I think you may be right."

The chaplain went on: "The name of the Lord is a strong tower; the righteous run to it and are safe." Then his voice rose in exhortation. I wasn't sure whether he was addressing the dead cross-country captain or the assembled congregation when he turned to First Corinthians and said "Do you not know that in a race all the runners run, but only one gets the prize? Run in such a way as to get the prize."

"I can't believe this," Beth said.

"Dear boy," continued the chaplain, quoting from Galatians, "You were running a good race. Who cut in on you and kept you from obeying the truth?" That startled me; did the chaplain have some clue that Randy had been murdered? Apparently it was just a chance reference, a mere water stop in the marathon that led to Hebrews: "Therefore, since we are surrounded by such a great cloud of witnesses, let us throw off everything that hinders and the sin that so easily entangles, and let us run with perseverance the race marked out for us."

A member of the cross-country team offered a briefer and much more affecting eulogy, then we sang a hymn I'd never heard before, "Join all the glorious names," presumably chosen by the chaplain, for it contained the phrase "O let my feet ne'er run astray." As we left the chapel I heard no sign of anyone else being bothered by the service so I held my peace.

The South displays a wide range in matters ecclesiastical. One Sunday early in the fall I stopped in, more or less by accident, at the Church of Eternal Bliss. I arrived early but not early enough to bypass the huggers, who occupied the spot held by greeters in more tactilely challenged churches. A jazz singer was rehearsing "The Sunny Side of the Street" (the prelude) and "I've Got the Sun in the Morning and the Moon at Night" (the offertory), accompanied by sax, bass fiddle and drums. The service proper included "Solitudes"-style music on the harmonium to accompany the meditations, upbeat hymns with lyrics projected on a screen, and the entire congregation singing Malotte's "Lord's Prayer," an unforgettable, and somewhat unbelievable, experience.

The undergraduate French Club barbecue on the lawn in front of the French building saved me from having to cook dinner. I have always wondered about the connection between posture and mental acuity. Specifically, how is it that people seated at a dinner table, as I was in January at a party hosted by Prof. Plowright, can be witty, urbane and well-informed, whereas the same people, standing around at a cocktail party or, as in this case, a barbecue, can be vapid, distrait and downright boring? Although the dinner party was composed mostly of faculty members from the French Department, when the conversation turned to Middle East politics, they spoke with an intimate knowledge of technical terms for religious leaders that left me astonished. At the barbecue things were different. Now it may have been that Prof. Plowright had simply had too much to drink—how else explain his spouting Lamartine to anyone who would listen, and to not a few who wouldn't?—but he wasn't even the worst. To avoid further embarrassing members of the department to which I was at least peripherally associated, in the words of Mark Twain, "Let us draw the curtain of charity over the rest of the scene."

Chapter 18

AFTER THE BARBECUE I OCCUPIED myself with French phonetics, readings for Prof. Trente's course in French civilization, and the inevitable fifty pages of Proust, and still had time to get over to Clearwater for a special showing of Jean Cocteau's film *La Belle et la bête*. You could always spot the freshmen, or first-time film-goers. Some maniac had designed the auditorium with descending stairs that alternated steps perhaps a foot and a half long with shorter steps about six inches long. Concealed lights illuminated the longer steps but not the shorter, so that once the main house lights dimmed there were regular crashes and cries of surprise from the unwary. I wouldn't have been surprised if more than one Magnolia romance had begun with one person inadvertently landing in another's lap, all the result of an egregious error in design.

Prof. Nelson appeared onstage to introduce the film. He hadn't even mentioned the event in class—I happened to see it listed in the *Reynolds Rap* events calendar. He was a funny man, Nelson, incredibly modest and yet in command of a vast quantity of knowledge. His love of film had endeared him to me when I made a preliminary visit to Magnolia the spring before the start of my study year. He knew Cocteau's films intimately and had spent several afternoons interviewing Cocteau during one of his regular visits to France. Nelson also admired the work of François Truffaut and was fond of mentioning that whenever he stayed in the Hotel Victoria in Nice he always occupied the room used by the director of *Day for Night*, a large portion of which was filmed at that hotel.

Nelson's brief lecture preceded a screening of the film, a remarkable piece of cinema. I particularly admired the scene where Beauty walks down a long corridor in the Beast's castle, illuminated by candles held by human arms extending from the walls.

It was 10:30 by the time I arrived at the Computer Center. This time Bridget didn't seem particularly pleased to see me. "I'm not sure it's a good idea to be seen with you, Axel," she said.

"You make me sound like a murderer," I said, trying to ingratiate myself.

"No, you're doing what you think is right," she said. "But I'm just a computer geek, not a spy. If you want to carry on James Bond adventures that's fine with me, but I don't think I want to play anymore."

"Oh." I wasn't sure how to handle this. "Could you give me just a couple of minutes? I think we may have been looking at this wrong."

"You mean you think Sheila's death was an accident?"

"No; I still think she was murdered. But I don't think it was the work of a professional hit man. Why would he go to the trouble to make it look like the lapse of a drunken teenager? And in broad daylight where anybody could have remembered his face? That's not how hit men work."

"I see. So you've had a lot of experience with professional assassins?"

"Just what I see in the movies."

"That's what I thought. You're not exactly reassuring me, Axel."

This wasn't working. I guess I hadn't thought of what might happen when I got Bridget involved; I just needed her expertise. Trouble was, I still needed her help if I was going to find Sheila's murderer. I recounted my conversation with Carlton Wick and my visit to the bank. Returning to questions of public key encryption seemed to put Bridget more at ease.

"I think I see where you're headed," she said. "This gang may not be operating out of Malaysia at all; they could be local."

"That's the way I'm beginning to look at it."

Bridget thought some more. "You know, Axel. That's even worse. It's one thing if the Hacker and his evil employers are breaking into computers from far away. But if they're nearby …" She didn't finish her sentence but gave me a worried look and asked whether I'd see her home.

We walked to her apartment in silence. I was feeling really badly that I'd gotten this agreeable girl into a perilous position, but there didn't seem to be anything that I could say to make things better. I hated moments like this and recalled times in high school when I swore to myself that it would be better not to have anything to do with women at all rather than endure a situation in which neither of you had anything to say. We said good night and I watched Bridget let herself in at the front door.

The magnolias from which the university took its name had just begun to bloom that morning and somehow it seemed that, in anticipation of the annual arrival of tourists seeking Kodak moments, cardinals had come to light on each blossoming branch. I scarcely noticed the heavy aroma as I tried to figure out what to do next.

I was only a few blocks away when I heard the explosion. The concussive force of the sound pushed me off balance so that I watched at a cockeyed angle as flames began to shoot into the night sky. I couldn't see which building was on fire but a sick feeling in my stomach told me it had to be Bridget's house. I ran in the direction of the flames, feeling the air becoming perceptibly warmer as I approached. People started coming out of neighboring buildings as the blaze turned into a full-fledged conflagration. Before I had a chance to take in the full extent of the damage I became aware of a small figure sobbing against a tree. As I put my arm around Bridget's shoulder and led her away from the horrible scene I heard sirens in the distance.

Beth didn't stop to ask questions. In no time she had a blanket wrapped around the trembling girl and a cup of tea in her hand. I sat on the sofa beside Bridget and Beth took a chair facing her and we waited for her to become calm. The walls mercifully muted the sound of approaching sirens, but we could not avoid thinking about Bridget's ordeal.

"I'm still alive," were Bridget's first words. Beth and I just nodded and smiled at her. Bridget's analytical mind seemed to be drawing her protectively away from the scene she had just witnessed. "I was feeling really crummy when you dropped me off, Axel, so instead of going to bed I went to the all-night convenience store to get some chips. I was just coming back to my house when …" Bridget seemed determined not to cry again but took a couple of deep breaths and began to sip her tea.

"It's going to be all right," Beth said. "You can stay here tonight; I even have an extra toothbrush."

Bridget grinned. "Good thing. Sharing toothbrushes really grosses me out." We sat quietly for a few more minutes, the silence interrupted from time to time by more sirens: fire, police, probably an ambulance. The street in front of Bridget's house was probably getting pretty crowded. At length Bridget said, "Okay, let's figure out what happened. Was that a bomb in my house?"

"Sure sounded that way," I said.

"But how would anyone know where you lived?" Beth asked. "I thought you guys were doing all your snooping from Sheila's PC in the Computer Centre."

"You're right," Bridget said. "The Hacker must have traced the Network Identification Card on the computer to that location then sent someone to watch the building."

"He could have noted the time that the computer was shut off and then sent word to watch for the next person to leave the Computer Center," I said.

Beth remained silent for a moment and then asked, "Do you guys know about Occam's Razor?"

"Oh no," I said, "Are we in for more murder techniques?"

"It's not that kind of razor," Beth said. "My father explained it to me once. He actually made me memorize the Latin: *Entia non sunt multiplicanda praeter necessitatem.*"

"'fraid my Latin's a little rusty," Bridget said.

"It came from a 14th-century English logician named William of Occam. It means when trying to explain a phenomenon, avoid all unnecessary assumptions, or more briefly, simple explanations are the best."

"Okay, so now we've gotten our Latin lesson out of the way, what's that got to do with my house blowing up?" I was glad to see that Bridget was getting something of her characteristic feisty spirit back.

"You keep talking as if we're up against an evil empire. First there's a Hacker working in Malaysia for an organized crime syndicate that flies hit men to North Carolina to murder Sheila and Randy. Then there's this cabal of cyberspace bank robbers that have infiltrated Reynolds. Wouldn't the simplest explanation be that there's just one guy?"

"No, there had to be at least …" Then I stopped. Sheila's hit-and-run looked like an amateur job. Randy's murder was ingenious but didn't seem like the work of a gang of criminals. Hacking into the SETI network or the First National bank files didn't require a team. "You could be right," I said. "But what about the Malaysia connection?"

Bridget said, "I can answer that. You don't have to be physically present to establish a computer presence. It requires a bit of computer savvy, but we already know the Hacker has that."

Beth went on. "But if there's just the one guy, he would assume that Bridget died in the blast, at least until the newspapers report that no body was found."

"So Bridget's safe so long as she doesn't show herself," I said.

"Can you stay here tomorrow?" Beth asked.

"I only have one class on Fridays," Bridget said, "and I guess it would be all right to miss that."

"What about you, Axel?" Beth asked.

"I don't think the Hacker has any idea what either of us looks like," I said. "It was just a matter of following one of the regular inhabitants of the Computer Center."

"I don't think the Hacker considers a musicologist to be much of a threat," Bridget said. Then, seeing my face drop she added, "No offense intended."

"None taken," I said.

"But what are we going to do after tomorrow? I can't stay here forever, although I guess I don't have anyplace else to go for the time being."

"Shouldn't we tell the police what we know?" Beth asked.

"And what exactly is that?" Bridget demanded.

"Well, we know that someone hacked into the SETI network," I said.

"Not really," Bridget said. "We've just found one contraption on one machine that happened to be part of the project. It's not exactly convincing proof."

"Well we know that a prime number turned up on Sheila's computer and then she died," I said, but just putting it into words made me see how ridiculous it sounded. "Okay. But until we can figure out who the Hacker is, Bridget's just going to have to be a prisoner."

"Oh, it's not as bad as that," Bridget said. "I could do with a bit of a break. All this business has been costing me sleep. Speaking of which," she said, turning to Beth, "If I stay here, where are you going to sleep?"

"Oh, I'm going with him," Beth said, turning to wink at me.

So Beth pulled out an extra pair of pajamas for Bridget then took my arm and we headed to my apartment. The scent of the magnolia blossoms wafted clearly through the breezeway connecting the apartment units. When I tried to bring up the Hacker, Beth just touched a finger to my lips and once inside my apartment we didn't talk a lot. The evening ended with Beth introducing me to things I'd never experienced north of the Mason-Dixon Line.

Chapter 19

I DON'T KNOW WHETHER THE events of Thursday night had just put me in a bad mood, or whether my frustration at not being able to identify the Hacker had left me ready to attack anybody, just for the sake of doing something. One way or the other, things did not go well at the Alternative Curriculum meeting. Marla, the girl whose madrigal report I'd criticized, had told everyone how mean I'd been to her. Gloria, the head of the program, was attending the Faculty Senate meeting so I was the only adult present. Todd, who had always seemed suspicious about my allegiance to the AC, decided to take charge of Marla's defense. "Axel, I think you owe Marla an apology."

Oh no, I thought. Anything I say is going to be wrong, but I had to say something. "I didn't mean to offend Marla," I said. "I was just trying to make a case for academic integrity."

"Hmph," said Jeff the projectionist.

"'Academic integrity?'" Matt said in a mocking tone. "That's not a phrase we hear a lot around here."

"Well what standards do you respect?" I asked. "It seems to me that you folks are willing to question every assumption about university education except your own."

"What are those?" asked Cam.

"That freedom forbids discipline, that rapping is better than research, that nobody older than thirty knows anything worth learning."

"If you don't believe those things," Matt demanded, "what are you doing in the Alternative Curriculum?"

"That's something I've wondered from the beginning," Todd said.

"You don't seem like the same person who wrote that article on teaching music," Marla said.

"Maybe he's an impostor," said Jeff, the first words I'd ever actually heard him utter.

"Why don't we talk about this some more next meeting?" I said.

"Don't run away so fast," said Todd. "Marla's not the only one you've upset."

"What are you talking about?"

"You got Bridget's house blown up."

"How did you …"

"Computer people stick together. I heard about your amateur sleuthing. How naïve can you be?"

"What do you mean?"

"Do you think you can poke into the affairs of criminal gangs and not get your fingers burned?

"Well I just …

"Personally, I don't care if you get yourself blown up. I sometimes wonder what you're doing down here in the first place. But getting a student in trouble—don't you people up North have any sense of shame?"

I didn't know what to say, but Todd didn't seem to be waiting for an answer. "Today we're supposed to be planning the retreat. Tell you what, Axel. Why don't you do your research while we 'rap'?"

It seemed like an inglorious retreat, but I guess I should have considered myself lucky to be given an out before things really started getting ugly. I forced a smile and left the group to its deliberations.

As I headed toward the French building I reflected on the teaching styles I had seen at Magnolia and wondered whether I could adopt any of them as my own. I knew I'd never be comfortable with the anarchical aspects of the Alternative Curriculum. If the "grown-up kindergarten" approach had suited me in California, it no longer fit. Unlike the AC students, I valued organized learning above "sharing the experience."

I admired Prof. Plowright's erudition, but his manner of beating around the bush, refusing to organize his ideas into sensible presentations, offended my sense of orderliness. That may have worked for him—he always seemed to have full enrollment for his courses—but it wasn't going to work for me.

Prof. Trente was organized—you had to give him that. But he read the same notes every year, to the point that his lectures seemed to come from a tape recording rather than from a real person. I had heard of Parisian professors like this. Their students kept two notebooks, one blank and one borrowed from someone who had taken the course before. Then they would take notes with colored pens, knowing that the words coming from the professor's mouth had to be virtually identical to those previously recorded. Not my style either.

Mme Cointreau represented another aspect of French pedagogical practice: memorizing dialogues, copying passages from classic French literature, imitating the masters as a means of developing a decent sense of prose style. It might work as a way of teaching French but I had doubts about its applicability to teaching music history, and it certainly didn't fit my own personality.

The university abounded with models for would-be teachers, and they weren't limited to the French department. The musical director at the university chapel was a choral conductor of the "Success Through Intimidation" school. The technique of keeping singers in a state of unholy terror naturally has a certain appeal to insecure conductors, but one wondered why more singers didn't simply quit. Last Sunday the worthy Kapellmeister, in an effort to inspire greater rhythmic vitality, asked the chorus to stamp the main beats as they sang. "That's not stamping," he roared, "that's tapping! You!" he said, singling out a poor freshman soprano (funny that he never picked on the men). "Let's hear you stamp." Two hundred pairs of eyes fastened on the embarrassed girl. "Now stamp!" If she'd had more spirit she might have responded, "Get off my back, you pig!" Instead she did her best to stamp with her rubber-soled shoes. "Now," the director's voice turned unctuous. "Let me hear you tap so that I know you understand the *difference!*" Red with humiliation, the girl tried to manage a wistful tap.

Arriving at the French building, I entered Prof. Nelson's classroom and took my seat. I had come to admire this wise old man for so many things—his encyclopedic knowledge of French literature, his devotion to Proust, his passion for cinema, his remarkable output as a writer, his consistent embodiment of the life of a scholar—perhaps he also held the secret to teaching.

Chapter 20

THE FIRST DAY IN LEON Nelson's class I was amused to notice that all the desks were firmly bolted to the floor. No touchy-feely "share the experience" education in this classroom. The students were here to learn, the professor was here to teach.

At precisely the appointed hour, Prof. Nelson rose from his desk, began pacing the room, consulted his notes, and chose a student to recite, in this case, answering questions on points covered during the previous class. Nelson's students quickly learned that it wasn't enough just to take notes in his classes; you had to reread them in the evening, consult the anthology if any points were unclear, and then commit the ideas to memory. It wasn't difficult—every point had three sub-points, every maxim had been finely crafted.

Nelson's clientele seemed ideally suited to his teaching methods. His classes drew on the entire population of the university. Indeed, it had been said that you didn't really have a Magnolia education unless you'd taken at least one course with Leon Nelson. So when he posed a question on virtually any subject, there would be a history student or a divinity student or a classics major to contribute some piece of knowledge which Nelson would lovingly place into the pedagogical structure he was creating before our eyes, after which he would polish it to a fine expository sheen and pass it on for us to copy into our notebooks.

But woe betide the student who hadn't memorized his notes from the previous class. Nelson would never raise his voice or express the slightest irritation, but neither would he let the hapless student off the hook. He would continue to ask questions, always offering the student the possibility of redemption. Nelson compared us, his students, to Prometheus, chained to a desk while an eagle (in this case an American bald eagle, Nelson having long since lost his hair) came to extract our liver.

As the lesson continued, it occurred to me that Nelson was putting us through a daily catechism. A lifetime of scholarship, pedagogy and devout Catholicism had produced an ordered world-system, its tripartite organization everywhere apparent, ruled by a benevolent pontiff who entertained student responses to his endless interrogation, then formulated the appropriate dogma in maxims of elegant French prose for us to commit to memory.

It dawned on me that the secret to teaching is knowing who you are as a person, and then being that as a teacher. Having immersed myself in the literature of radical education alternatives before starting my teaching career in California, I had given students my very best imitation of John Holt. At Monongahela University I had done my best to impersonate my thesis advisor, turning my undergraduate survey course into a graduate seminar, with dismaying results for all concerned. The lesson from Magnolia was not to imitate Prof. Nelson, or any of my other teachers, but to know myself. I enjoyed learning, arranging what I had learned into a coherent structure, and presenting it enthusiastically. If this be lecturing, then so be it, and devil take the hindmost. If I could lecture successfully to my fellow students in Prof. Trente's civilization course, why not to the students enrolled in my classes back home? The idea struck me like a thunderbolt.

Then I noticed the empty seat beside me, formerly occupied by Sheila McCormack, and realized that I had more urgent business than working out my pedagogical plight. After class I went for a run to try to get my thoughts straight, a mistake as it turned out. I took a wrong turn at the Nexus and ran several miles out of my way before discovering the misstep, then compounded the error by trying unsuccessfully to retrace my steps.

At one intersection I encountered Carlton Wick and decided to run with him. I thought I owed him an explanation and an apology for impersonating him at the bank.

"That was you?" he asked. His laughter relieved my apprehension. "When the assistant manager called I didn't know what to think. First the phony VISA entries and now this. I was being to wonder whether I was the victim of identity theft."

"Did he tell you that you weren't the only victim?"

"No. In fact, he didn't even mention the VISA bill."

"I'm not surprised. He seemed pretty embarrassed about it when

I talked with him. Here the bank has been putting out flyers telling customers about the impregnability of their new encryption system. I think they'd just as soon keep you quiet if they could."

"Now this is beginning to make sense," Carlton said. "Oh, we need to turn here." He led the way down a narrow side path I'd overlooked.

"How do you mean?" I asked.

"He said the bank was prepared to offer me a special rate on my mortgage renewal and that I was one of five finalists on the drawing for a new car. I don't remember even entering the contest in the first place."

"What do you want to bet that the other four so-called finalists are customers who have suffered 'irregularities' in their VISA bills?"

"Naw. You mean the bank would set up a phony contest just to buy us off?"

"If you happen to refer to the First National Bank anytime in the next week or so, don't you expect to mention the car?"

"Well …"

"The bank has a big PR problem on its hands until someone figures out how their system is being compromised. The price of a new car is nothing next to what they'd lose if people started getting their VISA cards at another bank?"

"But if someone could beat the system at First National couldn't he do the same thing elsewhere?"

"Sure, but that's not the way people reason when it comes to their money." I was keen to know more about the SETI project but wasn't sure how to introduce the subject. With nothing to lose, I just jumped in. "Do you know if many of your students belong to the SETI network?"

"A lot of people signed up when Hewitt first announced the project. I think they had the idea that they would be receiving personal messages from Martians, or something to that effect."

"Is that what Prof. Kilby promised?"

"Oh, no. The actual announcement was very serious. In fact, I don't think anyone would have bothered to volunteer until the student paper got hold of the news and made it sound like something out of the *National Enquirer*."

"So that got things going."

"I'll say. It started out as an 'in' thing but pretty soon students started making fun of those who hadn't joined the network. This turn will take us off the course." Carlton led us onto a main trail. "Can you get home from here?"

"This is great. I really appreciate getting untangled. I'm over in the University Apartments."

"Good. Well, I guess I'll see you in class." He ran off in the direction opposite mine. I would have liked to ask more questions about Hewitt Kilby, but they would have to wait.

Chapter 21

AFTER DINNER I MADE MY way to Beth's apartment. She gave me a long hug and we just smiled at each other for a few moments before turning to the business at hand.

"I didn't know how to reach you, Axel," she said. "I have some news about Bridget's house."

"Don't tell me they've found the bomber."

"Well the police don't think it was a bomb, or at least not the way you're thinking. The way my brother's friend described it, someone turned the entire house into a bomb by turning on the gas in the kitchen and then igniting it."

"Wouldn't that take a long time?"

"They estimated that an hour would be enough, if you blew out the pilot light and closed all the doors and windows."

"But how could anybody set it off without being killed?"

"They guessed that the perpetrator may have hooked up an alarm clock to a device that would produce a spark, but there's no way of knowing for sure because whatever it was got destroyed in the explosion."

"But if that's the case, Bridget's even luckier than we thought."

"That's right. We'd imagined the Hacker waiting outside the building with some kind of radio-controlled detonator. The whole thing could have been much simpler than that."

"Where is Bridget, by the way?"

"She got tired of being cooped up and went to the convenience store for a snack."

"Listen. I was thinking about what you said about Occam's razor. What do we know about the Hacker?"

Beth bit her lip as she thought. "He hijacked the SETI network in order to crack an encryption system so that he could steal money from credit card accounts."

"Right. Now all along we've been attributing huge powers to this guy. If Occam's razor tells us to minimize the assumptions, why did we assume he'd hacked into the SETI network?"

"Well he had to. We saw the number on Sheila's computer." Then Beth stopped, opened her mouth in the surprise, and turned it into a smile. "Kilby?"

"Why not? He wouldn't have to hack into the network. He had access to it as supervisor of the project."

"He might have been getting publicity from the project, but he wasn't getting any money. Do you think it's as simple as greed?"

"You're the one who said to keep it simple."

"You mean this fiendish mastermind could really be just a professor?" Beth looked at my expression. "Sorry, but you know what I mean."

At that point Bridget burst into the room. "It's Kilby! I tracked him to his house."

At that point everyone began speaking at once, but after we sorted out our protestations over the risk Bridget had incurred by returning to the Computer Center and Bridget had explained that she'd tracked the hacker using his Network Identification Card the same way as he had tracked her to the Computer Center, we had to decide what to do next.

Bridget had apparently worked it all out. "You have to confront him, Axel."

"Oh, yeah," I said. "Just walk up to a homicidal maniac and accuse him of two murders and an attempted murder."

"What's he going to do?" asked Beth. "You're a university professor same as he is. He isn't going to just shoot you."

"That's right," said Bridget. "The whole point in the other killings was not to show his identity."

"Why don't you come along to look at his computer?"

"Oh, no," said Beth. "He hates women. It has to be you, Axel."

"This still doesn't seem like much of a plan," I said.

"Here's the way it works," said Bridget. "You find his computer, and then blink the lights somewhere in the house. We'll be waiting outside. I'll come in to confirm the evidence and Beth will call the police."

"How's she going to do that?" I asked.

"With this," Bridget said, pulling out a small device. "It's a cellular phone I borrowed from a guy at the Centre."

"But it's so small," Beth said.

"That's the way they're making them nowadays," Bridget said.

What little confidence I had faded as we walked the several streets to Prof. Kilby's house on campus. The dim streetlamps made the Victorian dwelling look like the one house you avoided every Halloween, and I told my companions, "This reminds me of the scene in *The Wizard of Oz* when the Cowardly Lion tells the others that he has just one request."

"What's that," said Bridget and Beth, picking up the cue.

"Talk me out of it!" I said.

They just laughed and Beth made a remark about the bravery of Yankee soldiers that just made me feel worse.

Hewitt Kilby opened the door in response to my knock and when I explained that I was interested in the SETI project admitted me into the house. Kilby, though not a tall man, projected a fierce intensity accentuated by a thick shock of silver hair combed straight back, like conductor Herbert von Karajan but without the charm. Beth told me that since his wife's death of cancer some years before, Kilby had not remarried, or even dated, but had thrown himself entirely into his work. When he smiled, the curve of his lips never crossed the horizontal, as if he carefully measured the amount of energy he was willing to devote to social matters.

We went into the living room, an agreeably furnished room with chairs facing a fireplace and built-in bookcases on two walls. I tried to figure out what was missing and decided that it must have been the complete absence of any female presence: no flowers, no throw rugs, no jar of colored pebbles picked up at the ocean. It looked as though Kilby, after his wife's death, had simply removed all traces of her from his life without troubling to put anything else in their place.

Kilby, after outlining the general principles of the SETI project, waited for questions, his professorial style evidently carrying over into his private life. "I'm particularly impressed by the link-up of hundreds of computers into a single network," I said.

"We might as well put all these kids' computers to some profitable use," Kilby said in a sound that resembled a growl.

"The student newspaper said that your network could be compared in power to a supercomputer," I said.

"Unh," said Kilby in a tone of vague disdain.

"Properly directed, that power might even be used to find prime factors."

"Could do, but what that's got to do with SETI?"

"You could break the encryption code of, say, the First National Bank and make a tidy sum without ever leaving your computer," I said.

"What are you suggesting?" Kilby said with an angry snarl.

"I'd really like to see the master computer that controls the network," I said.

"That isn't here—it's in the astronomy building."

"But we traced the computer to this address."

"That's quite enough!" Kilby's voice rose to a roar. "I don't know who you think you are, barging in here and making vague accusations. As I understand it, you're just an academic visitor. I think I have enough influence to get your invitation cancelled and send you back north where you belong. Now I'm going to ask you to leave my house, and don't come back!" Kilby's face had become flushed, with the center of redness at the tip of his nose, a sight I might have found comical in other circumstances but somehow I didn't feel like laughing. I thought about Sheila, Randy, and the shattered remains of Bridget's house and left as quickly as I could manage.

Beth and Bridget were waiting for me in the shadow of a tree. I was in the middle of recounting my unprofitable conversation when we heard an anguished cry come from the house. A moment later I saw a slim figure emerge from the side entrance carrying an object about the size of cigar box. "Call the police," I told Beth.

"What will I tell them?" she asked.

"Say you heard a blood-curdling scream," said Bridget. "That should get their attention."

"Where are you going?" asked Beth.

"I think we may have gotten the wrong Hacker," I said. The young man caught sight of us and broke into a run; I took off in pursuit. It looked a lot like Jeff, the quiet denizen of the Alternative Curriculum, but he wasn't headed in the direction of the AC. I ran as fast as I could but didn't seem to be gaining any ground. As we crossed the campus in near darkness I thought I knew where he was headed. The students had told me that he served as projectionist for the Clearwater Film Festival, and the theater seemed to be our destination. There was a flash of lightning followed quickly by a crash of thunder and a deluge of rain, no gentle spring shower this but sheets of water that made it difficult to follow the path through the gloom. If I hadn't guessed where the Hacker was headed I would probably have lost my way altogether. By the time I reached the building I was thoroughly drenched.

Chapter 22

I LOOKED AT MY WATCH. It was later than I thought. The last show would have ended perhaps half an hour ago. The place looked deserted, but Jeff presumably had a key. As I entered the building I could hear footsteps ascending the stairs to the projection booth. The rain continued to pound on the roof of the building. I found the narrow stairway and began the ascent.

I paused at the top of the stairs. Jeff had presumably led me here for a reason. I had a choice of entering the projection booth cautiously, into a possible trap, or to make an explosive entry. Careful planning lay behind the dual murders and the destruction of Bridget's home. A trap seemed to be the most likely alternative. I opted for the explosive entry and, sure enough, I blew right past Jeff, standing with an electrical cable in his hands ready to use as a garrotte. He turned off the tiny maintenance lamp beside the projector and the room became almost completely dark. Darkness gave the advantage to Jeff, who knew the room well. Before the light went out I caught a glance of a shade covering the room's only window. I stumbled over what felt like discarded pop bottles on the floor, ripped the shade from its rod and then ducked as a bar stool came flying toward my head. Even with the window covering removed the room seemed pretty dark. Then the rain let up and for a brief moment a bit of moonlight filtered in through the window. I picked up an empty film canister and hurled it across the room to create a disturbance. This place seemed to have an awful lot of junk lying around. I wasn't sure what Jeff had in store but the longer I stayed in this place the more likely I was to get in trouble. My only hope lay in somehow disabling my opponent.

The only weapon I could think of lay close at hand. I removed the reel from the projector nearest me. A brief ray of moonlight showed me where the boy was standing and I shifted the projection reel to my right hand. It was a lot bigger than a Frisbee but not appreciably heavier. It looked easy when Odd Job did it in *Goldfinger* but who knows how many takes he had to get it right. I wasn't going to get more than one chance at this. I waited for the darkness and then flung the reel where I thought Jeff's neck had been. I felt the metal cut my fingertips as I put the last spin on the projectile, then heard a cry of pain and a thud as the Hacker fell to the floor.

With any luck I'd knocked him out. I realized that Jeff was between me and the door. I'd been lucky to escape the garrotte and I wasn't really interested in learning what other skills the guy had learned. The room went dark again as the moon disappeared behind clouds, but I could smell the odor of, what was it, turpentine? Then flames appeared near the door and quickly spread toward me. The trash on the floor rapidly caught flame and I realized that Jeff had rigged this room as a lethal firetrap. The door opened and quickly closed again as he made his escape. Guess the Odd Job trick didn't work so well in real life. My imagination had clearly run away with me. "Intrepid Professor Fells Felon with Frisbee." What could I have been thinking?

Keep calm, I told myself. There was probably a fire extinguisher somewhere, but I didn't know where to begin looking. That tiny window wasn't going to be any help. Stay close to the ground where there's still oxygen. I began crawling toward the door but I seemed to be moving awfully slowly. The flames grew higher. Too late I thought about all the plastic in the room and the material of the upholstered chair in the corner behind the projector. Dioxin … poisonous … heavier than air … I shouldn't be near the floor.

When I came to I found myself lying on the ground outside the theatre with Todd slapping my face. I got the impression he was taking a certain amount of pleasure in the exercise. I saw Beth and Bridget standing behind him with worried expressions on their faces.

I tried to get up but Todd said, "Just lie still. You breathed in a lot of bad stuff up there."

"How did you …"

"I was coming out of the library when I saw Jeff running across the campus with you in pursuit. You're in pretty good shape for an old guy." I tried to get a full breath of air. "I was curious so I decided to tag along."

"The police caught Jeff," Beth said, "but Todd's the one who dragged you out of the projection booth."

"I saw two people go into the theater and only one come out. Even I could do the math, Axel."

"I'm really grateful ..." I began.

"It's nothing," Todd said. "Randy Preston was a friend of mine. I'm glad somebody was doing something about his death."

Now I was really beginning to feel cold in my wet clothes. I managed to get up, shook Todd's hand, and then walked back to my apartment with Beth and Bridget as escorts.

Chapter 23

THE NEXT MORNING BETH MADE French toast and the three of us sat around the kitchen table and tried to make sense of the week's events.

"What happened to Jeff?" I asked.

"The police got to the theatre just as he was running out," Bridget said.

"Here we were so concerned with finding evidence to show the police," Beth said, "and he practically handed it to them."

"Apparently the hard drive he was carrying contained not only the data he'd stolen from the bank but also information on digitalis and how to rig a gas blast," Bridget said.

"Who is this guy, anyway?" I asked. "I'd seen him all year at the AC Centre but never stopped to think about why he was such a loner."

"When his mother died, his father evidently gave up parenting," Beth said. "Jeff dropped out of Magnolia after two years but still hung around campus with the AC and the film society."

"Sounds as if he wanted to get away from his father but still stay close," I said.

"So close that he hacked into his father's computer network," Bridget said.

"What happened last night, anyway?" I asked.

"According to my brother, Jeff zapped his father with a taser and then maced him," Beth said. "Seems as though he'd already worked out a plan to defend his lair if anyone got too close."

I felt a brief shiver as I thought about the plan he had set up for me. "I guess after Prof. Hewitt threw me out, he remembered what I'd said about tracing a computer to his address and realized that the only computer in the house was his son's."

"So what's going to happen to the kid?" Bridget asked.

"They'll probably lay charges for bank theft and blowing up your house, and now arson, but I doubt they'll ever get him for the murders," Beth said.

"But why would he kill people?" I asked.

Bridget said, "If you were a computer hacker and imagined yourself an anarchist, like a bunch of the characters at the AC, you might get to the point that eliminating obstacles was like removing bugs from a program."

"I don't know," Beth said. "My guess is that the hacking and code-breaking wasn't so much for the money as to earn his father's respect, but somewhere along the line things just got out of hand. I think there was probably something twisted inside him that we'll never understand."

Outside a cardinal's familiar "Huit, huit" call struck me as an ironic summary of the past week, a repeated number pronounced in French. I turned to Bridget and asked what she planned to do now.

"My dad sent me some money to buy clothes and replace my books. After they settle the insurance claim he's going to come down and help me find a new place to live. In the meantime, I was sort of hoping we could continue the current arrangement."

I looked at the two girls in bathrobes. Bridget didn't seem to mind the Minnie Mouse nightshirt Beth had lent her or the Goofy slippers. Beth gave me a heart-melting smile.

"Suits me," I said.

Whene'er I to the passing moment say
"Tarry awhile, thou art so fair!"
Then, mayst thou me in fetters lay,
And to destruction sweep away!
Then, may the death-bell toll for me—
From thy engagement thou be free—
The clock be done, its index fast,—
For me be Time forever past!

—Goethe, *Faust, Part I,* translated by Robert Talbot

TARRY AWHILE

Chapter 1

THE EASTER SERMON AT THE Cathedral had burgeoned with images of new beginnings—blades of grass, tulips, Easter eggs—with the obligatory theological references shoe-horned self-consciously into place, as if the young bishop had not completely made his peace with Christianity's central conundrum. I had marveled at the presence of this Gothic edifice in the midst of a modest Midwestern community—a university town, to be sure, but by no stretch of the imagination a city, much less a metropolis. A brochure in the narthex supplied the answer: a wealthy Hoosier, visiting Europe for the first time as an adult, declared that "we should have one of them cathedrals back home." (Perhaps that wasn't exactly the wording.) But so it happened.

The plan seemed to have been taken from one of the illustrations in David Macaulay's book *Cathedral*, presenting an archetypal version rather than imitating any actual structure. Twin crenellated towers rose at the front of the building, with stained glass windows down both sides and twin transepts at the front. Inside, one saw the classic ogive construction invented by medieval builders, even though here the stonework served as decoration for a modern steel skeleton. The organ, at least, was a true pipe instrument, the handiwork of the thoroughly American Aeolian-Skinner firm. All in all, an American version of Gothic—towers not spires, four-square attachment to reality in place of aspiration toward the divine.

That afternoon, as I walked across the campus of Frangipani University—or "eff you," as irreverent undergraduates liked to call it—I had difficulty summoning the requisite optimism for new beginnings when my career seemed to be coming to an end. My years at Chihuahua State College had ended ignominiously. After two years of academic odd jobs in Boston, and a stint at Brook University, I had landed the position at Monongahela University from which I had recently been fired (or "denied tenure," if you cultivate a taste for academic euphemisms). While completing my doctorate I'd never pictured myself stuck in the middle of a cornfield, just one Visiting Professorship away from the unemployment line. Approaching my fortieth year, I began to have difficulty seeing much point to my continuing existence: every promising start seemed to end in disappointment.

The Brobdingnagian proportions of the university provided ample opportunities for soulful introspection. Upon my arrival in June I had had to hike nearly a mile to pick up my mailbox key, my apartment in the graduate housing complex being near the town end of the sprawling campus and the maintenance department that handled keys at the opposite end near the vast football stadium which, though modest by Big Ten standards, rested on the plains like a mighty Leviathan. Sounds from the FU carillon interrupted my bleak musings. At 161 bells it ranked fifth largest among the 130 carillons in the country (the university displayed an unnatural enthusiasm for self-serving statistics). More to the point, the carillonneur (or –euse) really knew how to play, and the gentle tintinnabulation made it impossible to keep moping.

After all, wasn't Charlotte Wagner waiting for me in her office? We had met improbably at the annual Christmas Banquet held in the world's largest Student Union. (Two hundred hotel rooms, seven banquet rooms, and six public dining rooms, in addition to the usual facilities.) From the outside the building nearly defied description. Colossal, to be sure, but where to go from there? An enormous, stolid tower rose in the middle, between a five-story Tyrolean structure on one side and a cathedral-like torso on the other, as if one had taken the mid-section of Notre Dame and stripped away the flying buttresses. On the far end stood a section resembling an Italian villa, if villas ever rose to three stories, while in front one could see a low series of Georgian porticos. In ordinary circumstances, of course, one would never obtain such an encompassing view: I had had to climb the bell tower hill in order to see how the pieces fit together.

As a visitor, and feeling lonely, I hadn't known any better than to attend the banquet. Charlotte, emerging from an unpleasant divorce, had been looking for an agreeable night out. We found ourselves in line together, eventually took a table together, and discovered that we shared an ironic perspective on the air of unabashed boosterism propelling the event. The "Holiday Fabulous Forty Smorgasbord" promised "prime rib carved to order, a complete salad bar, specialty entrees, vegetables, breads and desserts: at least forty items in all!" Well, there were forty items all right, and each one tasted different, but none of them tasted very good. In the background, one could enjoy "Christmas Music by the Tom Moeller Trio," featuring "O Holy Night" in a *bossa nova* rhythm. (I also noticed that in stores, all the Christmas carols in triple meter—"The First Nowell," "Away in a Manger," "What Child Is This?", "It Came Upon a Midnight Clear," "We Wish You a Merry Christmas," had been forced into duple meter to accommodate the disco backbeat.)

The baronial Tudor Room had been gaily decorated with tiny white lights and a small portable fountain. Red-clad hostesses seated guests at round tables, three couples to a table. The random distribution placed us among strangers, hearing the odd conversations that take place when people don't listen to each other. Thus on one round, the woman beside me mentioned that her mother kept kosher, and on the next round the woman across from me turned to her and inquired brightly, "Do you have ham at your house at Christmas?" Fortunately, my own partner was somewhat more attentive, and happy to continue our conversation in the clear winter air after we had sated ourselves with authentic Hoosier cooking.

Shared laughter led us to seek out other common interests—movies, literature, sports. I had never been much of a basketball fan—a heretical admission at a university that bragged about its national championships in the sport—but Charlotte explained the fine points of the game to me and our dates frequently took us to the gymnasium (along with more than seventeen thousand other fans).

Charlotte taught German literature so, partially as an excuse for spending more time together, we created a course, "Faust in Literature and Music," that we managed to have approved just in time for spring term. We'd thoroughly enjoyed the experience of team teaching but recently it had become painfully clear that our students had only a marginal understanding of Goethe's masterpiece, hence this Sunday afternoon meeting to put together a one-page synopsis for their benefit before we turned to the music based on the play.

I carried echoes of the Easter bells with me as I entered the Humanities Building.

Chapter 2

CHARLOTTE SMILED AT ME AND took off the rimless glasses that she wore for reading. Her light-brown hair fell in bangs over her forehead, with one long lock tucked behind her ear and the rest gathered in back. Her blue eyes, attentive in concentration, sparkled with mischief when she saw me.

"Are you sure we really need to spoon-feed the students this way?" she asked after we had embraced.

"You saw the quizzes," I said. "At least three of them thought that 'Tarry away, thou art so fair' refers to Gretchen."

"I guess you're right," she said. "But we can't possibly squeeze all twenty-five scenes into one page."

"Suppose we just hit the highpoints," I said.

Charlotte walked to the small blackboard between the bookcase and the filing cabinet and began writing. I glanced about the office. Above a work table, covered in almost obsessively neat stacks of papers and books, hung a portrait of her favorite poet, Rainer Maria Rilke. When she first identified the picture for me I commented that he had written in French as well as German, incidentally supplying texts for six choruses by Paul Hindemith. An air fern on top of the filing cabinet and a rubber tree growing in one corner added a bit of natural life to the scholarly surroundings.

Today the window supplied ample illumination, the sun casting the shadow of an elongated cross along the floor. A severely angular floor lamp could be counted on for cloudy days. Charlotte had bought it at her own expense rather than use the overhead fluorescent light supplied by the university. When I looked at the blackboard again I saw the list of headings Charlotte had created.

Easter Bells

Faust and Mephistopheles

Auerbach's Cellar

Gretchen and the Jewels
Duel
Cathedral
Witches Sabbath
Dungeon
Gretchen's Redemption

"I guess that should do it," she said, "although it means omitting some of my favorite scenes."

"We should probably add a few sentences for each heading," I said.

"I've been writing for an hour before you got here," she said. "Suppose you take notes."

I sat down at Charlotte's desk and began a fresh sheet from her stenographic pad. I marveled at how she managed to keep such a neat desktop. I could always find what I needed on my desk but could never achieve the geometrical orderliness that Charlotte maintained as the norm.

"Faust, a medieval scholar and alchemist, contemplates ending his life," she said. "Then the sound of Easter bells makes him think of his childhood and he regains his equilibrium. Your turn."

"Mephistopheles appears and strikes the famous bargain: if he can get Faust to say of the passing moment, 'Tarry awhile, thou art so fair'—in other words, if Faust ever abandons his constant quest for new knowledge in order to remain in the present moment, he will have to surrender his soul."

"And, of course, Faust, Type A man that he is, swears it will never happen—he will always want to move on to the next great thing."

"Did you want me to write that?" I asked.

"Just editorial comment," Charlotte said. "Okay, Mephistopheles takes Faust to Auerbach's Cellar and fetes him with wine, women and song, none of which tempt Faust to abandon his quest and settle for the present moment."

Charlotte continued, "Then Faust sees Gretchen—not an experienced courtesan but a naïve girl—and asks Mephistopheles how he can win her hand. Mephistopheles obligingly produces a chest of jewels which the poor girl initially resists but whose luster eventually overcomes her scruples. You might want to put an ellipsis in there somewhere—after all, Faust impregnates Gretchen and she gives birth to a baby girl, even though the text never says so specifically."

"Okay," I said. "Then Gretchen's brother comes along to challenge the man who has debauched his sister, and Faust, presumably with Mephistopheles' assistance (academics aren't known to be great swordsmen) kills him."

"That's the second death on his conscience. He's already poisoned Gretchen's mother." Charlotte's judgmental tone made it sound as if she had an almost personal interest in the situation.

"I'm not sure that counts—Mephistopheles told him they were just sleeping pills, so that Faust and Gretchen could get it on without being disturbed."

"We'll leave the question to our students' moral sensibilities. I'd say that at the very least he was an accessory after the fact. Okay, now we're at the Cathedral. Evil spirits condemn Gretchen for killing her baby while the 'Dies Irae' sounds in the distance. You may have told me about the 'Dies Irae' but I've forgotten."

"It's Latin for 'Day of wrath,' part of the liturgy for the Requiem Mass. Pretty terrifying, if you ask me. The opening lines go: 'Day of wrath and doom impending, David's word with Sibyl's blending! Heaven and earth in ashes ending!'"

"Even if students don't know that Sibyl was a prophetess, even her name sounds somehow menacing."

"Then comes Walpurgisnacht, the Witches Sabbath," I said.

"We're getting pretty close to the real date," Charlotte said. "It actually falls on April 30."

"Mephistopheles takes Faust to a perverse celebration of the mass, with witches, goblins, and evil powers."

"Next we find Gretchen in a dungeon," Charlotte said, "condemned to death for murdering her child."

"Then in the final scene a chorus of angels announces Gretchen's redemption—in their eyes it was all Faust's fault—and she rises to heaven. End of Part I."

"I think there'll be some space left," Charlotte said. "Would you like to list the musical pieces we'll be studying?"

"Sounds like a good idea," I said, and went to the blackboard, where I wrote:

Schubert, *Gretchen am Spinnrade*

Schumann, *Scenes From Goethe's Faust*
Berlioz, *The Damnation of Faust*
Liszt, *A Faust Symphony*
Gounod, *Faust*
Mahler, Symphony No. 8, second movement

The room seemed suddenly still. I realized that the carillon concert, whose sounds carried faintly into the office, had come to an end.

"What about you, Axel?" Charlotte asked.

"What do you mean?"

"What Faustian bargain would tempt you?"

"You mean tenure in exchange for doing research along approved lines?"

"Something like that."

"It seems as if there's an unwritten rule that musicologists are supposed to stick to manuscript studies. Look at my colleagues here at the university: transcription of a codex of medieval substitute clausulae (don't ask); translation of a treatise on Baroque performance practice; manuscript study of Haydn string quartets; manuscript study of Mass movements of an obscure Polish Renaissance composer."

"Couldn't you do that with Debussy?"

"Other people are already doing that, but I can't even decipher his musical handwriting. Besides, I find that kind of work boring. I'd much rather investigate the relationships between poetic and musical structures in Debussy's music."

"Even though that kind of research doesn't find favor?"

"My last chairman said my work was too speculative."

"And you didn't take that as a warning?"

"You surprise me, Charlotte. I don't think of you as being bound by convention."

She blushed slightly. "You're thinking of last night. I may be wanton and abandoned in bed but here in the department I work to please my boss. I should think you would do the same." She paused for breath and then continued. "Sometimes you seem like a boy who thinks that life is just fun."

"You may be right, but I keep thinking of that line from the film *A Thousand Clowns*: 'You've got to goose the world every now and again to prove that you're a human being and not a chair.'"

"Even if it costs you your job?"

"And saves my soul? Somehow I thought you'd be on my side on this one."

"I support you whole-heartedly, Axel, you know that; but sometimes you have to be practical."

I couldn't see that this discussion was going to get us anywhere so I changed the subject to movies and we made plans to see the latest Woody Allen film, "Hannah and Her Sisters," that evening.

Chapter 3

FROM A SCHOLAR'S PERSPECTIVE A year at Frangipani University represented a kind of nirvana. Only a handful of institutions could top its impressive statistics. The music library contained some 300,000 volumes, listed 1200 periodicals and related serials, held 3000 opera scores and boasted a record collection of 60,000 recordings, with 55 listening booths equipped with headphones. Whenever I needed a particular article for my research I could request one of my graduate assistants to make a photocopy for me, confident that the required journal could be located among the library's vast holdings.

The musicology faculty consisted of six scholars of national, and even international, reputation: no dead wood here. I was told that each of them believed himself to be the only really sane person in the department and that his colleagues ranged from slightly whacko to stark raving bonkers. This may have accounted for the uniformly pleasant mood of the faculty meetings: they were all humoring each other.

On Monday morning I had intended to look up some books on Debussy that I hadn't been able to find anywhere else but I was deflected by an animated discussion between Thomas Waterdown, the director of the Collegium Musicum, the university's early music ensemble, and Lucinda Dumont, a diminutive but feisty voice teacher. Waterdown, tall, sandy-haired, earnest-looking, dressed in a dark gold turtleneck and matching slacks, spoke so softly that I could understand no word until I joined the conversation. Elaborately coiffed black hair—surely dyed at her age—added several inches to Miss Dumont's diminutive stature, and her regal bearing contributed to her physical presence, but she would always be considered petite. Nonetheless her voice, that carefully honed instrument, projected with the force of an operatic soprano. "I think it's outrageous! A disgrace!"

Seeing me approach Waterdown explained, "Poundstone's dead."

That would presumably be J. Watson Poundstone, the stage director of the Music Arts Centre.

"Killed on the very stage of his production!" Miss Dumont continued indignantly.

"Hoist on his own petard, if you ask me," Waterdown said.

"I'm having a bit of trouble understanding this," I said. "What exactly happened?"

"That infernal chandelier—the only really interesting detail in *The Phantom of the Opera*—fell on him on Friday night and, needless to say, killed him."

"I can't say I know much about the *Phantom*, but isn't that chandelier supposed to stop six feet above the stage?" I asked.

"Not in this production. Poundstone insisted on a chandelier that would fall to six *inches* above the stage," Waterdown said.

"Wasn't that dangerous?" I asked.

Waterdown frowned as if talking to a small child. "Of course it was dangerous. That was the whole point. Poundstone even painted a large circle on the stage that he liked to call the Ring of Death."

"But surely there must have been elaborate safeguards to prevent an accident. Doesn't the chandelier weigh more than a ton?"

"2.2 tons," said Miss Dumont. "It's the centerpiece of the production." (Was everyone at this school mesmerized by impressive statistics?)

"I still don't get it," I said. "Wouldn't there be a member of the technical crew assigned to operate the apparatus?"

"You mean you haven't heard about Jay's toy?" Waterdown must have noticed the look of puzzlement on my face because he went into a patient explanation. "The chandelier represented just one feature of the production. Poundstone got his start on the technical side and he added dozens of special effects to *his* version of the *Phantom* that didn't even appear in the London production."

"That must have required an expanded technical crew," I said.

"In performance, yes," Waterdown said. "But J. Watson Poundstone was a control freak who liked to try out his little games without having to keep a crew always on call. So he had a remote control gadget cooked up so that he could play with the technical effects to his heart's content whenever he wanted."

"'Whatever you do,'" Lucinda Dumont intoned, lowering her voice to mimic that of the deceased director, "'Don't press 33 while I'm standing in the Ring of Death.'"

The music librarian appeared at the desk, observed that we didn't require her assistance, and returned to her small glass-walled cubicle. Students walked past us, either too polite or too uninterested to try listening in.

"So a lot of people knew about this remote control device?" I asked.

"Everybody knew. The students even joked about it," Miss Dumont said. "Someone would shout '33!' and the others would duck or run."

"This sounds more and more like murder," I said.

"And it couldn't have happened to a nicer guy," Waterdown said sarcastically. "Seducer, megalomaniac and general all-around bastard."

"And he overstrained young voices. I would never let my singers participate in his productions," Miss Dumont said self-righteously.

"You mean he never chose any of your students," Waterdown said.

I had to marvel at the way a diva carried off spontaneity. A carefully controlled intake of breath, always from the diaphragm, preceded the expostulation. "Well!" the little woman exclaimed. "I don't need to stand here having my integrity impugned!" She stalked off with all the dignity of a *prima donna*. I felt badly for her. Had Waterdown just been thoughtless, or didn't he care? But my mind returned to the matter at hand.

"Was Poundstone as bad as all that?" I asked.

"It's not just that Poundstone was a rotten scoundrel. It's that he reveled in it," Waterdown said. "He openly bragged about the women he seduced and the men he screwed. And those rings he wore on every finger! I've never seen a more colossal sense of entitlement. I don't think of myself as a particularly religious man, but I look at this as the wrath of God." He didn't wait to find out how I looked at it, but glanced at his watch and made his excuses. I stood alone and concluded that I still had a lot to learn about the School of Music. Then I descended into the stacks in search of Debussy.

Chapter 4

AN HOUR LATER I WAS sitting in my office, perusing the books I'd brought back from the library. The collection having long since outstripped the available space, the music library had recourse to a system of sliding stacks to house the older books. You turned a large wheel—roughly the size of a sports car steering wheel—to separate adjacent stacks enough that you could slip in to inspect their contents, all the while hoping that other patrons would check for possible casualties before turning the wheels in the opposite direction to close the gap. Happily, the works I required could be found on stationary shelves.

Of course it wasn't really my office. As a Visiting Professor I occupied whatever space happened to be vacant each semester. I had not met the man whose absence provided me with a temporary home but an orange basketball perched proudly on top of the bookcase suggested a former athlete who perhaps still enjoyed a pick-up game to stay in shape. I hadn't troubled to rearrange the furniture, so the desk still served as a kind of protective barrier against students hoping to petition for a better grade or glean some hint of the questions on the next test.

The contents of the bookcase indicated a member of the music theory department rather than a musicologist. The musicologists at Frangipani U. considered teaching to be an unpleasant and unwarranted intrusion on their research time. Some taught with a lofty attitude of *noblesse oblige*, others with scarcely disguised distaste for the students and everything they represented. The students, not surprisingly, picked up on these attitudes and avoided attending class as much as possible.

The theory teachers, by contrast, considered teaching to be their primary mission and embraced me as a kindred spirit. Word spread about my passion for teaching and, as a rule, nearly all of the one hundred seventy members of my music history survey attended lectures.

Their enthusiasm further kindled my own as I taught this fundamental course for the first time.

Those familiar with the ways of academic music departments may wonder how this could be. As a rule musicologists detested the survey course and regularly assigned it to the youngest member of the department, a new arrival with no say in the matter. How could I have missed out on the process? The answer lay with the ersatz university organist at Brook University, Seth Chichester Nelson, whom I secretly called Professor Twinkletoes. Given the wretched assignment upon his arrival many years earlier, he had simply recycled notes he had taken as an undergraduate and, unwilling to prepare a new course, had foisted his long-outdated material year after year upon unsuspecting music majors.

In the first half of the music survey at Frangipani, Music Before 1750 (which the students derisively dismissed as "pre-music"), I drew on their status as performers to give live renditions of medieval plainchant and simple motets, and even had the class parade around the room to perform liturgical procession music. Now, in the second term, Music Since 1750, when I myself performed a piece by Chopin or Liszt to illustrate a lesson, I received appreciative applause from would-be professional musicians who understood exactly how many hours had gone into mastering those works. I couldn't count on students doing the assignments, but the sound of an auditorium full of laughter at jokes understandable only among musicians left me exhilarated (and raised eyebrows among my musicologist colleagues who considered zest for teaching an obvious indication of scholarly weakness).

A knock on the door interrupted my thoughts. Gretchen Spindler entered and took a seat. A tall, rather plain young woman, brown-haired, dressed in an oversized brown sweater worn over black legging, she seemed even more ill at ease than usual. For performers, the School of Music at Frangipani represented perhaps the most challenging experience of their careers. No competition they faced in their professional lives would exceed the fierce struggle for recognition at the School of Music. Tales of tendonitis abounded among instrumentalists practicing seven, eight or more hours a day, knowing that their compatriots were doing the same. One cellist among my students talked of finding a practice room among the brass students to avoid snide remarks from other string players lurking outside the door and listening to her work.

Singers like Gretchen had it the worst. With their instruments actually located in their bodies, they proved to be unusually vulnerable to jibes directed at their fragile egos. Singers in each "stable" loyally defended the vocal technique advocated by their teachers and denigrated other teachers' methods and other students' performances with the venomous intensity of high school cliques.

The student-teacher relationship often extended beyond matters of musical technique so that voice teachers ended up serving as personal advisors in affairs of the heart or any other crises emerging in this hothouse of combative activity. So I was surprised when Gretchen opened up to me rather than to her teacher, Miss Dumont.

"I don't really know how to begin," she said, looking down at the floor and hunching her shoulders unattractively.

"Have you read *Alice in Wonderland*?" I asked, eager to relieve her discomfort by directing her attention away from it.

"Yes, of course," the young woman said a bit nervously.

"The Queen of Hearts tells Alice, 'You should begin at the beginning, proceed until you get to the end, and when you get there, stop.'"

Gretchen made a brave attempt at a smile then abandoned the effort. "I'm not sure I want to do that," she said.

"Well then," I said, "suppose you begin wherever it seems easiest."

"I've had an abortion," Gretchen blurted out.

"You're not the first," I said. I felt nearly as uncomfortable as Gretchen but I tried not to let it show. Gretchen looked confused, so I changed tack. "How do you feel about that?"

"I thought I'd feel relieved, but instead I feel guilty."

"The two often go together, strange as it may seem."

"They do?" Her confusion seemed to increase and I felt distinctly out of my depth. Why couldn't she just talk to her voice teacher like the other singers?

"Do you feel you did the right thing?" The young woman nodded. "And if you had to do it again, would you do the same thing?" Gretchen hesitated then nodded again. "Then you have consistency and good instincts on your side," I said. "That counts for a fair bit. Who is telling you that you did wrong?"

"I was raised Roman Catholic," Gretchen said. "So this must have been a sin."

Ah, yes. Black and white thinking seemed to go with the colors of priests' robes and nuns' habits. "Do you believe in your heart that you were right to terminate your pregnancy?"

"Oh yes," she said. "It would have been awful to have that baby." She squeezed her eyes shut as if trying to force the unwanted vision from her imagination.

"Have you been thinking about this for a long time?"

"Yes. I've been wrestling with it ever since I learned I was pregnant. Then … well, something happened … and so I had it done right away." Gretchen looked at the floor.

"Have you tried talking to a priest?" I asked. Maybe confession had its benefits.

"Oh, I haven't been to church for years. I don't think I believe that stuff anymore."

"But ancient lessons still hold their strength."

"Something like that."

"If in your heart you believe you did the right thing, I'd suggest listening to your heart."

"You're not going to tell anyone." Gretchen looked nervous again.

"My lips are sealed. I'm a musicologist, not a gossip," I said, adapting a favorite line from the movie version of *Harvey*. Gretchen seemed somewhat more relaxed but didn't make any move toward leaving her chair, so I tried to steer the conversation toward a neutral subject. "Do you sing in the Collegium Musicum?"

"No," Gretchen said. "Professor Waterdown said my voice isn't pure enough."

"I've heard you sing in class," I said, "and I can't agree with him." Gretchen smiled for the first time since she had come into the office. "Still, I guess that means you won't be making the trip to Carnegie Hall."

Gretchen looked surprised. "Didn't you hear?" she asked. "That trip was cancelled."

That was news to me. Thomas Waterdown had, over the years, raised the reputation of the early music ensemble to the point that students began coming to the School of Music with the express purpose of playing the recorder, viol or sackbut here. Students of traditional instruments who had begun by looking down their noses at instruments whose mere existence constituted a novelty for them, eventually had to recognize the possibility of genuine virtuosity even from such an unexpected source. The addition of small choral group had allowed the Collegium Musicum to enlarge its repertoire.

Yet a New York recital remained an obligatory cachet as much for an early music ensemble as for a solo artist. I had heard talk of the planned appearance of the Collegium Musicum at Carnegie Hall—the small recital hall, not the main concert hall—ever since arriving at the university. I could only imagine the effect of the cancellation on the morale of Thomas Waterdown and his band of early music performers.

Gretchen must have read the surprise on my face. "Some problem with funding," she said.

I asked whether she was enjoying rehearsals for Gounod's *Faust,* the next production in the school's active opera schedule. Her face brightened. "Miss Dumont is so pleased," she said. "It's the first time one of her students has had the lead in an opera production."

"Is that the reason you signed up for the Faust course?"

"Yes. I thought it would be a good idea if I learned something about the background of the story."

"I guess it wouldn't be fair to ask if you're enjoying the course."

"I am. But that's partly what made me come to see you. Gretchen in the play is tormented by evil spirits after she murders her baby. Isn't abortion just another form of murder?"

So she just couldn't leave that topic. I cast about for a suitable response. "I'm no expert on ethics, Gretchen, but I'd be happy to share my opinion on abortion for what it's worth."

"Please do."

"I once had a friend who'd had an abortion and described it as simply removing a bit of excess tissue from her body. I've known other people who insisted on legal protection for an embryo from the moment of conception. I'm sure that I reject both of these extreme positions. I believe the truth lies somewhere in between, but pinning down that point requires more wisdom than I have and I suspect that there may be no universally applicable lesson—you have to judge each case on its merits."

"So you don't think I'm a murderess?"

"Not for a single second."

Gretchen's smile transformed her plainness into something that might be called pretty, an attribute that probably served her well on the stage. "Thanks, Professor Crochet," she said. "I really appreciate your listening."

My raised palms suggested the inadequacy of my assistance as I watched Gretchen depart. Martin Baxter must have been waiting outside my door because he entered almost immediately after Gretchen's departure. Martin, a clarinetist—actually, a very fine clarinetist—lived across the hall from me in the graduate student apartment building that served as my living quarters for the year. With the physique of a basketball guard, blue eyes and a cherubic expression, he looked like the sort of guy you'd expect to be at ease in any situation. Instead, he seemed totally lacking in self-confidence, even in music, which didn't make sense at all. He invariably wore a red FU baseball cap, which made him look rather sporty even though I knew he did it to cover a premature bald spot.

Martin came in, looked around nervously, and seated himself on the very edge of the chair in front of the desk. "I don't know what I'm going to do, Axel," he said. This seemed to be my day for listening to other people's problems. Perhaps the musicologists had a point in keeping as far away from students as possible.

"What seems to be the trouble?"

"Look at this," he said, thrusting a letter in my face. I scanned it briefly.

"So what's the problem? They're asking you to an audition."

"That's the step just before they can you—I'm going to lose my scholarship and have to leave school."

"I've only been here a short time," I said, "but that doesn't sound like that the way the School of Music operates."

"They can do it, too," he said. "I flunk the audition and it's good-bye FU."

"Have you received any complaints about your playing in the orchestra?" I asked. The School of Music sustained five complete symphony orchestras, with increasing levels of competitiveness. I wasn't sure which one Martin played in.

"No—that's just how they do it," he said. "They lull you into complacency and then, bang, they throw you out of school."

"Aren't you letting your imagination run away with you a bit? Have you ever known anyone to be dismissed from the orchestra?"

"It happens all the time."

"But don't they just get reassigned to another orchestra?"

"Most of the time, yes, but you never can tell."

"May I offer you some advice?"

"Yes! Please! Anything."

"When's the audition?"

"End of the afternoon—right before rehearsal."

"Do you have anything important between now and then?"

"Not really."

"Eat lunch. Take a walk. Have a nap. Then play your best and let the devil take the hindmost."

"That's easy for you to say." Martin seemed determined to rule out all possibilities but the bleakest.

"Okay. What would you suggest instead?"

"I could always quit school right now and avoid the embarrassment."

"Martin—give yourself a break."

"Maybe I should spend the afternoon practicing scales."

"Martin—don't touch your clarinet before the audition."

"Really?"

"Really."

Martin looked at me skeptically, then shrugged his shoulders and walked out of the office.

Chapter 5

MONDAY AFTERNOON FOUND ME AT the Technical Services Office hoping to resolve a problem with Janice Fraser. I still hadn't worked out her position in the complicated constellation of responsibilities. Whenever I wanted anything, she seemed to be sufficiently in charge to resist my requests. Whenever she wanted anything, it seemed as if she lacked all authority and needed me to rescue her.

A counter separated the public from the work area of the office, with filing cabinets on one side, a work table with a tape editing station in the middle, and on the opposite side a 16-millimeter projector evidently undergoing repair. Reels of film sat in a neat pile on a shelf; nearby stood overhead projectors, film-strip projectors and a portable projection screen. Against one wall someone had rolled a trolley containing turntable, amplifier, and two loudspeakers.

I recalled our conversation just before the beginning of term. I had brought Janice the handouts I wanted made for the first week of the history survey.

"What's this?" she demanded. Janice was a stern-faced older woman with gray hair arranged in a complicated pattern. No crossed knitting needles actually protruded from her coiffure, but they would have looked entirely appropriate. Janice always had a way of making me feel as if I were about to receive a reprimand, to the point that I had to brace myself every time I approached the Technical Services Office.

"Handouts for the history survey."

"What do you want me to do with them?"

"I need 170 copies."

"No way!"

"But this is how we operated all summer."

"That was summer. This is the real thing. And in the summer you had a class of twenty. Now you're talking 170. Forget it."

"But it's really important that the students have these pages."

"Then do what all the other professors do. Gather the materials you need for the term, we'll send them out to get printed into a Maxipak, the students will buy them along with their textbooks, and you're good to go."

"But I don't have materials for the whole term. This is the first time I've taught the course. I'm lucky if I can stay two weeks ahead of the students."

Janice looked at me suspiciously. "You seem a bit old to be teaching the history survey for the first time."

I considered trying to explain about Professor Twinkletoes and thought better of it. "If it's a matter of cost," I said, "couldn't I send the students in here every couple of weeks to buy each new set of notes?"

"We're not equipped to handle money in this office."

"How much do you think it would amount to per student over the term?"

"That depends on how many pages of handouts you intend to make."

I counted the sheets in my current handout and extrapolated and Janice estimated a sum. "So that works out to around $2 a student," I said.

"That should cover it," Janice said.

"But if I collected $2 a student and gave you the money, you couldn't take it?"

"Nope."

"There's got to be a way to make this work. Who officially runs this office?"

"We answer to the Dean of the School of Music and operate under the budget he sets."

"So if I could get my handouts as a line item in your budget, we'd be all set?"

Janice frowned as she considered the situation, which apparently had no precedent. "I guess that would be all right," she conceded, as if reluctant to be party to any bending of the rules.

In the end, I collected $2 from each student and wrote a check to the School of Music. The dean's office sent a memo to Janice, and it all worked out. Over the course of the year we had worked out more than one unconventional arrangement but I never knew how Janice would react.

Finally Janice appeared, holding a sheaf of pages in her hand and waving them at me accusingly. "Why is this handout thicker than usual?" I told her that I'd taught that piece before and was including notes from my previous lecture into the handout. "You mean, every time you teach the course, the handouts get thicker?"

"I hadn't really thought about it that way. I figure that rather than making students take notes on what I said in the lecture, it would be easier if I could supply the information to them in written form."

"So then you say something different in the lecture?"

"Well, sure. I wouldn't want to just repeat what they already had in front of them."

"And then the notes for that lecture go into the handout for the next time around?"

"Yes."

"So the handouts just get thicker and thicker."

"I think of it as enriching the material."

"How do you think the students look at it?"

"I'm not sure."

"It just means more stuff for them to read. I can see why they complain about your course."

I didn't have much to say to that so I mumbled something about trying to average out the number of pages in the handouts and left.

Chapter 6

As a Visiting Professor at "the largest school of music in the world"—a title the S of M had no intention of ever surrendering—I thought it appropriate to make use of student performers whenever possible, a policy that pleased the students and provided nearly professional-level renditions of the works we studied. Gretchen Spindler, the only soprano enrolled in the Faust course, had agreed to perform Schubert's "Gretchen am Spinnrade" (Gretchen at the spinning wheel) for our next class meeting, and she appeared at my office on Tuesday morning to rehearse the piece with me.

This office, a good deal larger than the one I had occupied during fall term, actually had space for my grand piano. I had paid to have it moved from my apartment to the office, secretly imagining that its presence would assure my obtaining a permanent position in the School of Music. After all, you can't very well evict a person with a grand piano in his office. ("Magical thinking," Charlotte informed me when I confessed the move. "Not worthy of you, Axel.")

Gretchen performed the song with a remarkable intensity of feeling. At the words, "My poor head is deranged, my poor mind is distracted," she conveyed a sense of utter desperation. When she sang of the character's infatuation with Faust, I felt the full force of her adolescent idealization of the older man. Her voice had a certain thrilling quality but also a perfect clarity. I couldn't imagine why Thomas Waterdown had rejected her for the early music ensemble.

After we finished practicing the song Gretchen leaned on the piano to share an idea with me. Her eagerness seemed almost palpable. "I remember how you said that the running sixteenth notes in the accompaniment represented the movement of the spinning wheel," she began.

"All the commentaries mention that symbolism," I said, "and

judging from other accompaniments representing brooks or millwheels, it's presumably what Schubert intended."

"And you suggested that the repeated refrain represents Gretchen's growing obsession with Faust." I smiled. What teacher doesn't like to have evidence that a lesson has been absorbed? "But I was wondering about the melodic motive in the left hand of the piano part. It appears during most of the piece but then it stops when Gretchen gets all rapturous about Faust's face."

I nodded and Gretchen continued. "So I decided to talk with my grandmother and she told me that her grandmother really had a spinning wheel. There's a foot treadle that keeps the wheel spinning, but you have to keep moving your hands to feed the material into the machine to make thread."

"Go on," I said.

"When you see people in movies or historical villages, it always looks so easy, but evidently there's more to spinning than you might think." I nodded again. "Well, if the constant motive in the accompaniment represents the foot treadle, couldn't the other motive represent the hands?"

"No reason why not."

"And if that's true, then when Gretchen starts exclaiming over Faust's face, her feet keep going but her hands stop and she just makes a mess of the thread-making."

"I don't think I've ever read an analysis of the song that accounts for that second motive. I'd be pleased if you'd share your description with the class next time we meet."

I thought of my dissertation showing how Debussy created musical structures for his songs that seemed appropriate to the poetic structures of his chosen texts. Speculative? Perhaps, but the individual structures were demonstrable. Was it so irresponsible to suggest that the relationship between the two might be intentional?

Gretchen looked pleased, but then her face clouded and one of her legs twisted nervously as she continued to lean on the piano. I waited for her to continue and eventually she spoke, though with a good deal less animation than before. "There's something I didn't tell you the other day, and now I'm really in trouble."

"You mean feeling guilty about your abortion?"

"It's even worse than that." I tried to imagine the cause of her distress but came up blank. Now that Gretchen had gotten over her initial reluctance, the words poured out. "The police think I killed Professor Poundstone. Yesterday they came to ask me questions and I'm afraid I'm going to be arrested!"

"I'm not following this very well. I think you're really going to have to follow the Queen of Hearts' advice this time and start from the beginning."

"I guess you're right." Gretchen bit her lip as she tried to gather her thoughts. I guess I shouldn't have been surprised that she approached the subject obliquely. "You can imagine that practically every soprano in the school auditioned for the part of Marguerite."

Indeed I could. In fact, while I admired Gretchen's voice in singing Schubert's song, she hadn't seemed like the most obvious choice for the operatic lead in *Faust*. She had the vocal agility for the part but not as large a voice as one might have expected for the role.

"So when Professor Poundstone called me back for a second reading I was pleased but also a little surprised. But nothing compared with what I felt when he told me his plan."

I began to have a sinking feeling in my stomach, remembering Poundstone's reputation as an unabashed womanizer. Gretchen must have guessed my thoughts. "It's not quite what you're thinking—not just sex anyway. Professor Poundstone wanted a baby. I think he was having a hard time with the adoption agencies, being a single father, but I believe he really wanted his son to have half of his genes."

"His son?"

"I know. I guess he really thought he could control a child's gender through an act of will. That's just the way he was. So he made me a proposition: I could have the lead in *Faust* if I'd have a baby for him."

Gretchen's words took me aback. Even with everything I'd heard about Poundstone's manipulations, I found myself unprepared for this idea. What a colossal ego this man had! "I don't suppose he believed in artificial insemination?"

Gretchen blushed. "No, he wanted to do it the old-fashioned way, and so we did."

"Sounds pretty businesslike."

"Oh, it was. He made me sign a contract and everything. The police found it when they went through his papers and so they came to me."

"This was just after the abortion?"

"Well, yes. I arranged it as soon as I heard about his death. I mean, why should I give up nine months of my life if he wasn't even around to raise the child?"

"But you're still going to sing the role in the opera," I said.

"Now you're beginning to sound like them," she said. I suppose my question had sounded judgmental, but this whole development offended my sense of the rightness of things.

"So the police think you killed Poundstone to get out of your contract?"

"Something like that."

"Didn't you think the contract would eventually turn up?"

"But I didn't kill him!" Gretchen's eyes filled with tears. "I thought you'd understand."

Once again I wished that Gretchen were having this conversation with her voice teacher rather than with me. "I'm still trying to make sense of this," I said. "You heard that he was killed by that infernal chandelier?"

"Yes."

"And you knew how to operate that silly gizmo."

"Everybody did. It was a standing joke around the school."

"Where were you Friday night?"

"Studying in my room."

"I don't suppose you can prove it."

"No; I was alone." My heart sank as I considered this girl's plight.

"So from the perspective of the police you had motive, means and opportunity: the fatal triad."

Gretchen made a whimpering sound and stared at the floor. We remained silent for several moments. "Will you help me?"

"Have you thought about consulting a lawyer?"

"If I did that I'd have to tell my mother."

"What about your father?"

"He disappeared when I was little."

"How about Miss Dumont?"

"That's even worse! I don't want anybody to know about all this. I'd have to leave the School of Music and give up my career and everything."

That sounded a bit extreme to me but I decided not to mention it. "I don't make any promises," I said, "but I'll see what I can do."

Gretchen suddenly came over to the piano bench where I was sitting and hugged me, then dashed out of the room before I could frame an appropriate response.

Chapter 7

MUSICOLOGY REPRESENTS A RELATIVE NEWCOMER among academic disciplines. The term first appeared in its German form—*Musikwissenschaft*—in 1885. American musicology dates from the period during and after the Second World War when German émigrés brought the "science of music" to the United States. Most musicologists in that era devoted their energies to editing complete works of major composers or, once those spoils had been divided, of successively more minor composers. Often government funds could be found to support the publication of works of composers from that country. Each new generation of musicologists scoured European libraries and monasteries in search of manuscripts that could be edited and published in the interest of general scholarship and their particular careers. The emphasis on manuscript studies seemed to pre-empt all other considerations.

After Gretchen's departure I mused on my conversation with Charlotte on the inappropriateness of my own research. My musing must have turned into daydreaming because I imagined myself sitting at a giant spinning wheel with a complicated mechanism beyond my capacity to comprehend, while Charlotte's voice rebuked me: "Axel, you've broken the thread of scholarship."

"Axel, Axel …" I opened my eyes to see Charlotte herself standing before me, dressed in a chestnut-colored sweater, slightly darker than the color of her hair, over a dark brown skirt. A necklace of tiny shells prevented the outfit from seeming too severe. She leaned over to kiss me, then said, "Pleasant dreams, I hope." It took me a moment to clear my head. Then we went over plans for the next meeting of the Faust seminar, which included works by Schubert and Schumann. "I'd like you to hear something," I said, and located the band for the last six minutes of Mahler's 8th Symphony.

We sat beside each other and listened to the chorus and orchestra perform a musical setting of the final words of *Faust*:

What is destructible
Is but a parable;
What fails ineluctably,
The undeclarable,
Here it was seen,
Here it was action;
The Eternal-Feminine
Lures to perfection.

Words that sounded awkward and pedestrian in translation seemed to make more sense in the original German, and Mahler's rapturous setting transformed "the Eternal-Feminine" from a sterile abstraction into a spiritual verity.

When the echoes of the last chord had finished reverberating Charlotte turned to me, her eyes full of tears, and said "That's the most beautiful thing I've ever heard." Happily I had the good sense not to ask if she didn't find it a trifle overdone. The embrace that followed felt so precious to me that I reflected on the Faustian bargain and thought that I myself might have wanted to say of that particular moment, "Tarry awhile, thou art so fair."

Then I thought of Gretchen's predicament and the awful responsibility I had somehow accepted. When our hug ended I turned to face Charlotte.

"You've heard about the death of J. Watson Poundstone?" I asked.

"Well that's one hell of a jump. You mean the legendary lecher?"

"Yes. It seems as if the whole campus has nothing better to do than speculate on which of the dozens of people he's damaged might have done the deed."

"Don't tell me you've gotten involved."

"It looks that way. One of my students—our students, actually—has fallen under police investigation and expects to be arrested."

"I guess it shouldn't surprise me that Poundstone would include students among his conquests."

"She claims not have done it, but swore me to secrecy on the incriminating details."

"So now you've become a man of mystery." Charlotte smiled at me.

"I feel pretty helpless," I said. "I'm an academic, not a detective. The only thing I can think of to help her is to furnish a more convincing candidate as murderer."

"There are legions of people at the university who thought the world would be a better place without Jay Poundstone in it, but I don't imagine many of them would actually go to the trouble of killing him. Academics may talk a good game but the proverbial 'life of the mind' doesn't usually lead to a lot of action, and very seldom to violence." Charlotte seemed to have overcome her initial distaste for the subject and brought her analytical mind to bear on the question.

"Suppose we set aside ancient grievances for the moment. Who has he harmed recently?" I asked.

"One name that comes to mind is Ronald Holton."

"Who's he?"

"You usually hear him described as 'the distinguished Ronald Holton.' He holds an endowed chair in the history of science."

"What's his connection to Poundstone?"

"His wife. Or ex-wife. Holton's, that is. She had a brief but destructive affair with the opera director."

"I don't mean to sound blasé, but aren't a certain proportion of extramarital amours considered more or less normal in academia?"

"They are if they remain discreet. As you must have learned by now, discretion wasn't part of Poundstone's lexicon."

"What happened?"

"The consensus of the campus gossip has the wife inadvertently catching Poundstone's eye at some faculty function. He invents an excuse to invite her for an innocent lunch. He times a dinner invitation with her husband's absence at an out-of-town conference and eventually beds her."

"I never thought of Poundstone as a particularly attractive man."

"Men always think of looks first. That's not what it takes. It was Poundstone's intensity of energy concentrated singlemindedly on a vulnerable woman that turned the trick.

"So she was indiscreet."

"Oh, no; she always feared her husband would find out. She was completely mortified when Jay Poundstone publicly hung the horns on her husband, humiliating him in front of his colleagues at the President's tea. Poundstone really had a diabolical sense of humor." I recalled Thomas Waterdown's characterization: seducer, megalomaniac and general all-around bastard.

Our conversation returned to *Faust* and the essay we'd asked the students to write on the character they found most interesting in the drama. "I've always been interested in Valentine," Charlotte said.

"Gretchen's brother."

"Yes. I find something noble in his behavior."

"How's that?"

"Well, you have to remember the importance placed in this era on preserving a woman's virtue. She has to remain pure for her husband-to-be, and it was up to the family to maintain that condition."

"Contain the raging hormones, you mean?"

"They wouldn't have used that language, but yes."

"No living together or trial marriages?"

"No way. Anyway, Faust deflowers his sister. Valentine can't reverse that action so he has to avenge it."

"Do you think he expected to die?"

"He probably thought he'd be an adequate match for Faust if Mephistopheles hadn't intervened. But I don't think it really mattered. Valentine took the action that honor required, and if he had to sacrifice his life, so be it. In a lot of ways he shows more integrity than Faust."

"You really think so?"

"Well, look at it. Faust professes to be concerned only with gaining knowledge. I can respect that, as a fellow academic. But what does he give it up for? A pretty face. I can imagine that some of the students in our seminar would call it 'thinking with his dick.'"

"Isn't that a bit harsh?"

"That's not the worst part. After he has his way with Gretchen, he abandons her, a pregnant, unmarried girl."

"He comes back at the end."

"But he's not the one who saves her. She receives heavenly redemption. Faust just feels guilty, not that it does Gretchen any good." In reading the play I'd always identified with Faust, but the way Charlotte portrayed the situation he seemed more scoundrel than hero.

"When would you say he lost his soul?" I asked.

"I don't know. I suppose at the moment that he says, 'Tarry awhile, thou art so fair.'"

"In other words, when he first catches sight of Gretchen and tells Mephistopheles he wants her."

"I guess that's right."

"Then from that point on, he has no soul, and can't be judged by moral standards. He's not responsible for being a cad."

"Only a man would construct an argument like that."

"But it's consistent with the terms of the story."

"I suppose you're right, but that's the most cynical reading of Faust I've ever heard."

"I didn't mean to offend."

"I don't take offense at you, Axel—you're the most moral man I've ever met. But I don't know how you can even see the story from that perspective."

"A scholar's relativism, I suppose." It bothered me that our discussions of Faust always seemed to involve our own personal relationship.

"Have you given any more thought to how you'd deal with the Faustian temptation yourself?" Gretchen asked.

"I've been considering it. I think that if I were going to sell my soul, I'd want to be pretty sure that I was getting full value."

"How do you mean?" Charlotte's frown suggested that this discussion was a good deal more than academic from her point of view.

"Let's take the bargain you proposed: carrying out conventional research projects in order to get tenure. During the years I taught at Monongahela, five of us came up for tenure, several stronger than myself, and I thought I was pretty good. Not one person got it. In particular, one ethnomusicologist published a lot, kept his head low at faculty meetings and fulfilled all his responsibilities diligently: they still denied him tenure."

"So what's your point?"

"I keep thinking about what my mentor at Cornell said: 'Go with what you love.' If you abandon what you love for the sake of tenure, and don't get it, then you've lost everything."

"So you're saying you'd want an ironclad agreement if you were going to sell your soul."

"Something like that."

"But don't you see, Axel: Mephistopheles always cheats. When you sell your soul, you never get what was promised."

"Sounds as if you're making a pretty good case for the opposition."

"I don't know. I see your point, but the way the system works, if you don't get tenure, your career ends."

I didn't feel particularly comfortable with this line of conversation so I turned the subject back to *Faust*. "I think you may be romanticizing Valentine?"

"How do you mean?"

"Well, as Valentine lies dying after the duel with Faust, he calls his sister a whore and curses her."

"Do you think those are his true feelings towards Gretchen?"

"You could make a case that Valentine is really defending his pride rather than his sister's honor."

"Isn't that a bit harsh?"

"At the beginning of the scene Valentine complains that he used to be able to boast about his sister's virtue, but now he's the subject of taunts and sneers. Note—he's the subject of sneers, not her."

"You may have a point." I still had the sense that Charlotte was taking this discussion personally.

"What bothers me is the Walpurgis Night Scene. What's the point of it, anyway?" I asked.

"What's the matter? You don't like naked witches?"

"Naked witches farting."

"Many versions of the text still read 'Witches f---ing." Makes it seem worse than it is."

"Guess that's one problem with censorship."

"Perhaps you've been spending too much time with Gounod's *Faust*. The opera tends to focus on Marguerite but Goethe's *Faust* really is about Faust. While Gretchen's busy offstage having a baby, drowning it, and generally going crazy, we're following Faust's activities."

"And what pleasure does Mephistopheles take from all these goings-on? It's as if his main purpose is to keep Faust from his scholarly work."

"Spoken like a scholar." Charlotte smiled at me.

"It seems a far cry from Marlowe's *Doctor Faustus*, where Faust surrenders his soul ...

" ... and body"

"Yes, and body—in return for twenty-four years of service from the Devil."

"And even farther from the historical Faust."

"You mean there really was such a man?"

"Yes. He was born near the end of the 15th century. He studied magic—you could do that in those days—and taught school."

"Sounds innocent enough."

"Not really. He used to sodomize the boys."

"What happened to him?"

"He became a university professor instead." Charlotte's tone underlined the irony.

"Then what?"

"He pledged his soul to the devil."

"And?"

"Evidently he attracted such a following that the church authorities got upset. They needed the devil to keep the congregation in line, but Johann Faust made the dark side look altogether too attractive, so they sent a priest to convert him."

"How did that go?"

"Faust wouldn't have any of it, so they expelled him from the city."

"No infernal distractions at FU—not for musicologists anyway."

"You're thinking of your colleagues?"

"Yes. I heard one bragging to a friend in New York about the amount of work he gets done here without urban blandishments to tempt him."

"Fifteen hundred concerts don't constitute a distraction?"

"Musicologists never go to concerts."

"Except for you?"

"Except for me."

Chapter 8

LATE TUESDAY AFTERNOON I MADE my way to the Ratskeller, where Ronald Holton's colleagues predicted I'd be able to find him. The place suggested a Disneyfied version of a Biergarten created by someone who had never set foot in Germany. Oversized steins decorated with Tyrolean heads stood in a row behind the bar, tended by a young lad clad in Lederhosen. Huge dark-wood beams divided the ceiling into sections while Bavarian "gingerbread" bedecked every window casing. Two gigantic Alpenhorns crossed on one wall opposite a frieze depicting blond-haired boys and girls at play in a scene that bore an uncomfortable resemblance to a propaganda poster for Hitler Youth.

I ordered a Coke and looked around the room. Two students, one male and one female, huddled in earnest conversation near a window. Three students sat around a pitcher of beer in the corner. Otherwise the place seemed pretty quiet. I carried my glass to a table where I found a man matching the description I'd been given: a grey-haired scholar wearing a grey Harris Tweed jacket with brown leather elbow patches. Ronald Holton probably once looked distinguished; now he appeared simply dissolute.

I introduced myself and, after suspiciously inspecting my non-alcoholic beverage, he invited me to sit down.

"Interesting décor," I said, gesturing around the room.

"It's so damned upbeat it feels depressing," Holton said. "I make a point of facing away from that horrid picture of young people disporting themselves." The constant sound of German polkas in the background would have driven me crazy if I worked there. I tried to put the annoying music out of my mind.

"I take it you spend a fair amount of time here."

Holton looked up at me sharply, then said, "Oh. You know who I am and you've come to talk with me. And here I thought you were just looking for company."

"I'm a Visiting Professor in the School of Music. No doubt you've heard about Professor Poundstone's death."

"That bastard!" Holton took a long sip of his drink. "But I guess if you've come to see me you know the story."

"I've heard rumors. I find it safer to consult primary sources."

"Always the scholar!" Holton's chuckle turned into a cough.

I wasn't sure how to proceed. This poor fellow clearly was not taking care of himself. It wasn't really my business but I couldn't help feeling sorry for a fellow academic in distress. "Have your friends talked to you about the basics: sleep, decent food, exercise?"

Holton dismissed the suggestion with a wave of his hand. "It's thoughtful of you to be concerned, young man, but for the time being this seems to be my second home." I waited for him to continue. In the background Elvis Presley sang a German language version of "Wooden Heart." "So you want to know about me and Jay Poundstone. You want to know what that J stands for? Jerk!" I took a drink of my Coke and tried to wait without appearing impatient. "Well I guess you know he seduced my wife," he said. I nodded. "I suppose that was bound to happen sooner or later—an attractive woman married to an old fart like me. But in my day faculty affairs remained behind closed doors and people usually ended up back with their proper partners."

"But not this time?"

"Hell!" Holton looked as if he'd just endured the ignominy all over again. "He had to announce his conquest in front of me, my wife, my colleagues, and even the president of the damn university. Unbelievable!"

"So you couldn't forgive your wife?"

"You've got it backwards, son. She left me. I guess she couldn't stand the thought of being tied to someone who'd been so thoroughly demolished in public."

"No 'for better or for worse,' eh?" The background music had moved on to yodeling songs. Holton must really have it bad if he could put up with this stuff day after day.

"You're all right," Holton said, and took another long pull on his drink.

I felt really badly about what I needed to say next, but I thought about Gretchen's pitiful expression and pressed on. "I guess you realize that this gives you a pretty good motive for killing Poundstone."

"Whazzat?" Holton focused his attention on me with apparent effort.

"Murder," I said.

"Wish I had," Holton said, a bit fuzzily.

"But you didn't?"

"Couldn't."

"How do you mean?"

Holton sat still for a few more moments. I wasn't sure whether he was collecting his thoughts or losing his grip on thought. Eventually he spoke again. "You must have heard the statistics about the Musical Arts Center." That I had. The stage at the MAC was the deepest in the world and wider than the Met's. Since 1948 the School of Music had produced 912 fully-staged, professional-level performances of 143 operas, all in English. "They may not have told you that it also has a state-of-the-art security system. During the day it's open to all, but after six you can get in there but I can't."

"How's that?"

"It's coded into your faculty ID card. Only School of Music faculty can get in after hours, except for public performances, of course."

"I didn't know that."

"When's the bastard supposed to have died?"

"Around nine o'clock, I understand."

"Then I'm in the clear." Holton patted the table with his palm, looked around, saw me, appeared to wonder who I was, and then managed to regain the thread of the conversation. "I do appreciate your circumspection, though. More than I can say for the police."

"Did you tell them about the security system?"

"Didn't want to muddy the waters. At nine o'clock Friday I was right here with three members of my department, getting sloshed to the gills. So I have an old-fashioned alibi. Seemed the easier route."

"I have to say I'm relieved."

"*You're* relieved! I may be down on my luck, but jail holds no appeal whatever." I thought of keeping company a bit longer with this unfortunate man, but the wailing clarinet of a recorded Klezmer band proved to be more than I could stomach, so I thanked Holton for his time and walked home to dinner. My path took me between two residence halls. A banner hanging from a window in the women's residence read "NO MEANS NO." Across the quad, a banner displayed on the outside of the men's residence read "NO MEANS TIE ME UP," and at the other end of the building another banner read "NO MEANS MORE BEER." Ah, the glories of American freedom of speech!

Supper sometimes consisted of fried eggs over corned beef hash, but I found that a casserole of ground beef sautéed in onions, canned tomatoes, canned corn, frozen peas, appropriately spiced and topped with cornbread, could last me for several days. I was just taking the Pyrex container out of the over when Martin knocked on my door. He seemed excited, so I invited him to sit down, tell me what was on his mind, and then join me in a meal.

"I didn't get thrown out of school," he began.

"Good news," I said. "What happened?"

"I got promoted to the philharmonic."

"That's the top level, isn't it?"

"Right."

"So you'll be playing for the production of *Faust*."

"That's right. I'd forgotten that."

"Congratulations!"

"I'm just hoping they haven't made a mistake."

"Come again?"

"Suppose they just sent me the wrong letter so when I go to rehearsal they'll say, 'Sorry—you were supposed to get the "being thrown out of school" letter?'"

"It isn't going to happen."

"How can you be so sure about these things? Isn't it possible?"

"Of course it's possible, Martin. Anything is possible. The question is, is it probable?"

"How do you mean?"

"Is it more likely than not to occur?"

"I don't suppose so."

"Forget the possibilities, Martin. Just worry about the probabilities and you'll be a lot happier."

Martin mused on my suggestion and an unaccustomed sense of relief seemed to pass across his face. I served the casserole and he began to eat. We enjoyed the casserole in silence for a few moments and then Martin said, "Have you heard about Professor Poundstone?"

"Yes."

"Everyone's talking about it as if it were an accident, but I don't think it's an accident at all."

"No?"

"No. I think he committed suicide."

"Surely you're joking."

"No, really."

"You think a person's going to stand under a 4400-pound chandelier and let it squash him?"

"It would be a fitting end to a sorry life."

"What's so sorry about it?"

"Professor Poundstone was always acting depressed."

"You're the first person to say so."

"You had to know what to look for, but I could see the signs."

"Such as?"

"Working late at night, being short-tempered with singers, always being discontent. He was basically a very unhappy man."

"It's a novel theory, Martin, but I don't think many people would accept it." I told Martin the story of *Faust* as a way of avoiding more lugubrious topics. By now I could summarize the plot in a few sentences.

"So you're telling me that the whole point of this bargain with Mephistopheles is that Faust bets he'll never be content enough to stay in one place?" Martin said.

"I guess that's one way of putting it."

"In other words, he has Attention Deficit Disorder."

"I don't think I've ever heard that phrase applied to Faust."

"Well it stands to reason. If Mephistopheles had just slipped him a few Ritalin pills, he could have won Faust's soul right away and saved everybody a lot of trouble." Martin's face brightened. "Or maybe Faust was bipolar?"

"Let me guess—you're taking abnormal psychology as an elective."

"How did you know that?"

"Just a shot in the dark." We finished the casserole and topped it off with a piece of lemon meringue pie that I'd baked a few days before when I'd invited Charlotte to dinner.

"Well, thanks for the meal. I'd better get ready for rehearsal."

After Martin departed I washed the dishes and prepared to attend an evening recital, one of my students performing Schumann's *Carnaval*.

Chapter 9

THOMAS WATERDOWN'S OFFICE MIGHT HAVE passed for a museum gallery, with vielles, sackbuts and serpents mounted on the wall and a large shawm resting gracefully on the top surface of a low bookcase. A framed page of illuminated plainchant hung on the wall beside a grave rubbing of a slender knight. As I passed through the open door on Wednesday morning Waterdown got up from the virginal, where he'd been playing what sounded like a Renaissance dance, and greeted me.

"What bring you back here to my medieval cloister?" he asked. "I thought you hung out in the 19th and 20th centuries."

"Your office is worth a visit in itself," I said, looking around at the collection of instruments, some of which I was unable to name. "I have to say I admire your determination for establishing an early-music program at a school so unabashedly devoted to the standard repertoire."

"Thanks for saying 'determined.' I've heard 'quixotic' and worse," he said. "Although I have to say, I don't encounter the term 'pre-music' so much anymore."

"I heard about the cancellation of your Carnegie Hall concert. That must have been disappointing. What happened, anyway?"

Waterdown's face darkened. "I guess you're familiar with the phrase *De mortuis nil nisi bonum.*"

"Make nice around the dead."

Waterdown snorted. "You'll have to put niceties aside if you want to hear this story." He gestured to a pair of comfortable chairs just in front of a pair of curved krummhorns and we sat. "The School of Music has a fair amount of money," Waterdown began. "On the other hand, it also has fairly high expenses."

"All those piano technicians."

"That's not the half of it. Opera is an expensive undertaking no matter how you slice it."

I thought of appeals from the Pittsburgh Opera Company, when I had lived in that city, pointing out that income from ticket sales covered less than half the costs of running the organization. "But presumably people operate within budgetary constraints." As soon as I uttered the words I realized my mistake, as I watched Waterdown's normally placid expression turn red with anger. "Maybe I said the wrong thing."

"No," he growled. "You've hit the nail on the head."

"Let me guess. Does this have anything to do with a certain *Phantom?*"

"Arggh!" Waterdown's exclamation resisted easy transcription but the pain on his face could have been described as eloquent. "I don't know how he managed it, but the day after Jay Poundstone got approval for producing that silly extravaganza, the Dean called me to his office to suggest that this might not be the best year for a trip by the Collegium Musicum. I could have killed that fat, egotistical bastard."

"And did you?"

Waterdown gave me a quizzical look. "So now you're playing Young Sherlock? No. If thoughts could kill, he would have been dead that moment, but I have thirty members of the Collegium Musicum who can tell you that I had a rehearsal that Friday evening." His voice softened. "You really should come to our concert Sunday afternoon at the Cathedral."

"I might well do that."

"Among other things we're performing the 'Dies Irae.' How many modern uses of that plainchant can you name?"

I'd known people like Waterdown back in graduate school, always eager to play "drop the needle" and challenge you to identify whatever work they'd put on the turntable. "Well, there's Berlioz's *Symphonie Fantastique*, and Saint-Saëns' *Danse Macabre* to begin with."

"Not bad, but you forgot Rachmaninoff's *Rhapsody on a Theme of Paganini.*"

"Right you are."

"I thought we'd perform the work in procession so that the sounds gradually travel all about the building."

"I like the idea. I'll plan to be there."

The School of Music produced more than 1500 concerts a year, more than in all of New York City, one of the students proudly informed me. Faced with the problem of deciding which concerts to attend, I considered a number of alternatives: (1) avoid concert-going altogether: as a musicologist, you don't listen to music, you only write about it. This seemed to have been the policy adopted by my colleagues, who never appeared at concerts. (2) attend concerts containing interesting music (but that included nearly all of them). (3) attend concerts in which your students were performing. This strategy, applauded by my students, enabled me to hear several remarkably competent voice recitals; a program of diverse pieces by a doctoral candidate in composition; a soprano, countertenor, and bass performing Handel arias, duets and cantatas (this to satisfy a *harpsichordist's* chamber music requirement); a performance of Bach Cantata 51 as part of a trumpet recital; and a noontime brass quintet recital, among others. And that was just during the summer term!

I could certainly manage to fit in a concert by the early music ensemble.

Chapter 10

I DIDN'T SEEM TO BE getting very far in my search for an alternative murder suspect to get Gretchen off the hook. A lot of people may have rejoiced at Poundstone's death but celebration didn't constitute incrimination. Then I thought about Gretchen's teacher, Lucinda Dumont, and her comment Monday about Poundstone's refusal ever to cast any of her students in operas (with the glaring exception of Gretchen Spindler). It seemed like a pretty thin motive for murder, but I didn't have much else to go on, now that Ronald Holton's explanation of the MAC security system had effectively limited the field to School of Music personnel. I figured that the easiest way to learn more about Miss Dumont was to visit the Publicity Bureau, and I directed my steps to the office in the School of Music administration building.

As I walked across the quadrangle I thought again about the seduction in *Faust*. Aside from the jewelry, the text doesn't tell us how Faust accomplished it. Gretchen's friend warns her about letting her head be turned by a chest full of baubles. Did Faust pledge marriage? Did Gretchen ever say no, or did she surrender immediately? I got so caught up in these questions that I missed the entrance to the Publicity Bureau and had to retrace my steps.

The walls of the waiting room were covered with opera production posters. Shelves contained bound volumes of all the concerts in a given year, each program headed by its number, as in "The 1374th concert of the 1980 season." When I requested information about Lucinda Dumont a pleasant woman attendant gave me three notebooks of clippings and other materials, an inventory as complete as any diva could desire. It occurred to me that no one had asked me for identification—I could be anybody. Then I remembered that unlike other bureaucratic offices, too many of which seemed devoted to guarding any information in their possession, the whole point of a publicity bureau was not to hoard but to disseminate. I took the notebooks to a table evidently provided for the purpose and began to peruse the materials.

Like many university voice teachers, Lucinda Dumont turned to pedagogy after the end of her active career as a performer. According to the evidence contained in the notebooks, Miss Dumont had enjoyed success at several opera companies, including the Met. Her signature roles included that of the Marschallin in *Der Rosenkavalier*, one of the most endearing characters in grand opera, a woman of a certain age who accepts the necessity of surrendering her young aristocratic lover to a woman closer to his age. Opera stars specializing in this role often continued performing it late into their careers. When I did the arithmetic, Lucinda Dumont seemed rather young to have given up a part so closely identified with her.

I continued poring through the clippings, photos, programs and reviews until I arrived at the final production in which Miss Dumont appeared. Reviewers had panned the stage direction but had singled out her portrayal of the Marschallin for praise. Yet there seemed to have been problems associated with the production. Subsequent clippings disclosed Miss Dumont's complaints of vocal strain—an unusual occurrence in such a familiar role, in which the singer had long since learned how to pace herself through the demands of the opera.

Continued searching revealed no evidence of subsequent appearances as an opera singer. For all intents and purposes, this production of *Der Rosenkavalier* had ended Lucinda Dumont's career. I flipped back to the program book and at the bottom of the page I found the words, "Stage Director, J. Watson Poundstone." I had discovered a motive worthy of murder.

Chapter 11

THE SCHOOL OF MUSIC ASSIGNED me four graduate students to help administer the history survey course, especially grading tests and exams. I wondered whether students appreciated the effort that went into judging their work, particularly their wrong answers. When someone cited a hemiola in the first movement of Brahms's Fourth Symphony, we went through the score measure by measure to ascertain that none existed. A similar search determined that there are no augmented triads in Liszt's *Orage* (the student had presumably been thinking of *Hamlet*). Occasional bits of unintentional humor relieved the tedium of test-reading. "*Ionisation* was the first piece to use all inaudible percussion instruments," one student wrote. "The octatonic scale was a scale composed only of octatones," claimed another. It had taken us an entire afternoon and evening and well past midnight, sustained by take-out pizza, to correct the Christmas exam, after which we felt confident that every paper had received due consideration.

On Wednesday afternoon, at the Technical Services Office for the second time in three days, I found Janice in a frazzle over listening tapes. Anyone outside the School of Music might take it for granted that if you were studying music history you'd probably spend a fair amount of time listening to music. In an effort to keep the task manageable I had compiled a listening list which I gave Janice at the beginning of the term to convert into cassette tapes that students could sign out to complete their weekly listening assignments. When Janice complained about the task I sent in two of my graduate assistants to compile a master tape. After that Janice only needed to produce copies for students to borrow.

I'd planned for the students to listen to roughly sixty minutes of music each week, mastering the material a little bit at a time. This unfortunately did not fit in with the students' plans—remember the eight hours a day of practice on their instruments. They preferred to cram all the listening into one night before a test and hope for the best. When the Technical Services Office couldn't provide enough copies of the tapes for every student on that one particular night, things got ugly, with Janice bearing the brunt of their ire.

"Professor Crochet," Janice wailed upon catching sight of me. "Your course is just killing me."

"What seems to be the problem?" I asked.

"It's your music tapes!" she exclaimed. "Nobody listens to them for weeks on end and then suddenly they all want them at the same time."

"Don't other professors have listening assignments?"

"They play the music in class, and they ask students questions from the textbook. They don't make students identify works and composers just by listening to them."

"If you were taking an English course wouldn't you expect to discuss excerpts from a piece of literature?"

"In an English course each student owns a copy of the poem or novel or essay or whatever they're studying."

"Students have copies of the scores in their Maxipaks."

"But they don't have copies of the cassettes. That's the whole problem."

"How much do cassettes cost?"

"Practically nothing—maybe a dollar or two."

"So it wouldn't cost too much to make a cassette for each student."

"Are you kidding!" Janice acted as if I had asked her to scale the outside of the university bell tower. "Who's going to make a hundred and seventy copies of a cassette?" Now Janice seemed alarmingly close to fainting. I had spent more time than I liked to admit dealing with this woman but I still couldn't make an accurate judgment on how much of her histrionics was deliberately created for my benefit. Every place I worked seemed to have someone like Janice, a constant test of one's resolve not to sweat the small stuff.

"I see your point. How many copies of the cassettes do you have available for the students to borrow?"

"We've made fifty copies. It took John and me three days to copy them all."

"You can still do your work while the machine produces the copies?"

"Well, yes, but still."

"Tell you what. Suppose I stagger the test over three days—I'll make three different versions of the test—so that you could handle each wave of students as it comes."

"That's more like it." Janice acted suddenly mollified.

"Well, it does seem to be one solution to your predicament."

"I wish some of the other professors would be as accommodating. Why, just last week Professor Waterdown asked me to ..."

I cut in to say that I was glad we'd come to an understanding, and beat a hasty retreat. Why did every encounter with Janice somehow end up making more work for me?

The "search for lost time" described life in the School of Music, where students never had enough time. Yet, one spring concert suggested that there was really plenty of time; it was just a matter of how it was used. Five symphony orchestras rehearsed every day--hours and hours of student time, devoted to what? Well, one concert opened with the Sibelius *Tapiola*, a composition which should be reported to the Society for the Prevention of the Abuse of the Whole-Tone Scale, and concluded with the Shostakovich First Symphony. Sandwiched in between was the Lalo Cello Concerto, performed by the winner of the string division in the annual concerto competition. For this event, perhaps 50 of the 80 cellists in the School of Music had spent countless hours perfecting the Lalo concerto, a piece of music without a single idea in its head. All this lost time could have been devoted to composing fugues, analyzing Bartók, reading Proust, learning calculus, listening to the Wagner *Ring* cycle, writing poetry or, as an absolute last resort, doing the listening assignments for my history course. But no, the students had no time, just never any time.

Chapter 12

I SHUDDERED INVOLUNTARILY WHEN I entered Lucinda Dumont's studio later that afternoon: the obligatory photos chronicling her opera career, apparently as essential to a voice teacher as the display of professional diplomas to a dental surgeon or psychotherapist, appeared not as a wall display but in free-standing frames covering the entire surface of her grand piano. Clearly no serious keyboard performance ever took place in this temple to the human voice. The accompanist existed only as a discreet, unavoidable servant, never as a musical partner.

The total absence of rugs, heavy drapes or wall hangings helped to create an acoustical setting designed to set off the human voice as a well-designed piece of jewelry might show off the features of a precious stone. I was a bit surprised at the absence of musical scores. Perhaps with such a well-equipped library near at hand, Miss Dumont found no need to maintain her own collection. Where one might have expected to find a bookcase there sat a long sofa and a pair of armchairs, perhaps the corner where the voice teacher exercised her other role as informal confidante and counselor.

"Gretchen said she might be slightly late for her lesson, but I didn't call you because I thought this might give us an opportunity to become better acquainted," Miss Dumont said graciously. "She seems to think highly of your teaching." She gestured me to a chair, not the standard issue of the School of Music but an armchair, obviously a personal possession, perhaps her mother's, though lacking the lace doilies that an earlier generation considered obligatory.

"Gretchen has been of great assistance in the Faust course," I said. "I much prefer to use live performers wherever possible."

Miss Dumont smiled. I had evidently given the correct response. "How are you finding it here at the School of Music?"

"I'm astonished at the level of accomplishment of the students, and lengths to which they seem to be willing to go in order to achieve it. I hear tales of pianists spending seven or eight hours at the keyboard."

"It does sometimes strike one as somewhat excessive," Miss Dumont said. "Of course the vocal students are enjoined from practicing more than two hours a day."

"Is that a school policy? I understand there's a fair amount of competition among singers."

"That's putting it mildly!" she said. "Yes—after a number of regrettable instances of young voices breaking under the strain of overuse, the School of Music put in a general rule for singers. They can spend as long as they want studying scores and thinking about their roles, but no more than two hours of actual vocal practice."

"What about the choirs?"

"No rehearsal lasts longer than an hour, although they may practice several times a week."

"How about opera?"

Miss Dumont's expression changed. "We voice teachers disagree on a great many matters, and I confess that many of us are loathe to attribute an iota of intelligence to our colleagues, but we speak as one in this area: students can "mark," or sing softly, during repetitions, but deliver only one full-voice rendition each rehearsal."

"And do the opera directors generally respect that policy?"

"All but one!" Miss Dumont's voice had dropped nearly to the level of a whisper but her voice had the painful intensity of fingernails scratching across a blackboard.

"I take it that would be the late Professor Poundstone?"

"You take it correctly."

"Forgive me for intruding, but wasn't he somehow connected with the end of your operatic career."

"There's no need to beat around the bush, young man," Miss Dumont said. "Jay Poundstone ruined my career." Her expression seemed to combine bitterness and regret.

"Again, I don't wish to be too inquisitive about a subject that you must find painful, but as I understand it, you had sung the role of the Marschallin dozens of times."

"*Hundreds* of times," Miss Dumont said, gesturing grandly at the photographs arrayed atop the grand piano.

"So you must have learned to balance your own stamina against the demands of the role. What happened that time, if you don't mind my asking?"

Lucinda Dumont sighed and frowned, as if reluctantly recalling a painful memory. "I take it you're familiar with the score of *Der Rosenkavalier.*" I nodded. "The overture has been described as one of the most erotic pieces of music ever conceived, depicting in detail not only the sexual frenzy between the Marschallin and Octavian but, even the young man's premature ejaculation." I recalled hearing such an account of the work. "The orchestral music is inspired, graphic, even explicit." I thought of the trombone passage usually identified with orgasm and nodded my assent. "Jay Poundstone had no confidence in Strauss, or perhaps more accurately, no confidence in the musical sophistication of the audience. He insisted on making us assume the most grotesque physical postures in performing the opening scene. Every time I tried to alter one of his stage directions to accommodate a more relaxed vocal delivery he would fly into a rage and force me into a more contorted position. I thought I could outwit him, never imagining that his contempt for the voice seemed to be without limits. In the end he got what he wanted and I was destroyed."

How like a singer so thoroughly to identify her ego with her vocal instrument! I didn't know exactly how to proceed. I paused for a moment and then plowed ahead.

"It sounds as though you had a strong motive to murder him."

"Is that what all this has been leading up to? My goodness—your ingenuous demeanor conceals a devious mind."

"I'm sorry; I didn't know any other way to ask the question."

"Oh, I don't take offense, mind you. It's just that you don't strike one as much of a detective." I felt a nearly overwhelming urge to tell Miss Dumont the reason for my impertinence but I remembered Gretchen's fearful expression and held my peace. "Well, all right. I confess that in the weeks and months following that fateful production I considered ways in which I might gain revenge on that monster. Now I've been more concerned with protecting young voices like Gretchen's."

I recalled the conversation between Miss Dumont and Thomas Waterdown and found this to be another case in which objective reality probably didn't exist; it all depended on one's perspective. "If you'll indulge me, do you have any idea who profits from Poundstone's death?"

"How do you mean?"

"I was thinking of all those rings I understand he wore. Who inherits his wealth?"

"Wealth!" Miss Dumont's laughter carried an overtone of contempt. "Like everything else about Jay, it was an illusion."

"But I hear he enjoyed a pretty lavish lifestyle."

"Jay Poundstone came from a European tradition in which families fawned over the son and ignored everyone else. His father left a substantial fortune that Jay had been frittering away. His sister must be furious."

"I didn't know he had a sister."

"She works in the costume department at the MAC. No expense was spared for his education; she was supposed to consider herself lucky to receive training as a seamstress. Theoretically she stands to inherit a tidy sum at her mother's death, but dear mama could never say no to her darling boy."

"So he's been gradually eating away at the family fortune?"

"Not so gradually of late. Last week, at his annual birthday bash, Jay announced that next year's celebration would take place in the Bromley Mansion."

"I can't say I know the place."

"The city was hoping to buy it for the Historical Society but Poundstone evidently outbid them."

"Without any money of his own."

"That was his genius. He never used his own money. I really think there was a certain hollowness at the center of that man." Miss Dumont looked at the clock and asked if I'd care for a cup of tea. I declined politely. "I've read your book on Debussy's songs, by the way. It gave me a lot to think about."

"I'll take that as a compliment."

"So it was intended. And when I subsequently learned that you would be coming here for the year I asked to read your *curriculum vitae*."

"Couldn't you have found a more conventional way to get to sleep?"

"You've put together a distinguished record of work, but if you don't mind my bluntness, you seem to have a hard time keeping a job."

"I appreciate your being direct—it makes it easier to talk." I tried to frame an appropriate response. "I love teaching. I love thinking and writing. Getting to spend hours in a well-equipped university strikes me as one of life's greatest pleasures."

"I take it that departmental politics occupies a lower rung on your ladder of values."

"I don't like it and I'm not good at it."

"I can understand your distaste. Goodness knows I've seen enough blood on the carpet in my time. The School of Music's list of superlatives sometimes includes astonishing nastiness. But if you'll permit a word of advice from an old woman, if you don't devote a certain amount of energy and imagination to protecting your job, you may lose the privileges and pleasures of which you speak." I couldn't think of any appropriate verbal response and settled for a grimace. "Ah, here's Gretchen. And just to conclude our earlier conversation, I spent the entire evening Friday dining with the Dean."

Gretchen came in for her lesson and we rehearsed the Jewel Song from Gounod's *Faust* that she would perform for the seminar later in the week. In the opera, Gretchen puts on the jewels that Faust, through Mephistopheles, has left for her as a tool of seduction, and sings, "Ah, I laugh to see myself so beautiful in this mirror." Gounod portrays the laughter in a series of coloratura passages quite at odds with the supposed simplicity of this innocent girl but which form the climax of this best-known aria in the opera. Gretchen summoned the technical agility that the piece required without ever losing the essential vulnerability of her character—an impressive performance. Miss Dumont made a few minor suggestions but mostly smiled at her protégée's accomplishment.

"That was lovely, my dear," Miss Dumont said, "and technically nearly perfect." Gretchen smiled. "I'm wondering," Miss Dumont continued, "if your performance wouldn't be still better if you thought a little more deeply about your character."

"How do you mean?" Gretchen reverted to her normal, slightly nervous expression.

"Think about Marguerite, the name that Gounod gives Gretchen. She has no father; she lives in poverty. Suddenly a young man shows interest in her. Remember, Mephistopheles has changed Faust's appearance from an aging scholar into a handsome swain. And he brings her jewelry that she would never in her life have imagined wearing. You can figure that the mirror in the aria is nothing grand—perhaps it's even cracked. But when Marguerite looks into it, she finds herself transformed, and the transformation is so incredible as to be laughable."

"You …" I started to speak but Miss Dumont shook her head as if to say, "Let her figure it out for herself."

When Gretchen sang the aria again it sounded remarkably different. I thought about the difference between instrumentalists and vocals. A piano teacher may adjust one's hand position; a string teacher may call for a different bowing. A voice teacher needs more indirect methods for evoking change. I now saw how dependent a singer could become upon her teacher, not only for improving her vocal technique but for helping her deal with the challenges of her personal life. And yet Gretchen for some reason kept from her teacher the awful secret with which she had chosen to burden me.

Chapter 13

AFTER THE LESSON GRETCHEN AND I walked toward the Music Library. Summer comes early in the mid-west and even though the calendar had not yet registered May, a number of students could be seen sunbathing on the quad, in apparent disregard of potential danger from several guys tossing a lacrosse ball. In the central circle a number of fellows with trick bikes were trying to outmatch each other with wheelies and, in one case, a handstand. I asked Gretchen what would happen to the production of *Phantom* after the death of Professor Poundstone.

"He was the stage director," Gretchen said, "and the staging had already been set before he died. So the musical director will continue to conduct the actual performances and the technical director will be sure that Professor Poundstone's instructions are followed. I understand he left very detailed notes."

"And what about *Faust?*"

Gretchen's face brightened. "The musical director will conduct the performances, of course, but Mr. Hollis, the director of the Musical Arts Centre, has agreed to step in to do the stage direction."

"Isn't that rather unusual?" I asked.

"Maybe so, but Mr. Hollis was a stage director before he took over running the MAC, so I guess it isn't that much of a stretch."

"But the Collegium trip is still off?"

Gretchen looked puzzled. "Well sure. Why wouldn't it be?"

I realized that I was about to divulge privileged information and changed tack. "So the students have accepted the loss?"

"They were a bit bummed out at first but they got over it. But I heard Professor Waterdown was so upset that he walked out in the middle of rehearsal—made his assistant take over."

"Which rehearsal would that have been?"

"Last Friday."

I was about to ask Gretchen another question when a large woman planted herself firmly in front of us and blocked our progress. She wore a dark sleeveless vest over a grey sweater, charcoal slacks and what you might have called "sensible" shoes. A wide belt buckle was decorated with rhinestones outlining the shape of a star. She wore her hair cut short, almost mannish, I thought, and she did not look happy.

"You!" she said, poking her finger into Gretchen's chest. "You killed my brother!" So this was the sister I had heard about. Gretchen gasped at the assault and pulled back.

"I never ..." The woman didn't give Gretchen a chance to complete her thought. She took another step forward and punctuated her words with continued jabs into Gretchen's chest.

"You harlot!" the sister continued. "You took advantage of my brother's weakness to promote your own interests." She took a step back and looked Gretchen up and down. "And look at you! You're not even good-looking enough to seduce him the usual way, so you exploit his most vulnerable spot—his desire for a son—and then force him to sign that infamous contract just so you could get the lead in the opera. I spit on you!"

The woman looked as if she were prepared to follow words with action so I tried to interpose myself between the two. The sister would have none of it and pushed me aside as if I were a child.

"Then you decide you don't like your side of the bargain so first you murder him and then you murder his baby! Oh, yes! I know all about that abortion. You cowardly slut! I could tear you to pieces." The woman seemed perfectly capable of doing exactly that.

"I think you're making a mistake," I said tentatively. The woman turned on me.

"Oh yeah? Ask her what she was doing Friday night? She got my brother to let her into the MAC and then she got hold of his device and killed him." The sister refocused her attack on Gretchen and resumed her jabbing. "What did you say to him, you shameless whore?" Her voice took on a seductively macabre tone that gave me shivers. "You're not going to get away with it. I'm going to see you fry!" She took another step toward Gretchen, who hid behind me. I had no more chance of stopping this large woman than of blocking a football linebacker, so instead I grabbed Gretchen's arm, pulled her to one side, and headed across the lawn in the direction of the Music Library and sanctuary.

"Go ahead and run away!" the woman shouted. "You're still going to fry!"

I thought Gretchen was going to faint. I put my arm around the young woman and half-carried her. For some reason no one considered this to be anything out of the ordinary: the girls kept sunbathing; the boys continued their lacrosse and bicycle tricks. When we reached the Music Library I asked Gretchen if she wanted to go to the infirmary but she insisted she'd be all right and disappeared into the rest room, leaving me to wonder whether her appeal for help might have been an act.

Gretchen had demonstrated her ability to transform herself on stage; was the innocent victim just another role? Had I been risking embarrassment with my colleagues for the sake of an artful murderer? I recalled the accusations I had made and flushed with shame. Surely this was conduct unworthy of a Visiting Professor, certainly one who entertained hopes of being offered a permanent position. Had my instinct to rescue a young woman in distress blinded me to my collegial responsibilities? I did what I always did when faced with imponderable personal issues and buried myself in work. No sooner had I discovered a vacant carrel in which to peruse some of the library's recent acquisitions than I heard a whispered voice.

"Psst! Axel." It was Martin Baxter.

"What is it, Martin?"

"I have an idea you should hear." I led him to a section of the Music Library where we would be less likely to disturb other people and asked him what was on his mind. "I figured out who killed Professor Poundstone." His smug tone suggested that the police, and I myself, might as well call off our investigation forthwith.

"So you don't think that it was suicide anymore?"

"No. I think you're probably right about the depression. Now I think he suffered from narcissistic personality disorder, but that isn't usually fatal."

"That's a relief."

"So do you want to know who really killed him?"

"I'm sitting on pins and needles."

"Mitchell Yarwick."

"I can't say the name rings a bell."

"He's the head technician at the Musical Arts Centre."

"Yes?"

"Well isn't it obvious? If stage directors are going to start operating special effects by remote control, where does that leave the tech guys?"

"As I understand it, they carry out their usual duties during performances."

"That's just to lull their suspicions."

"Really?"

"Yes. That remote control device is just a Trojan horse. Once the practice becomes accepted, it'll be easy enough to use it for performances, too, and then all the techies are out of a job."

"Have you talked with what's-his-name Yarwick about this?

"You don't think a master criminal is going to tip his hand to a clarinetist, do you?"

"Perhaps not."

"And nobody knows where he was Friday night."

"I'm sure somebody knows."

"Nobody I've talked to."

"I see."

"He's got motive, means, and opportunity. Isn't that enough for an arrest?"

"I think there needs to be a witness."

Martin looked crestfallen. "And here I thought I had it all wrapped up." I shook my head. I'd heard about taking an idea and running with it, but Martin carried the matter beyond all reason. Still, he looked so silly in that baseball hat that I couldn't take any pleasure in his discomfort and so I tried to distract him from it.

"How are you making out in the new orchestra?"

"I like it. I especially like the first violist. I even asked her out."

"Way to go, big guy."

"But she probably isn't going to like me."

"Why would you say that? She agreed to go out with you, didn't she?"

"But it might have been a trick. A lot of girls like to lead guys on and then dump them."

"Has that been your experience?"

"It's possible, isn't it?"

"Don't you remember our conversation about possible and probable?"

"Well, I figure if you always prepare for the worst, you're less likely to be disappointed."

"Less likely to be happy, too."

"You think?"

"Just go on the date and have a good time. Save the analysis for later."

"Maybe you're right." Martin seemed to have an unnatural reluctance to simply enjoy life. "By the way, last night I read *Faust*."

"You're kidding me."

"Well, Part One anyway."

"You really read it?"

"The orchestra is playing for the opera and you're teaching a course on it—I thought it might be interesting."

"And was it?"

"I've read worse. But what gets me is, Goethe calls it 'The Tragedy of Faust' but I can't see that anything especially tragic happens to Faust."

"No?"

"No. He just seems to glide along creating mayhem wherever he goes. Now Gretchen—there's a tragic figure. And her mother and her brother both suffer tragic deaths, essentially because they have the misfortune of being related to Gretchen. But Faust? For him it's all fun and games. Where's the tragedy in that?"

"Well, he dies in the end."

"Aw, right! At the end he gets carried away by a band of angels—not exactly what I'd call a tragic ending. If you ask me, Faust is some kind of monster: he makes the mistake of selling his soul but who suffers from it? Everybody around him." Martin glanced at his watch, realized he was late for class, and hurried off.

Perhaps without intending it, Martin had given me an idea, and I decided to pay another visit to Thomas Waterdown.

Chapter 14

"Why, it's Young Sherlock!" Thomas Waterdown said, the irony in his voice friendly but unmistakable, when I entered his office later that afternoon. "I'll bet you've just discovered that I didn't stay for the full rehearsal last Friday night and you can hardly wait to ask me to account for my actions." He thrust his hands toward me. "Put the cuffs on, officer. I admit it. I lied to you."

Now I felt thoroughly embarrassed, probably the effect that Waterdown had been aiming for. There didn't seem to be too much that I could say, so I remained silent and after a time he went on.

"Sorry. I didn't mean to come on so strong." We sat down and he continued. "I admit I had a plan in mind when I turned the rehearsal over to my assistant last Friday. I walked to the MAC, saw Wilma Poundstone heading for the entrance, and walked in immediately after her. I know you've heard that Jay Poundstone seemed impervious to attack—I sometimes think he enjoyed the fallout from his outrageous behavior—but I had some information on him that he wasn't going to be able to ignore. I thought I could extract a promise from him that might allow the Carnegie Hall trip to go ahead."

I nodded.

"I didn't really dislike the guy, you understand—he had an incomparable talent for getting publicity, and publicity's the name of the game in the music profession, don't let anybody tell you differently."

I nodded again.

"As I say, I planned to run a power play on the guy." Waterdown looked almost as satisfied with himself as if his plan had actually succeeded.

"But you didn't?"

"No. Instead of taking the stairs down to the costume department Wilma Poundstone walked right into the auditorium."

"And you naturally followed."

"I kept out of sight, but yes, I followed her."

"Then what happened?"

"She went up on stage, where Jay was working out some effect with that gadget of his, and wrenched it out of his hand. She was making a lot of noise but I was too far away to make out the words. Something to do with money, I gathered."

"Go on."

"Anyway, she did exactly what I would have done in the same circumstances. There's no way you could expect to make Jay yield ground physically in an argument, even if you were a head taller than he, like Wilma. Instead, she let him back her up until she had him in the middle of the Ring of Death. Then she pushed in the fatal code, and curtains."

"So to speak."

"So to speak."

"Have you told this to the police?"

"Axel, how can you have gotten this far in life and still be so naïve?"

I couldn't think of a satisfactory answer to that question—perhaps it didn't even have one—so I remained silent. People seemed to be asking me a lot of unanswerable questions lately.

"What's to prevent Wilma Poundstone from telling the same story, with our roles reversed? I have no evidence for what I've said—I didn't take photos, for God's sake. I'm just telling you what happened."

"So how are the police going to figure this out?"

"That's not my problem. You seem to have taken on this affair as some kind of extra-credit project—God knows why—but I know when it's in my best interest to keep my mouth shut."

"'And now, if that's all, I'd like the use of my office,'" I said in my best attempt at an officious British accent.

Waterdown said, "That's pretty good. Who said that?"

"It came from *The Private Patient* by P. D. James. It's followed by, 'And now, if you've nothing else to say, I'm sure both of us have work to do. I know I have.' Anyway, thanks for talking with me."

"I have no problem talking with you, Axel. Just don't expect me to play Boy Scout for you. It's not my style."

Chapter 15

ON THURSDAY AFTERNOON I FOUND myself back at the Technical Services Office, a place I visited entirely too often. This time it was about listening again, but not, thankfully, cassette tapes. Wagner's *Die Walküre* lasts upwards of four hours. I saw no point in asking students to listen to the work on their own—and knew that they wouldn't even if I asked—but the idea of assigning them to listen to a few disconnected excerpts seemed to do violence to Wagner's carefully-constructed musical architecture. This was one of the problems inherent in teaching a music history survey. Medieval and Renaissance music could be illustrated with brief, complete examples but if you intended to study Wagner at all seriously, you had to be prepared to invest a fair amount of time.

Instead I hit on the idea of a giant potluck supper. 170 students seemed too large a group for such a venture so a volunteer committee met with me, dividing the room into four sections named Earth, Rhein, Nibelheim and Valhalla, marked with appropriate posters, and each group leader assigned students in his or her section to bring food of various sorts for the meal. We planned to listen to Act I, eat the main course, listen to Act II, eat dessert, listen to Act III, and then go out for a beer (or root beer for an abstemious Visiting Professor).

Naively, I thought we'd handled the hard part. That was before I met with the perpetually frazzled Janice.

"The portable stereo system we wheel into the room works all right for brief musical examples," I explained, "but a four-hour opera needs a bit better treatment."

"What's wrong with the portable stereo? It's got a turntable, amp and speakers, doesn't it?"

"But the lecture hall is quite large."

"So just crank up the volume."

"That produces distortion. And even the turntable is fairly low-end.

242

I thought you might have something a bit more appropriate that we could move into the room for the occasion."

"So now you don't like the turntable."

"This is Wagner—there's a huge orchestra, great singers, and I'd like to do the work justice."

"I never cared much for Wagner."

"That may well be, but ..."

"You never get a cadence, for crying out loud. The music just goes on and on. Would it be asking too much to hear a perfect cadence once in a while?"

"Wagner thought of it as 'endless melody.'"

"That's just what I mean. Only a composer could think up a notion like 'endless melody.' When's a singer supposed to breathe, for God's sake? And *Die Walküre!* How can you make students listen to that?"

"I thought it the most accessible of the four operas in the *Ring* cycle."

"You call it accessible; I call it smut. The hero not only steals another man's wife, but it's his own sister! You've got adultery and incest all rolled into one. You call that art?"

"Well ..."

"And then Wotan imprisons his own daughter on a rock and surrounds her with fire. If that isn't child abuse I'd like to know what is!"

"I think we may be getting off the point here."

"I know perfectly well what the point is. You want me to find you a better sound system so that the students can spend four and a half hours listening to music in which there isn't a single cadence, where nobody has a chance to breathe, and where virtually every action on the stage violates Indiana State Law. Nothing doing!"

In the end I found a student willing to lend us a state-of-the-art high-end stereo system and another student with a station wagon willing to transport it to the potluck. After the party students asked why we couldn't do all the listening assignments that way.

Chapter 16

THE NOTE FROM THOMAS WATERDOWN asked me to meet him in the sacristy of the Cathedral on Thursday evening. I didn't know what he had in mind but thought that perhaps he was offering to make amends for our somewhat strained conversation the preceding afternoon. I didn't have anything else scheduled and figured that if he was extending an olive branch the least I could do was accept it.

Members of the Collegium Musicum entered the neo-Gothic edifice for their rehearsal, presumably the last before Sunday afternoon's concert. A balcony at the rear of the Cathedral held the organ loft where the choir would sit for Sunday services. For Sunday's concert the Collegium Musicum would occupy chairs at the front of the Cathedral to accommodate the audience's desire to see as well as hear the performance.

As I walked down the aisle toward the sacristy at the front of the church I encountered Gretchen, evidently headed in the same direction.

"We meet again," she said with a smile.

"Are you here to listen to the rehearsal?" I asked.

"Actually, I think Professor Waterdown is going to invite me to join the ensemble. His note asked me to meet him in the sacristy." As we continued down the aisle I heard singers and instrumentalists warming up. At the front of the nave we encountered a red and white sign reading "Private Area—Do Not Enter," with a life-size statue of an angel bearing a sword, presumably to deter the heedless. Undeterred, we continued to make our way to the sacristy. Collegium singers and instrumentalists took no notice.

"Do you think Miss Dumont was talking about me yesterday?" Gretchen asked.

"How do you mean?"

"When she was describing Marguerite's situation. After all, I don't have a father, or at least not one I can remember. And there was that business with Professor Poundstone."

"Acting teachers sometimes suggest that actors draw on experiences in their own lives to capture a character. I don't see why it shouldn't work the same way with singers."

Gretchen nodded but remained silent, as if trying to decide how large a change she would have to make to accommodate this new information.

The door to the sacristy took the shape of a rounded arch, imitating the contours of the stained glass windows. No sooner had I opened it and entered the small room than I felt a strong blow on the side of my head and I crumbled to the floor. When I regained consciousness I found myself seated in a chair with my hands bound behind my back. In front of me Wilma Poundstone was preparing some evil-looking sewing needles and talking in a venomous tone to Gretchen, bound as I was. The unpleasantness of my situation made unconsciousness seem like a preferable state. I tried to clear my head and make sense of things.

"I'm going to make sure you never have the chance to make the same mistake again," Wilma was saying. In the chapel I could hear the Collegium Musicum chorus practicing the 'Dies Irae,' the chant associated with the Day of Judgment. The otherworldly sound of the plainchant and the pain in my head made the bizarre sight in front of me feel even more disorienting. I tried again to focus my thoughts. If Wilma had bound me the same way as she had Gretchen, I was fastened not with rope but with heavy thread, which cut painfully into my skin. I especially didn't like the sight of those needles. Gretchen stared at me with a deathly pallor and I guessed that she was immobilized by fear no less than by her bonds. I had to get us out of here.

I didn't like my chances. Even if I could get free, the room didn't present much in the way of useful weapons. I knew that I could never hope to overcome Wilma Poundstone barehanded. Our previous encounter had showed that I was no match for her physically. The rule about guys being stronger than girls clearly didn't apply in Wilma's case, at least not against me. I might be able to claim the stamina of a long-distance runner but in terms of sheer strength I was totally outclassed.

I surveyed my surroundings. A closet along one wall presumably held vestments in various colors to suit the liturgical season. Beside me stood a mirror and sink and next to them a cloth-covered table with a cruet of wine and a plate of communion wafers. The heavy crucifix mounted on the wall certainly had enough heft but would be too unwieldy to maneuver in the confined space. No scissors, no knives—at least none that I could see. Even the waste basket looked much too flimsy to be of any use.

Wilma stood over Gretchen like an angel of death, or perhaps a cat toying with a mouse before ending its life. "Are you thinking about your sins, Gretchen? Do you pray for the soul of the baby that you murdered?"

The plainchant sounded in the Cathedral. "Dies irae, dies illa. Solvet saeclum in favilla." Behind it I thought I heard the sound of the organ.

Wilma continued. "Hear what the choir is singing: the great trumpet sounds, the graves tremble. And in your heart flaming tortures flare up." Where had Wilma learned Latin, I wondered distractedly? Then I saw a copy of Sunday's concert program, which presumably included a translation. She'd evidently been plotting this scene for some time.

Gretchen looked imploringly at Wilma. "Let me out of here. I can't breathe."

The choir continued. "Judex ergo cum sedebit, Quidquid latet adparebit, Nil inultum remanebit."

I refocused my thoughts on the problem at hand. My only advantage was that Wilma Poundstone had her back to me, but so long as I remained incapacitated it hardly mattered. I felt along the edge of the chair with my fingertips. Nothing but smooth metal. Then, wait, a rough spot. I leaned toward the corner of the chair, straining to bring the tough threads in contract with the imperfection in the surface of the metal. Would the roughness be enough to abrade the thread? Back and forth, back and forth. Wilma had used strong thread. Back and forth again. Did I feel one of the filaments separate? Back and forth. Yes; something had definitely given way.

Wilma continued her weird words of judgment. "Your sin and shame are now manifest. Woe unto you!"

The sounds of the "Dies irae" moved about the Cathedral. Evidently Waterdown was practicing the piece in procession, as he had mentioned to me. "Quid sum miser tunc dicturus? Quem patronum rogaturus? Cum vix justus sit secures."

Wilma's strange incantation at least gave me time to work on the threads. Back and forth; back and forth. "Your dead baby holds out her hands to you and makes you shudder. Woe!"

The choir sang, "Quid sum miser tunc dicturus?" In front of me I saw Gretchen faint.

Free. I rubbed my chafed wrists and tried to restore the circulation in my hands. But I still needed a plan. Wilma would hear any movement. Then I saw it—an unopened bottle of communion wine just to the side of the sink. How good was Wilma Poundstone's peripheral vision? I tried to estimate the angles but gave it up as hopeless. I wasn't going to get more than one chance at this. I rehearsed the movements in my mind until I thought I might have a chance at carrying it off: dodge to the side, grab the bottle, rise to my full height and strike Wilma on the back of the head. I didn't want to kill her but if I failed in the effort I might leave both Gretchen and myself worse off than before.

Take a deep breath. Concentrate. Execute. I slid from the chair as quietly as I could, took half a step to the side, grabbed the bottle, held it as high as I could reach and brought it down on Wilma's head. She fell noisily to the floor and I scrambled to Gretchen's side. As I cut Gretchen free with the scissors she regained consciousness and followed me down the side aisle to the front of the Cathedral. The heavy oaken doors that had seemed so difficult to open when we arrived now stood our last barrier to freedom. We crashed through the doors and into the arms of a policeman.

"Thank goodness!" Gretchen exclaimed. "She was going to …"

"Are you Gretchen Spindler?" the uniformed officer asked.

"Yes," Gretchen said. "But you've got to hurry before she comes to."

"I have a warrant for your arrest."

"You don't understand, officer. We were being held captive and she had thread and needles."

"I have instructions to bring you to the station," the man told Gretchen.

"But you're getting it all backwards," Gretchen said.

"You can explain that to the sergeant," the policeman said.

"Officer, there's been a big mistake. We're the victims here," I tried to explain.

"I'm not going to raise my voice to you, sir," the policemen said politely, "but unless you step to one side I'm going to have to arrest you for interfering with an officer of the law in the performance of his duty."

Further protest seemed futile. I moved aside and watched the policeman escort Gretchen to his vehicle. (It didn't take long in the presence of these guys before you started sounding like them.)

I watched the patrol car turn the corner and disappear from view. With no expectation that I'd fare any better with the station sergeant, and having no desire to share Gretchen's fate, I went back to my apartment to think matters over.

Chapter 17

I<small>MMEDIATELY UPON ARRIVING HOME</small>, I telephoned Lucinda Dumont to explain Gretchen's predicament without actually breaching her confidence. The feisty voice teacher assured me that she would send her attorney to assist the young woman in whatever way he could. On Friday night I really didn't feel much like partying, but I'd promised a colleague to attend her Witches Sabbath gala and I didn't like to disappoint.

The party took place at what looked like a university professor's house. Someone with a fair amount of imagination had evidently gone to a fair amount of effort to create an atmosphere that went well beyond conventional party decorations. To begin with, the lighting was subdued almost to the point of being nonexistent. A mysterious mist rose from various corners, dimly illuminated from behind. I supposed they might have made use of dry ice in water to achieve the effect but in the gloomy atmosphere I had no way of telling. My colleague and a few of her friends, presumably tipped off about the creative possibilities of such low illumination, had dressed entirely in black with strips of phosphorescent material in different colors creating eerie effects. Predictably, witch costumes predominated, with a goodly proportion of ghouls or goblins. I felt decidedly out of place in my hastily assembled costume as a minstrel.

Had they used black light to convert conventional party food into a sorcerer's repast? Shapes, textures, certainly colors appeared distorted beyond recognition. Again, the dim lighting made it impossible to know for sure how the effect had been created, only that one's sense of reality had been seriously undermined. A woman glided past me, apparently completely naked, but I had no way to be sure. On reflection, I decided that she probably wore a phosphorescent body suit—this was Indiana, after all.

A small rock band played at one end of what I supposed served in usual times as a family room, but something didn't sound normal and I tried to identify it. Guitars, keyboard, drums—up close, nothing out of the ordinary, but back several feet, a truly unearthly sound. I decided that they must have inserted a distorting element between amplifier and loudspeaker, the way television news programs sometimes disguised a voice in order to protect the identity of an undercover informant.

I saw a tall familiar figure emerge from the gloom. "Is that you, Martin?"

"Axel. Good to see you!"

"How are things going with your violist friend?"

"Just great! I never dreamed that such a beautiful girl would go out with me." Before I had a chance to respond, Martin said, "Ah, here she is," and gestured toward an old hag with one eye missing, the other bloodshot, a long pointy noise and a mouth missing several teeth.

Martin said, "I went to the library to learn more about *Faust.*"

"Why Martin—you show unsuspected depth!"

"What's the matter? You think clarinetists can't read? Honestly, Axel. If you weren't a friend, I think I'd be offended."

"Sorry, Martin. I'm just surprised when someone shares what seems like an esoteric interest. What did you learn?"

"Well, the librarian gave me a book of legends about Johann Faust—the real person behind Goethe's Faust."

"What do you think about old Johann?"

"I think Goethe ripped him off."

"Really?"

"Yes. For example, you know the scene in Auerbach's Keller, where Mephistopheles drills holes in a wooden table and out comes whatever beverage people want to drink?"

"Right."

"Well it turns out that it wasn't Mephistopheles at all. In the legends Faust himself performed the miracle. He was a noted necromancer."

"And sodomite, if you go by reputation."

"Well, that too, I guess. But the real rip-off comes at the end."

"The end?"

"The end of his life, I mean. In the legend, Faust has the Devil's services for twenty-four years—Marlowe got that part right—but at the end of that time he has to give up both body and soul to the Devil."

"He has to die, in other words?"

"But not just any death. At midnight on the last day of the twenty-fourth year, there's this terrific storm. When Faust's students come to investigate the next morning, they find his eyes on the floor, his brains on the walls, and his corpse lying outside on a manure pile. There should be a film of the story—it would be a lot better than that slasher film they showed here last Halloween."

"So you like that better than Goethe's version?"

"Are you kidding? Goethe has a bunch of angels taking Faust's soul away from Mephistopheles at the end. What kind of ending is that?"

A somewhat older witch approached and greeted me. "It's so nice to have you here, you," she hesitated, perplexed, "whatever you are."

"I'm a minstrel," I said.

She looked confused. "Aren't minstrels supposed to be in blackface?"

"You're thinking of a minstrel show. I'm a wandering singer of ballads. A sixteenth-century itinerant performer."

She still looked skeptical, then said. "Oh. You must be the music professor." I nodded. "Well, in any case, don't forget to sign the register." Presumably related to my hostess.

The word stuck in my mind as I continued to wander through the darkened room. A register! The thought struck me with the force of Wilma Poundstone's blow the night before. This might be just what I needed. All thoughts of partying left my mind. I gathered my things and made my way toward the front door. "Oh, Professor Crochet," a voice called. "You can't leave yet! We're just about to celebrate a Black Mass." I muttered a few lame excuses and hurried back to my apartment.

Chapter 18

ON SATURDAY MORNING CHARLOTTE, RETURNING from a three-day conference in Chicago, slipped into my apartment and into my bed. After a frolicsome re-acquaintance she came out of the kitchen with a mug of coffee, wearing one of my marathon T-shirts and nothing else. "I got in late last night and didn't want to wake you up."

"You might not have found me here," I said. "I managed to get Gretchen out of jail."

"Jail! How did she get there in the first place?" I recounted our misadventure in the Cathedral and its unexpected ending. "So was this the usual file-in-a-cake ploy or did you have recourse to dynamite?" Charlotte asked.

"Neither one. I had an inspiration from a witch."

"I like this better and better," Charlotte said as she snuggled beside me. "Bring me up to date."

"To begin with, there seems to have been no short supply of people happy to see J. Watson Poundstone dead."

"And you've talked to several of them."

"Yes. Anyway, it turns out that if Poundstone decided to get murdered after hours at the Musical Arts Center, only someone in the School of Music could have done the deed. From the outside it's a graceful pavilion but getting inside is a different matter—the security system may be discreet but it's very effective."

"Tell me about the witch."

"You mean the naked one or the other one?"

"You've been consorting with naked witches?"

"Only at a distance. The idea came from other one."

"And what kind of wisdom did this non-naked witch have to offer?"

"Not advice—an inspiration. Something she said made me wonder whether the hi-tech security system at the MAC includes a register of people signing in and out after hours."

"And does it?"

"To find that out I had to talk with Doug Hollis, the director of the center. He wasn't too keen to meet me last night but when I asked him whether he'd ever spent a night in jail and whether he'd wish that experience on the soprano lead in the opera he was directing, he changed his mind."

"But at this point she'd already spent a night in jail."

"Not an experience she was eager to repeat, I assure you."

"So how does this register system work?"

"It's not really that complicated. Once the security system is activated, usually at 6 p.m., every time someone swipes a card, the time and name get recorded on an advancing tape. Given the set-up, a single tape might last for a month before needing to be replaced."

"So it wasn't too difficult to locate the entries for last Friday."

"Right. Shortly before 9 p.m. we have Wilma Poundstone passing through the system, just the way Thomas Waterdown described it."

"But no record of him?"

"No—he slipped in just behind her so he didn't actually have to use his card."

"So that was enough to prove that Gretchen never went into the Musical Arts Center that night?"

"The tape register plus a letter from the director explaining how it worked and what it meant."

"So you just waltzed into the police station, waved this evidence at the man on duty and he fell over himself trying to release Gretchen, with profuse apologies, of course."

"Not exactly. He referred me to the arresting officer—happily he was still in the building—who referred me to the detective in charge of the case—these guys really work long hours—who saw that the evidence exonerated Gretchen, and he reluctantly signed her release paper."

"While a chorus of angels sang 'She is saved!'" I smiled at the reference to Goethe's Gretchen.

"Let's go back to Friday night." Charlotte had finished her coffee and piled a number of pillows against the headboard so that she could face me without craning her neck.

"You're still worried about the naked witch?"

"We'll come back to her. Did Wilma Poundstone then go ahead and murder her brother, the way Waterdown suggested?"

"Apparently not. According to Doug Hollis, Wilma sensed the presence of someone behind her and, concerned for her safety, went directly to the costume department office and telephoned him. He was about to call the campus police when they both heard the crash of the chandelier marking Jay Poundstone's demise. Hollis said he could hear it quite clearly over the phone."

"Thereby both establishing the time of death and providing an alibi for Wilma." Charlotte paused briefly. "So it was Waterdown, after all this?"

I nodded. "But he'll never be punished for the crime. There's no trace of him entering the Musical Arts Building—you don't need a card to leave it—and we have only the story he told me to place him there, a story he'll certainly deny if it ever comes to that."

"A perfect crime?"

"Looks that way. On the other hand, if you go by all the stories I've heard, Jay Poundstone richly desired to die."

"But murder is still murder."

No refuting that.

Chapter 19

THE SUNDAY AFTERNOON AUDIENCE FOR the Collegium Musicum concert at the Cathedral probably rivaled the morning congregation in size. Thomas Waterdown had built up a following in the town as well as on campus. The story of the cancellation of the Carnegie Hall trip had passed into general circulation and more than a few listeners seemed to have been determined to give the ensemble a public show of support, judging from comments I heard as I waited for the program to begin. With nothing else to do, I examined the interior of the Cathedral in greater detail, and the ways in which it strayed from its Gothic model, most notably the loudspeakers attached to every column and halogen bulbs in the light fixtures. A chapel, decorated in gold, occupied the front of the church on the right, while racks of votive candles stood on the left. A large stained glass window at the front of the building depicted Christ on the cross, with a thief on a cross at either side and a crowd of haloed spectators below. If the window followed the Renaissance model, the face of the donor would appear somewhere among the crowd, perhaps one of the centurions.

Sunlight streamed through the stained glass windows on the west wall, producing a pleasantly multicolored abstract pattern on the surfaces of the eastern columns. Beside me Charlotte studied the program, which indicated that the program would start with Thomas de Celano's plainchant for the Mass of the Dead, the "Dies Irae." I shuddered as I recalled the last time I had heard that music in this same place. When I recounted the misadventure to Charlotte she commented that Wilma Poundstone might not have been a murderer but she certainly seemed to be unhinged. At the same time she confessed a grudging admiration for the woman's loyalty to her brother and to her administration of justice as she understood it. I was more concerned with the trauma that Gretchen had sustained at Wilma's hands: the public accusations on campus, the malevolent private revenge that the sister had nearly succeeded in carrying out, and the ironic "redemption" that led to a night in jail.

Categories like "bully" and "victim" failed to account for the complex influences in these women's lives. Wilma Poundstone, through a combination of tradition and personality traits, had perpetually lived in the shadow of her flamboyant brother, who compounded the insult by draining away a family fortune that might have been counted on to allow her a more fulfilling life. Wilma a victim? A hard picture to reconcile with the physical presence of a woman who had no hesitation in employing physical violence. And what did she have against me, after all? I figured Wilma to be the source of the fake messages that had lured Gretchen and me to the Cathedral on Thursday night. Perhaps Wilma regarded me as some kind of accomplice after the fact. One could make a strong case for Gretchen as a victim—entangled into a morally dubious contract by the brother, then attacked in the most terrifying way by the sister. I suspected that you could carry the victim role all the way back to her abandonment by her father.

The low, resonant tones of plainchant put an end to my ruminations. Rather than greeting the audience or even asking for silence Thomas Waterdown had simply let the music begin, correctly calculating that the unfamiliar sounds would soon bring a hush over the crowd. The procession began near the sacristy and proceeded down the same side aisle along which Gretchen and I had fled. As a result, the performers remained out of sight for much of the audience, who heard only the monophonic tones of the plainchant amplified by the resonant stone surfaces of the building. "Judex ergo cum sedebit, Quidquid latet adparebit, Nil inultum remanebit."

Then the procession emerged into the wide area at the back of the nave and prepared to march up the main aisle of the nave. Like many other members of the audience I turned around in my seat to catch a glimpse of the performers, with their director leading the procession. What I saw next seemed so out of place that by the time I could make sense of the incident it had already ended. Proust may have had this kind of thing in mind when he maintained that we can never fully appreciate a moment in the moment itself but only in its recollection.

I saw the figure of Wilma Poundstone appear in the balcony directly above the procession, so tall that the delicate railing came scarcely above her knees. Above her head she raised a large heavy object that I subsequently recognized as the pulpit bible, an oversize volume encased in metal. For a brief instant she remained motionless, a biblical figure evoking the image of Moses holding up the stone tablets containing the Ten Commandments or, more accurately, the remembered image of Charlton Heston portraying Moses. Thomas Waterdown probably just had time to register her shouted words—"You killed my brother!"— before the falling object removed him from this life.

Singers toward the rear of the procession, unaware of the death of their leader, maintained the chant for a time so that the music provided a brief unintended requiem. "Quid sum miser tunc dictorus? Quem patronum rogaturus? Cum vix Justus sit securus." Only later did I recall that Charlotte had not turned around in her seat.

The School of Music, for all its procedures, evidently had no set drill for the death of a performer during a concert. The members of the Collegium Musicum, although shaken by the loss of their director, decided, after a hiatus during which police and ambulance attendants had been summoned and allowed to carry out their duties, to finish the performance under the direction of Thomas Waterdown's assistant.

At the end of the concert the assistant director offered a few impromptu remarks about the inspiring influence Thomas Waterdown had had on performers who were not always taken seriously by the rest of the institution. The simplicity of these obviously unprepared words carried a greater effect than a more eloquent eulogy might have done, and the audience responded first with respectful silence and then with prolonged applause.

Charlotte seemed unusually subdued as we walked away from the Cathedral. I broke the silence by sharing my own musings. "I'm still trying to figure out how Wilma found out that it was Waterdown."

A few moments passed before Charlotte said, "I told her."

A shock wave of conflicting thoughts and emotions prevented me from speaking.

"Justice must be done," she said. And when another moment had passed without a response, she continued, "Murder is murder."

During the next several weeks Charlotte and I talked a bit about justice and revenge, although our discussions become shorter and less frequent. We continued to teach the course together but spent less time together outside of class. Charlotte evidently thought me either squeamish or lacking in moral fiber for not endorsing her action. I had second thoughts about whether anyone with such fixed ideas of right and wrong could ever be a comfortable partner. But neither of us seemed to have the skill to bridge the gap between the abstract and the personal, so the question of our future remained unresolved and undiscussed.

Wilma finally received some financial assistance from her mother, who sprang for an experienced defense lawyer. Wilma escaped jail, though she did have to spend time in what would earlier have been called the loony bin.

Gretchen acquitted herself well in the production of *Faust*, an opinion shared not only by her teacher's other students but—even if somewhat begrudgingly—by other voice students, surely her most demanding critics. In May the School of Music announced, in a stunning piece of revisionism, that the Collegium Musicum, now under the direction of Thomas Waterdown's assistant, would make the trip to Carnegie Hall as originally planned, the School emphasizing that this project had always enjoyed "its full and complete support." And when one of the sopranos took ill, the assistant recruited Gretchen to sing with the ensemble.

Later that same month I received a manila envelope from Fleur de Lis University in Quebec offering me a position there. Accepting the invitation didn't really require a decision: a Visiting Professor, welcome guest for a year, no longer has a home when his term expires. I hired a tutor to help polish my everyday French. I had no difficulty carrying on a conversation about Debussy's uncompleted theatre pieces or rhythmic practices in French medieval motets, but still tended to freeze when someone asked me to pass the salt. When I subsequently received approval from the Canadian immigration authorities, I made plans to move to a new country, a new culture, a new language—a new life.

About the Author

Arthur Wenk loves music, mathematics, movies, mountains, mysteries, magic and marathon running. He has published books and articles on Debussy, music and the arts, music history and bibliography, programming graphing calculators, and the bookstores of Toronto. As a lecturer he has recently offered presentations on psychotherapy, film, and a history of western culture. Wenk's teaching career has taken him to southern California, Boston, Pittsburgh, Québec City and Southern Ontario, where he has founded a succession of *a cappella* choirs and served as a church musician in addition to academic duties. Axel Crochet, introduced in *The Quarter Note Tales* (Wingate Press, 2006), and reappearing in *New Quarter Note Tales* (*iUniverse,* 2010) represents a nod to Claude Debussy's alter ego, Monsieur Croche, the dilettante-hater. You can learn more about the author at his website, www.arthurwenk.com and about the series of novellas at www. axelcrochet.com.